ARIA FOR GEORGE

NORA LONDON

ARIA FOR GEORGE

E. P. DUTTON NEW YORK

Published in the United States by E. P. Dutton,
a division of NAL Penguin Inc.,
2 Park Avenue, New York, N.Y. 10016.

Published simultaneously in Canada by
Fitzhenry & Whiteside Ltd., Toronto.

Library of Congress Cataloging-in-Publication Data

London, Nora, 1924–
Aria for George.

1. London, George, 1920–1985. 2. Singers—
Biography. 3. London, Nora, 1924–   . 4. Musicians'
wives—Biography. I. Title.
ML420.L865L6   1987   782.1'092'4 [B]   87-516
ISBN 0-525-24536-7

W

DESIGNED BY EARL TIDWELL

1 3 5 7 9 10 8 6 4 2

First Edition

For my children
Andrew, Philip, Marina, and Marc,
whose love and support gave me
the strength to persevere

Acknowledgments

This book owes a great deal to the many friends who helped me to reconstruct the sequence of George's career.

I am particularly indebted to Dr. Howard B. Gottlieb, Director of Special Collections of the Mugar Memorial Library in Boston where George's memorabilia has been collected. Thanks to Dr. Gottlieb, George's hundreds of letters to his parents have been preserved. There I read for the first time what he wrote about me over thirty years ago.

I am very grateful to Robert B. Tuggle, director of the archives of the Metropolitan Opera, who gave me the list of George's performances in the old house and was most helpful in choosing the pictures of George in costume. With Wolfgang Wagner's permission, Dr. Oswald G. Bauer provided information about the Bayreuth Festival performances, and Gottfried Kraus obtained schedules of the performances at the Theater-an-der-Wien.

I want to thank Ruth Sickafus for her support at the very beginning and Lillian Schiff for her patience in copying my endless revisions.

Most of all I am indebted to Richard Marek, who made this book possible. His encouragement, gentle prodding, constructive criticism, and great sensitivity gave me the courage to complete my story.

Contents

Photographic inserts follow pages 116 and 148

ARIA FOR GEORGE

Prologue

Day after day, he sat in the big recliner, his beautiful hands stretched out on the armrests. He sat very straight, radiating strength in spite of his handicaps. His shiny black hair was just slightly streaked with gray, his skin was smooth, soft almost without wrinkles. The full lips were slightly parted and at times the black eyes still had the imperious look that reached the last row of the opera house. But mostly the eyes roamed aimlessly about the room and not a single word passed his lips.

I spoke to him every day. Every day for nearly eight years I talked to him as if he were well. He never answered. He could not speak. In 1977 he had suffered cardiac arrest. It took too long to revive him and, as a result, his brain did not get enough oxygen for more than fifteen minutes. He survived but remained brain damaged.

He was not paralyzed; he could move his arms and legs, but his brain could not give appropriate commands. He did stretch out his arms toward me and he could put weight on his legs if we helped him to stand. But he did not walk. He could not get up from his chair without help.

How much did he understand? I believe that he recognized me

and that he was always pleased to see me. He always turned toward me when I entered his room and screamed in anguish when I was gone for a long time.

Every morning I went into his room several times, until I saw that his eyes were open, for I knew that he could not call me. Then I would sit on the bed and say good morning to him and ask him how he felt and if he wanted breakfast. Every few months he would answer a loud and very clear yes. I would tell him that breakfast would be ready very soon. I embraced him and told him how much I loved him. I gave him messages from friends who called the previous night. Then it was time for him to get up.

I summoned the male nurse who helped me to take care of him. The nurse would get him out of bed, wash him and dress him while I prepared his breakfast. He was always dressed with care—a pretty-colored shirt and slacks—for he had been a fastidious dresser. Then he was taken to the dining room in his wheelchair, and as he arrived I put on a classical recording. He had been accustomed to playing music every morning for himself, and I tried to choose pieces he liked: baroque music, Schubert chamber music, Mozart symphonies, or Beethoven sonatas. I avoided vocal music at meals, for sometimes that excited him too much. He would become agitated and not eat any more.

I prepared a big breakfast—toast, egg, cereal—for this was his best meal and he was painfully thin. It was essential for him to eat well, at least in the morning. We had to feed him but he ate with gusto—it was the only thing that still gave him pleasure. Sometimes he would consume as many as six slices of bread with jam. He preferred sweets and I tried to prepare only dishes he liked.

After breakfast he was wheeled back to his room and transferred to his recliner. This was a moment when he was more attentive. He really listened to what I said and often acknowledged my words with a groan. "Do you want to hear more music?" I would ask. "Do you want orchestra or singing? Do you want to hear your own recordings?" I would ask this when I sensed he was particularly alert and when I was emotionally up to listening to his singing voice, which I loved so much but sometimes found too painful to hear again. But after all, singing was his work and mostly I managed to be detached about it.

[2]

I had to play his records; it was considered good therapy. Often he really enjoyed them. He tried to make some sound. Sometimes, miraculously, he articulated clearly the greater part of an aria in German or Italian.

After a while he fell asleep. I could leave him, for I knew that he would sleep for several hours. By the time he woke up it was midday. The nurse and I took him for an outing in his wheelchair, accompanied by our dogs, an Airedale and two dachshunds; we were a strange procession on the country roads around our house in Armonk, New York. When we got back, the nurse transferred him to a tilt table, which put him in a standing position. He carried his full weight on his legs. I liked to see him erect—all six feet two inches of him—towering over me as he always had. I could imagine that he was standing on his own. I drew close to him on the tips of my toes and embraced him.

But he could stand only because he was strapped around his chest and above his knees to the table. I worried that the straps might hurt him, for he was not able to tell us whether he was in pain, yet I knew that standing was essential for his circulation. He stood for twenty minutes. We played ball with him to distract him. Sometimes he could catch the ball but he rarely threw it back.

Then it was time for lunch, which was never as successful as breakfast. Again he had to be fed. Lunch was in the kitchen for a change of scenery. I think he enjoyed watching me move around preparing the meal. I tried to think of good desserts. He fancied custards, crêpes, most pastries; his friends sent him a steady flow of Sachertorten from Vienna. For these, he always had an appetite—his taste buds were unharmed.

After lunch he slept again until late afternoon. Sometimes, perhaps once a month, when he woke up at that time, he smiled and suddenly looked at me in the tender way that had kept me spellbound for over thirty years.

I lived for these fleeting moments, always hoping that there would be more. I gave him a kiss and told him that I had been shopping while he slept or that an old taped broadcast of his would come out as a new record. "Are you satisfied? Many of your recordings are coming out again," I said. Or "Si called from Washington to inquire about you and send his love." (Years had gone by since his cardiac arrest and still every day a friend called to wish him well.)

Later he was exercised on a mat. He did not move voluntarily. The nurse turned him left and right—we always hoped that he could learn to turn himself in bed. That would be a great achievement and make him more comfortable and independent at night. After half an hour of exercises interrupted by rest periods, he was lifted back into the wheelchair. Soon it was time for dinner. We could not wait too long, for when he was tired he did not eat well. There was a main dish and always ice cream for dessert, which he was sure to finish. While he was eating dinner we watched television. I tried to ascertain if his eyes followed the picture or just wandered around the room, but I never could be sure.

After dinner he returned to the recliner. I hugged him and then I sat next to him holding his hand until he fell asleep. The nurse put him to bed. He slept in a special extra-long hospital bed. A night nurse turned him twice in the course of the night. I could not do it because he was too heavy for me.

But every night I went to his room several times to make sure that he was comfortable and breathing regularly. I kissed him good-night and stroked his cheek when I was ready to go to bed. He lay on his side, apparently healthy. I fantasized about his waking up the next morning perfectly well and recovered.

Often I dreamed that he was walking, talking to me, laughing in his infectious way, displaying his unique zest for living that made everybody else seem dull. Finally I came to realize that the dreams would not come true, and year after year I lived outside of time in an agonizing twilight where George's physical presence was real and where his spirit was forever escaping my grasp.

Once a week I went to the city, among people, my friends, vaguely surprised to find that the rest of the world lived normally. I went to concerts and to the opera. I went to recharge myself and returned to George with renewed energy and love.

How did this happen? How did the joys, the tears, the enchantments, the frustrations lead me to a room at night watching over the sleep of a man who gave me so much and from whom everything had been taken away?

Let me tell you.

1

My Background

I was almost born on a train, thus clearly destined for traveling from the very beginning. My mother had miscalculated. She had prolonged her Christmas holiday in the Swiss resort of St. Moritz and the labor pains started on her way back to Germany.

My arrival, in Berlin on January 8, 1924, interrupted her life of leisure. Jeanna was the daughter of a wealthy Russian Jewish merchant and had been married off, as was the custom, to Jacob, a promising young engineer of similar background who had gone away to engineering school in Germany.

He came back to Russia, to his home town of Odessa, to find a wife. She was nineteen, he was ten years older. He took her with him to Germany where he had started to work for a manufacturer of automobiles. The year was 1911. Jeanna, as befitted well brought up young ladies, spoke German and French fluently and played the piano rather well, but had only vague notions of cooking or anything else of practical use. She told me much later how miserable she had been in the beginning of her married life, all alone with a strange man in a foreign country.

World War I broke out a few years later, and she was completely cut off from her family. Toward the end of the war, the Russian Revolution forced her parents to flee from Russia with her younger brother, Senia. Although her parents died of typhoid fever within a week of each other after their arrival in Poland, at least Jeanna now had the company of her brother, and soon she had her first daughter, Gabriele. In the beginning she was in love with her husband. He was dashing with his bright blue eyes, blond moustache, and charming smile. She had a languorous beauty, auburn hair, creamy white skin, and light-brown eyes. But after a few years the difference in their temperaments created conflicts and they drifted apart.

However, when my mother discovered that she was pregnant again, they decided to patch up their differences. My father hoped fervently for a boy. When I was born he was disgusted to have another girl and for a while he did not look at me. As I grew into a cute two-year-old with a striking resemblance to him, he became extremely fond of me and developed a benign fatherly attitude toward me. Later on he would be very proud of my scholastic achievements and enjoyed discussing mathematics with me.

My father had graduated at the top of his class from engineering school and his career had been remarkably successful. He became one of the directors and a large stockholder of the Daimler-Benz automobile company, later to become Mercedes-Benz. He could give his wife and children anything they desired.

In Berlin we lived in a huge, red brick house with a pointed roof coming down in a steplike effect, surrounded with two large terraces on which I pedaled in a special toy automobile that my father had given me. On one side, there were two separate apartments, one for the chauffeur, one for the cook and the maid, and an indoor swimming pool in the basement, which we never used. For the children and nurses, the house had a special wing. My sister, who was six years older than I, had a French governess, and a German nurse whom I called Deti took care of my needs for eight years.

I remember best the beautiful garden behind the house and a mysterious willow tree where we played hide-and-seek. Years later, after World War II, when I returned to Berlin with George, I looked for the house on the Ruhrstrasse and found that it still existed. But the garden was gone. An apartment house had been built on its location and our villa had become a brewery.

One of my earliest recollections is sitting for a portrait in my father's study where I was not normally allowed. The painting showed a serious little girl with neatly parted blond hair and limpid green eyes wearing a light-blue dress with two big bows on each shoulder and a bodice with smocking and tiny pink roses. Another time I remember sitting in ecstasy next to my mother on the piano bench while she played tunes from Johann Strauss, Jr.'s, *Gypsy Baron*. Still another time I opened the door to the upstairs dining room, all decorated in yellow chintz, and watched with horror my parents screaming and throwing things at each other.

When I was six years old, the truce was definitely over and my parents were divorced. My father remarried very quickly a short, very thin blond woman whom I called Tante Ida. Soon thereafter my mother married the man she had been seeing for some time, whom I called Uncle Choura. After their marriage, she followed him to France and settled down in Paris, where she had always wanted to live.

Although it seems incredible by today's standards, I did not suffer from the divorce at that time. Perhaps I was too young, perhaps I was sheltered by my devoted Deti, a very affectionate, no-nonsense person who made me perfectly happy. The only dark memory is that one scene in the dining room, which left a deep impression, for I have abhorred any kind of shouting throughout my life.

At first I found Paris alien and disquieting. We moved from one big hotel to another, without my sister, who stayed in school in Germany a year longer. Then we moved into an apartment on the avenue Kléber and finally my mother bought a house in the rue Jasmin, not too far from the Place de La Muette in the sixteenth district of Paris.

My mother was evidently very happy with Uncle Choura, a good-looking, dark-haired man who was very nice to me. He knew how to handle her moods and her fantasies, and they went out frequently with Russian friends to fashionable restaurants and night-clubs.

When Deti left after my eighth birthday, she was replaced by a succession of governesses to whom I did not become as attached. Instead I became very close to my mother. She did not care much about my schoolwork or other practical matters, but she was extremely loving and affectionate. I grew up secure in the knowledge that she adored me and thought that I was just wonderful.

In our house in Paris, my room and my study were on the fourth floor, one flight above her bedroom. Every night, no matter how late she came home, even when I was already a teenager, she would come up to kiss me good-night. I can still recall the scent of her perfume, the touch of her perfect white skin, and her elegant appearance.

After an unsuccessful year in different schools where I learned very little, my sister Gaby, more efficient than my mother, chose a good private school for me, the Cours Sainte-Clothilde, which she also attended. At first, I found it very difficult to adapt. I did not have any friends and my knowledge was not up to the school's curriculum. I had to have some private tutoring until I caught up with the other students.

Later I loved my school. It was a girls' school, as was customary then. I had two best friends with whom I spent all my free time. With one, Maïthe, I walked twice every day the five blocks to and from school (we had morning and afternoon sessions). With the other, Gigi, I competed for highest grades in the class. After school all three of us did our homework together. On Thursday afternoons there was no school and we went to the Comédie Française where we saw all the French classic dramas and comedies. We all loved Molière and argued about the merits of Corneille versus Racine. I preferred Corneille with his heroic and virtuous heroes and did not yet understand the subtle beauties of Racine's tragedies. We were forced to learn great amounts of poetry by heart. I was the best at reciting in class, and wallowed in the rhythmic Alexandrines of romantics like Musset and Vigny.

On Saturday or Sunday mornings, during the winter months, we went ice skating at the Molitor skating rink at the Porte d'Auteuil. We skated around, we three girls, holding hands, and tried to flirt with the boys who zoomed by on their hockey blades trying to scare us. I had no chance of being picked up. Between the ages of ten and thirteen I was overweight and clumsy and was not allowed to wear makeup to help my appearance. Anyway, I was much too shy to respond to any advances.

All my school friends were Catholics and studied the catechism.

I was the only Jewish girl in my class but this did not trouble me in the least, and I did not mind being different. At home we had no Jewish instruction or tradition of any kind. In fact, if anything, I was more self-conscious about having divorced parents, which was still an oddity in the 1930s, than I was about my religion.

When I was ten, I begged my mother to let me take piano lessons. At first she resisted, thinking it was just a whim and that I, like my sister before me, would not practice. However, I insisted so much that she gave in. I started going twice a week up the avenue Mozart to the Conservatoire de Musique where Mademoiselle Catelin gave her lessons. I adored her; she opened the world of music for me. I was quickly able to play easy pieces and progressed to the point where I could play some Chopin mazurkas and preludes with great emotion, imagining that I would become a great pianist someday. Eventually it turned out that I did not practice enough, and world events interrupted my piano studies, but I had developed my knowledge of music and started to go to concerts regularly.

We had a Marconi radio and a phonograph with a record changer and I started to collect records together with Gaby, who, being older, received a larger allowance. I discovered Gershwin's *Rhapsody in Blue* and Rimsky-Korsakov's *Scheherazade* and played them over and over. I also discovered singing with records of Mado Robin, then a well-known French soprano, and Feodor Chaliapin, the Russian bass who lived in Paris and was an acquaintance of my mother.

Little by little, my interests led me away from my school friends and closer to Tania, a new friend of Russian origin like me, who was the daughter of a friend of my mother. Through Tania I met a number of other young people, and after I was fourteen I acquired my first boyfriend, Paul Gerson, with whom I spent most of my free time. He was also of Russian origin and went to the prestigious Lycée Janson for boys.

We read voraciously the same books, Balzac and Proust. He gave me Kahlil Gibran's *The Prophet*. There was no more skating rink, but once a week, a foursome comprising Tania, her boyfriend, Paul, and I went to dancing school, which was considered the proper place to learn the latest steps, including rumbas, tangos, and waltzes. I was certainly never the epitome of gracefulness but I enjoyed myself immensely and felt very sophisticated whirling around in the arms of a young man. Our flirtation never went farther than kissing even though we went on two skiing vacations in the French Alps with a supervised group of friends.

Eventually Paul's parents, who had more foresight than my own, moved to the United States with him, and for two years we wrote each other long letters with ardent romantic promises that we knew to be meaningless, but I nevertheless looked forward to his letters each week with great anticipation.

Hitler had come to power in Germany and my father, who had remained in Berlin, foolishly convinced that his prominent position would shield him from persecution, was obliged to leave with extreme urgency. During the same period Uncle Choura suddenly fell ill with gallstones, which had not been diagnosed in time, and died within three weeks. My mother was devastated and I was heartbroken for her. At the same time I was also concerned for my father, who was in fact fighting for his life.

The winter of 1935 was a somber one for us. We waited anxiously for news of my father's escape. Finally we heard that he and his wife were on their way to Paris. He had managed to get out a good deal of his money, and although not as wealthy as before, he was able to live a very comfortable life in a new apartment near the Place de l'Étoile.

From then on I got to know him better. I had lunch with him every Sunday, sometimes at his home, sometimes at the best Russian restaurant in Paris, called Korniloff, where he was received with great deference and would invariably order large amounts of caviar and a pastry filled with meat or cabbage, our favorite Russian dish called *kulibiak*. Having recovered from his disappointment that I was a girl, he was delighted with my good report cards and evidently amused by my great resemblance to him. I continued to speak German with him, French with my mother. Everybody else around me spoke Russian as all the relatives and their friends were Russian. My schooling and my friends were French. From an early age I was used to shifting from one language to another with the greatest of ease. This was to be an asset later on in my life.

Another crucial change was the arrival of Miss Williams, an English governess, who came to supervise me when I was twelve years old. Somewhat reluctantly I learned to speak English quite fluently although I retained an accent about which my children tease me to this day.

Our wonderful life in France was coming to an end. World War II started in 1939. In May 1940 the last happy event was Gaby's wedding, which took place in Paris while the invasion of France was starting at the northern borders. Gaby married a young Frenchman, Jean Terrail, from a Catholic family. In order to marry, and possibly because she genuinely felt the lack of religious feelings in our family, she converted to Catholicism. I was profoundly shocked by her decision. Although I had never set foot in a synagogue, I was strongly attached to my Jewish background and felt, especially at that time, that turning your back to it was a betrayal of your heritage.

Shortly before the wedding, I had accompanied Herr and Frau Hauser, the couple who supervised our skiing vacations, to Paris's Vélodrome D'Hiver, the equivalent of Madison Square Garden, which was now being used as a detention center. The Hausers were German refugees who had fled the Jewish persecutions in the mid-1930s to make their home in France, where they made a living teaching gymnastics and organizing ski trips for adolescents. They were wonderful, enthusiastic, and decent people and they had permission to reside in France, but they were stateless aliens. The French government had decided to round up all German refugees and put them into special centers in the provinces. (Later the Nazis transformed many of these centers into concentration camps.)

The first mustering station for aliens was the Vélodrome D'Hiver. Our little group decided to escort the Hausers whom we loved dearly, and we said long tearful good-byes at the entrance. We were not allowed any farther. But I was overwhelmed at the sight of thousands of people herded together like cattle without the slightest concern for human dignity.

I could not forget what I had seen. The stories I had heard about Germany took on a burning reality and I suddenly developed a feeling of kinship toward my fellow Jews.

Gaby's wedding was nevertheless a stylish and joyous affair for me, but the next day the situation in Paris became so dangerous that my family thought seriously about evacuating, just slightly ahead of the government.

My father and his wife went to Bordeaux and a year later managed to go to the United States. Gaby and her husband left for their honeymoon in the South of France, and stayed in France unmolested during the rest of the war. We were not reunited until 1945.

But our small group, composed of my mother, her brother, my uncle Senia, me, and my dog Peter were on the run. We were luckier than most for we had a car, money, and my uncle's determination to get us out. By then I was also determined to leave France for, through the Hausers, I had some small idea of the Nazi persecutions.

Our last stop in France was the sea resort of Biarritz near the Spanish border. The morning we arrived Marshal Pétain announced the armistice with Germany. The defeat was disastrous for France. I walked on the beach, my long hair dripping wet under the drizzle. Nothing mattered anymore. Tears streamed down my cheeks. France was lost and my happy childhood was gone forever.

We had a difficult time getting a visa for Portugal. Thousands of people had fled just ahead of the advancing German army and most of the Jewish refugees were trying to leave France. The line in front of the Portuguese consulate extended into the street and well around the block. My uncle and I took turns standing on line. While I was waiting in the narrow cobbled street, the French policemen who watched the crowd decided to have some fun and paced back and forth dangling a dead rat in front of us as close as possible to our faces. I was outraged by their behavior and their cruel laughter and realized that we had to leave this country at all costs.

Fortunately, my uncle had been aware of the situation for some time and succeeded in securing visas for all three of us with the help of a young Portuguese friend who had connections at the consulate. In turn he promised to take the young man to Lisbon in his car. I think my uncle saved my life by taking me with him.

We were crowded in the car. Now, four people, my Airedale, and all our earthly belongings, but I did not care how uncomfortable I was as long as we got away. At the last minute in the hotel in Biarritz, I had to abandon my books, my most precious property, which I had managed to take from Paris but now, with an added passenger, there was no more room for them. But I refused to give up my dog, despite great pressure to do so. My mother finally gave in. She did not know where we were heading, but she understood my love for the animal and my need to keep him.

Once in Lisbon, we joined hundreds of refugees who were assigned to a resort town, Figueira da Foz, four hours away from the capital. There we waited for three months until we finally received our immigration visas to the United States. Uncle Senia had been the representative of Parker Pens in France and received affidavits from Mr. Parker personally, so we were able to get the visas fairly soon. Some people waited nearly a year and some went to any South American country that would accept them.

For me the wait was really not painful. We were close to a lovely beach and I loved to swim. I quickly made friends with other refugees and with some Portuguese families. It was summertime, beautiful weather, I had lost my baby fat. Blond, light-eyed, and suntanned, I seemed to be just the right type for the dark-haired Portuguese. In any case, I had a good deal of success among the young men and my mother watched carefully as they danced with me a little too closely during frequent soirées at the casino. I was pleasantly surprised with my sudden success with men, as I had thought of myself as unattractive. However, I was not attracted to anyone, and there was nothing but good-natured banter between the boys and me.

We flew to New York from Lisbon on the Pan American Clipper, the first plane to make regular transatlantic flights. On board I ate my first apple pie and cheese, which I found delicious. I was to love everything in my new country, and to this day I am a most patriotic American, forever grateful to have been allowed to come here.

My dog was not permitted on the plane and had been shipped on a merchant-marine boat. He arrived some weeks later, after we had settled down in the Hotel Bolivar on Central Park West. New York knew hardly anything of the war, seemed unconcerned by the fate of France, and felt strange to us. Soon we found many friends from Europe who had also arrived recently, and inevitably life went on. I went to school to perfect my English, then was admitted to Barnard College for the following fall.

In the summer of 1941 my mother and I drove, with our friends Lydia and Boris Chaliapin, across the United States in eleven days, visiting everything from an Indian reservation in South Dakota to Yellowstone National Park.

Lydia and Boris were the children of the famous Russian bass Feodor Chaliapin whom I had admired in Paris many years before. During the whole trip, as there was no radio in our Plymouth, we entertained ourselves by singing arias from any number of operas. I remembered my piano lessons and felt sorry that I had not played for so long. Now Lydia was telling me that I had a lovely soprano voice. She was a singing teacher and offered to give me lessons. I was the right age to start, she told me, just over seventeen. I was enchanted, for I had become infatuated with opera and went to performances at the Metropolitan as often as I could.

Once we arrived in Hollywood, my mother, Lydia, another Russian friend Rita, and I rented a house for the summer on El Camino Drive just behind the Beverly Wilshire Hotel. We had a great time entertaining the Russian Hollywood crowd, the actors Akim Tamiroff and his wife Tamara, Leonid Kinski, Gregory Ratoff, and others. It seems that I had really grown up and changed into an attractive girl. One of our friends, a well-known movie director, thought I was very much a type like Ingrid Bergman and wanted me to make a screen test. But I was not interested. My passion was books, not movies, and I wanted to go to college back east. I wondered later what would have happened if I had stayed. Would I have met George then (after all, he was living right near me in Hollywood)? Would I have entered into my first marriage? Anyway, I went to Barnard College in New York and I continued to live with my mother. I felt I could not leave her alone, so I lived at home and rode the Broadway trolley to school every day.

At Barnard I majored in government, as a result of my constant concern about European affairs and the war. But my most enjoyable course was advanced French literature. It was a graduate course taught by Mademoiselle Marguerite Mespoulet, a brilliant, elderly spinster who had a tremendous influence on my thinking. All her students worshiped her and the privileged ones, including me, were invited to her house for coffee and inspiring discussions about art and poetry. She introduced me, among others, to the poetry of Baudelaire, whom she considered France's greatest poet, and told us that great writing and great art would outlive the destruction of war.

Meanwhile, my father and Ida arrived in New York in December 1940. I found him changed and looking old. He had always been an optimist, but now he was depressed and saw no way that Hitler could be defeated. He died a broken man in 1942, unable to adjust to yet another country.

Our financial situation became worse after my father's death. He had paid for my tuition, but once his debts were paid there was nothing left for me, and I could no longer afford to go to college. I went to work as a French-English translator for the Voice of America at the Office of War Information. By then the United States had entered the war, and we worked in three shifts, in great excitement, broadcasting news twenty-four hours a day to occupied Europe and North Africa.

At that time I met another French-Russian refugee, whose family had known ours for many years in Paris. He was thirteen years older than I, athletic, amusing, intelligent, at the head of a prosperous meat-canning business. His name was Gene Garvin. He started courting me. We had the same background, I liked to listen to him, I accepted his advice. He was older, wiser, secure; he replaced the father I had lost. We were married in July 1943.

There was a small gathering for lunch at the Plaza Hotel, attended by his mother, his uncle and aunt, my mother and my uncle, and some close friends. It was wartime, we had lost contact with my sister and many other relatives, and it was no time for great celebrations. I was only nineteen and Gene, my new husband, was thirty-two. I wanted to appear sophisticated and worldly, neither of which I really was nor ever would be. I was in love with him. I trusted him and felt safe with him, a man so much older, who knew so much.

He liked to be my mentor and taught me much about living and about relationships between men and women. But there was a bit too much in his talks about freedom for each individual and not enough about love and romance. I should have been suspicious, but at the time I did not know enough to be. Everybody around us thought it was a good match, two people with the same background who were well suited to each other. Looking back, it amazes me that I stayed married to Gene for over ten years.

At first I was happy and enjoyed my new life. We lived in a

comfortable apartment on New York's Fifth Avenue. I had a car, lovely clothes, diamond jewelry, my first mink coat by the time I was twenty-two. In July 1945 I was fulfilled when my first son was born. It was the eternal incredible miracle of giving birth to a new human being, so wonderful and so complete. I was particularly delighted that it was a boy; there had been just the two girls in my family. Two years later I was just as thrilled with a second boy. I loved Andy and Philip totally and swore to myself that I would give them a happy, secure childhood. As it turned out, this was not such an easy formula to follow.

Once the war was over, we took frequent trips to France. There were joyful reunions with relatives who had survived, particularly my sister Gaby and her beautiful son Patrick, now three years old, about whose existence we had not known. Gene had a spectacular duplex apartment in Paris, overlooking the gardens of the Trocadéro and the Eiffel Tower, and it was there that we stayed.

We first went back to Paris in the winter after VE Day. The trip was full of emotion. There I was, back after five and a half years, no longer a child but a married woman with a child of my own, an American citizen but still loving this beautiful city that miraculously had been spared by the war. I walked over my favorite streets, along the quais, the Champs Élysées, my old neighborhood near the Muette, past my old school. Nothing had changed: I was particularly comforted that the bookstore near school was still owned by the same little lady who had been its proprietor when I was a student. The Nazi monsters were gone and suddenly everything seemed possible. I remember the fabulous New Year's party that winter at a friend's house on the Ile Saint-Louis, the ancient center of Paris. I was wearing my first made-to-order evening gown, and I felt mature and sophisticated. This was my first exposure to Paris's cosmopolitan society; the rooms were crowded with elegant women. I felt quite pretty, and the admiring glances of the other guests confirmed my feelings. I needed this support, for my husband was grudging with compliments. Occasionally he would say that I looked all right; it was meager approval for a young girl as unsure of herself as I was.

He was always rushing off somewhere for business or for some sports event. When he stayed home, it was usually because we entertained friends or business connections. On the rare occasions when we were home alone we talked about family, friends, and our next vacation plans, rarely about anything more personal. Only once in a great while he would complain about not being really interested in the meat-canning business. Then I would tell him that I understood and I would try to encourage him to go into politics, which he loved and for which I thought he was well suited. I told him that I did not mind living with less money if a different life-style would give him more satisfaction.

However, these reflective moments were rare, and most of the time he kept up a frenetic pace of business and pleasure pursuits. This life-style seems terribly shallow to me now and I understand my tolerance for it at the time only in the context of the widespread thirst for pleasure after the somber war years.

That winter we resumed the skiing vacations in Switzerland interrupted by the war. Mostly we went to Davos, Gene's favorite resort, which provided perfect slopes and cozy hotels for us. We were good skiers, especially Gene, who was an outstanding athlete.

We started spending more time in France, and after Philip was born I took the two children with their Swiss nanny, Klara Buchler, to live part of each year in Gene's apartment in Paris. It was a large duplex but I had a maid and a great Russian chef, so it was comfortable to live there. We started giving parties. We organized a costume ball, transforming the downstairs living and dining rooms into a nightclub. All the most attractive young Parisians came and we danced through the night. I was costumed as a Chinese; Jacques Fath, the couturier, had made a pale-green silk gown for me. I wore a black wig, and a makeup man had come to give me an Oriental look.

In the spring I won the first prize at the automobile elegance competition that took place every year in the Bois de Boulogne. Custom-built cars of various makes driven by elegant women competed along the avenue des Acacias in front of a stern and knowing jury to earn prizes for the drivers and publicity for the builders. I presented a light-green convertible Delage with a beige leather interior. I wore a matching green chiffon dress with a wide-brimmed hat of the same color. I received a beautiful gold and silver compact and a Sèvres vase from the City of Paris, and my picture was all over the papers and the newsreels for one week. Gene was very proud of his wife and for once seemed very pleased with me, which was more important to me than the prize and my success during the competition.

During the summers we rented a house in Deauville, a resort on the Channel, which had a beautiful beach and a famous casino where people gathered around the tables to gamble. Everyone went to a big ball for the Fourteenth of July, the French national holiday. I hated the gambling crowds and smoke-filled nightclubs, but I loved the beach life and the days watching my two little boys as they played in the sand and took their first tentative steps into the water. The weather was often overcast, with that gray-blue sky so beloved by French painters.

My life, which seemed so glamorous, was in fact empty of love outside of my two boys. Little by little I noticed that Gene was going out a lot by himself or that he was in France when I was in New York and in New York when I was in France. I caught him lying about his activities, there were strange calls for him from women, and finally I found some unknown woman's underwear in our apartment in Paris when I returned after some months in New York. I realized that his absences were not entirely caused by business obligations. He was having affairs with other women, not only from time to time but as an ongoing way of life. Everyone, except me, knew about it. I was even courted by the husband of Gene's current mistress. He assumed I would be ready to have an affair as well. Furious, I slapped him in response. When I confronted Gene, he had the nerve to suggest that I have some fun of my own. After all, he said, "You have everything you want. Why don't you enjoy yourself, too?"

I was miserable. I did not want to have a lover. I wanted a husband who loved me, who wanted to be with me, who enjoyed the things I enjoyed and who wanted to spend time with the children the way I did. It became clear to me, as the years went by, that Gene and I had grown completely away from each other.

I loved to be with my children and, although we had a nurse, I spent much time taking care of them. Nanny, Miss Klara Buchler, was a woman in her fifties when she came to work for us. She stayed until Andy was seven and Philip five, and came back to take care of Marina when she was born years later. Miss Buchler was an experienced and intelligent woman. She taught me about children but understood that I was the mother and that I wanted to be with them as much as possible. As the years went by we became real friends and stayed devoted to each other until she died in 1966. She knew that I was suffering because Gene paid so little attention to the boys. He spent almost no time with them, and even when he was home he hardly ever played with them; mostly he found reasons to criticize shortcomings that only he could see. They were both healthy, charming, vivacious, very bright children, but I don't think he ever understood what joy, what a blessing this represented. Often I begged him to go out with them or talk to them, but with little success.

I managed to take them along wherever we went—to Europe, to Paris, to the seashore, and back to New York. Those first trips after the war, by transatlantic ships, were far from simple. Everything had to be taken along, from baby food to toilet paper. But the boys and I were together. They went to French kindergarten and spoke perfect French and English right from the beginning. When they reached school age, we moved back to New York where we spent the winter months and went to France only for late spring and summer. We lived on Park Avenue at Eighty-third Street and I watched with apprehension from the window as Andy, now eight, walked alone down Park Avenue to school. He was going to Allen-Stevenson, a private school for boys, where he was one of the top students of his class, and it was incompatible with his standing, he explained, to be accompanied to school by an adult. So he went by himself and, a bit later, I would walk to the same school with Philip.

Now that the children were both going to school, I had a lot of time to myself. For a while I took singing lessons with Lydia Chaliapin, which I enjoyed very much. Through her I learned a great deal about opera. I even participated in a student concert, and sang fairly well. I met the other students at the studio, many of whom were much more advanced than I and were starting serious careers. We often went to the Metropolitan Opera where we were fortunate to listen to performances of Lauritz Melchior and Kirsten Flagstad. I loved grand opera and soon realized that my light soprano would do only for operetta at best. So I gave up singing and concentrated on playing the piano, which I had started again. But I did not give up going to the opera. I had a subscription—two seats in the Grand

Tier—and went regularly with one or another of my friends, because Gene did not care much for opera. During the winter of 1953 I saw a performance of *Don Giovanni* with a new star of the Metropolitan, the bass-baritone George London. My girl friend was ecstatic. "Look how handsome he is, so elegant, and such gorgeous legs." I agreed and also marveled at his beautiful voice and perfect musicianship in this difficult role.

Away from the magic of opera or the great joys I found at concerts (Jascha Heifetz or Vladimir Horowitz, Artur Rubinstein, Nathan Milstein in their prime), my life became increasingly aimless. I wondered if material security was not too high a price to pay for a life-style that gave me none of the things I really yearned for. I was deceived by a husband who no longer cared to be my lover, who was not eager to participate in any of my intellectual interests, and who would not consider having another child, something I asked for repeatedly over the years. I had to admit that he was right on this last point. Gene was hardly ever with me; what kind of future would this be for the children? I began to wonder if a divorce would harm them.

In fact, I was living alone with the children and the governess who had replaced Nanny Buchler. After ten years, it was hard to admit that my marriage had fallen apart, my lofty dreams about love and togetherness were destroyed. I had turned into a superficial, frustrated woman leading a meaningless life.

I stayed home with frequent migraines and no longer went out with Gene even when he was around. During February 1954, on my way to a skiing vacation in Davos, I again found another woman's clothing in our Paris apartment as well as an amorous note to Gene signed "Henriette." I had a long talk with my sister, opening up for the first time to anyone about my unhappiness and about a possible divorce. Gaby, who lived in Paris, was understanding and supportive. Like everyone else, she knew of Gene's numerous adventures and was furious at him, but she told me I should think about it some more and decide what was best for me.

I went back to New York troubled and vacillating. I spent days in bed or walking in the park with my beautiful setter, Banco, who had replaced the Airedale. I was just thirty years old and, except for my children, I was convinced that my life was a failure.

2

George's Background

George rarely spoke about his childhood. I asked him many times about his home and about his schooling, but he evaded the subjects. I did know that he went to school in Montreal. The school was a strict English-style institution, and on weekends the boys relieved the harsh discipline by playing rough games in the street near their homes.

During a speech to young singers in 1968, George told this story, which he had told me many times as if it were the only important event of his first fifteen years:

> I grew up like a typical Canadian boy interested in hockey and sports of that kind. There was no special musical background in my family, except for a wind-up Victrola. My mother had been a music lover in her youth and had heard Caruso. We had a number of records and I knew these records backwards before I could talk.
>
> A big change came into my life in 1931, I was just a young boy then [eleven years old] and that was the year the Metropolitan started broadcasting on Saturday afternoon. When I

heard my first opera I was simply overwhelmed. Now this caused an enormous upheaval in the neighborhood because I was a cherished left-wing player on the neighborhood hockey team on Saturday afternoons. I stopped going to the hockey matches, I was listening to the opera. Can you imagine what this did to my reputation? I was strictly a "gook." But I persisted, I read up on opera, I read all the stories, I knew all about the singers, I wrote out for autographed pictures.

George told me that in this way he received an operatic education. He heard and remembered all the stars of the 1930s. On other days he played baseball or went skating in the winter, but on Saturdays he always listened to the radio. His childhood was sad and lonely. He did not seem to fit in with anyone.

Once he was invited for the weekend to New Jersey by an aunt on his father's side. There was no extra room and he slept on the couch in the living room. During the night he woke up with an uncontrollable urge to go to the bathroom. When he saw a large plant standing in a corner, he relieved himself in it. The plant died within days and his aunt, guessing the truth, never invited him again. But he still laughed when he told me about this years later, hiding his lasting bitterness about his family's lack of affection and support.

He had a large family in Canada and shortly after our marriage he introduced me proudly to over twenty cousins, tall handsome young men and their attractive wives who were all the offspring of short Russian émigré parents. I attributed this miraculous transformation to the virtues of the North American soil. George's parents, Louis Burnstein and Bertha Berdichevsky, came independently from Russia at the beginning of the century. Louis had first settled in the United States, in New Jersey, and became an American citizen in 1911. After he met Bertha in New York, working like himself in millinery, they decided to go to Montreal where she had many relatives also in the clothing business. They married there in 1919. Although they were not very religious, they were married by a rabbi, partly because they were deeply aware of their Jewish background and partly out of consideration for Bertha's devout Montreal relatives. Louis was thirty-nine and Bertha twenty-nine. They were good workers and soon they had their own thriving millinery business, The Mabelle Hat Company.

Their only child, George was born on May 30, 1920, in Montreal. He was a big healthy baby, according to existing photographs, obviously well groomed and well fed by his mother and a housekeeper who helped her.

There are no more photographs of the young George after the baby pictures. As he grew into a boisterous young boy, his parents' business became less and less successful while at the same time their health became more precarious. They lost all their savings in the crash of 1929, and by 1935 the doctor told them that Louis would not survive if they remained in the harsh Canadian climate.

They sold the business and with what little money they had bought a car, engaged a driver, and after a short stop in New York to visit Bertha's brother and nephews, they drove to California.

They settled in Hollywood. George was fifteen years old and, thanks to the excellent Canadian schools, he was able to skip a grade in Hollywood High, where he graduated when he was seventeen. He told me that there were many great-looking girls in his class, one of them Lana Turner. "I was very tall and terribly skinny and burning to ask her out, but I had no money at all and could not even offer her a soda, and she never looked at me." He had to be content with going to the movies, where he could watch gorgeous girls to his heart's content. He went as often as he could, and when I met him he could still remember the names of all the stars and supporting actors of the 1930s.

At about that time, a neighbor heard him sing in the shower and told his mother that she thought he had a beautiful voice and should take singing lessons. George was thrilled by this advice. He remembered: "To my amazement when my voice changed it sounded like something serious, something whereby people would say 'my goodness, he should sing, he should study.' For me to study opera which I already was in love with was just about the most wondrous and miraculous thing that could ever have happened and that is just the way it was."

At first George took lessons from a good baritone, Nate Stewart, who was recommended by a friend. To pay for his lessons he worked at a fruit market, and years later he could still pick out a good melon.

In the fall of 1937 he matriculated at Los Angeles City College where he went for two years. There he auditioned for the director of the opera workshop, Dr. Hugo Strelitzer. This was the very first opera workshop in America. Dr. Strelitzer, who had fled the Nazi persecution in Germany, was able to bring his vast experience to young singers. Forty-three years later, three years before his death, Hugo wrote to me of his meeting with George:

He was one of more than a hundred students who came to audition for me and qualify for acceptance in this new unit. When he sang for me he was terribly nervous—who isn't? He was so terribly eager to be accepted and he sang like most young and unexperienced auditioners a song that was too high for his voice, and he cracked at the top and felt miserable. He asked me if he could audition a second time, go to some room, practice some more and then sing again for me. (Then and there I felt his burning ambition and some of the inner drive that has characterized his entire career.) Something in this young boy moved me. I liked him at first sight and felt his great sincerity. After some time he sang again for me with the same results. He cracked on the top notes but revealed in his middle range and in the lower part of his voice some extraordinary quality— a natural and God-given velvet quality that could lead this youngster to untold heights. So, I accepted him in the opera workshop.

When he came to us, he was, musically speaking, absolutely untrained, without any musical experience during the years of his childhood, not playing any instrument, no musical and artistic environment in his parental home that could have developed his innate musical instincts. As a matter of fact, when he sang in our chorus he sweated blood to keep up with the rest of the group. He sang at that time—in order to make some money—at the WPA Music Project in the chorus—and a few of the chorus members who later sang with George in my Hollywood Bowl Chorus told me how hard George had to work to learn music up to that date totally unknown to him.

In other words, George had to work from scratch—the gods did not drop the musical "goodies" into his lap.

But something else happened in those first few years when he was at the opera workshop—he outgrew his young adulthood and became a thinking human being, with an ever growing love for the tasks set for him and a genuine love for the music to which he devoted every bit of his life. He was ambitious as all talented men are—but with him there was more than that ambition—it was an almost *missionary zeal* to build and develop his many talents and setting for himself the highest goals.

His first roles in our opera productions were small but he grew very fast into bigger and then even leading parts in which he revealed an amazing sense for the stage and a dramatic instinct that was in his blood and cannot be taught.

I believe that those years with me at City College laid all the foundations on which years later a man named George London conquered the musical and operatic world.

It can be argued that Hugo wrote with hindsight because he knew all about George's career when he wrote this letter. But having had a long operatic career in Germany before he came to California in the early 1930s, Hugo knew what he was talking about. He did teach George an invaluable repertoire, music, languages, and voice, and George studied with him for close to eight years. He told me that he was immensely indebted to Hugo Strelitzer and the opera workshop.

In 1968 George recalled:

I sort of became the local baritone, the local bass-baritone around L.A., and lo and behold the glorious moment arrived when I made my debut, that is, when I made my first solo appearance before a public. It was in a production of *The Vagabond King* by Rudolf Friml. It opened on Christmas night 1939 and I had been assigned the role of the Herald of Burgundy who had a short but energetic scene in which he comes in with a huge broadsword and announces to François Villon and his followers that the Duke of Burgundy is just going to burn the hell out of them unless they surrender. This is all done very forcefully with all of the power and conviction of a nineteen-year-old.

By the way, I got interested in makeup at this time because I had a beard and a moustache which had been put on by the makeup artist, and from that day on I realized the importance of makeup because I was transformed from a callow youth of nineteen into somebody with a beard and a moustache looking at least twenty.

I entered and I planted my broadsword firmly down onto the stage and I thundered out my lines and then I had to leave. Now, in order to leave I had to take my sword with me but what had happened, this is God's honest truth, the sword went into a crack between two planks and I couldn't get it out. It took at least twenty seconds to get it out and that seems like two hours when you are in a spot like that. Of course the audience collapsed in gales of laughter, but this was the baptism of fire because it prepared me for all the horrors that would happen to me in opera later on.

That same year I was demoted but there was a financial reason for it. I was better paid for singing in the chorus at the Hollywood Bowl than I was for the solo job and it gave me wonderful experience. I sang in the chorus of *Prince Igor,* I sang in *Aïda,* I sang in *Carmen.* As one of the priests in *Aïda,* I remember waiting for the moment of my entrance and the part of the basso, the part of Ramfis, was sung by a young American bass by the name of Douglas Beaty. He was a tall imposing man; he had a fine voice, and with the kind of a studied bon-homie that an arrived singer sometimes displays toward a tyro he said, "What is your ambition?" and I said, "My ambition is one day to sing the title role of *Boris Godunov,*" and he replied rather wistfully, "Ah! that is the ambition of us all."

Little did I realize at that time that approximately ten years later in Vienna, I would indeed have the honor and the thrill of singing *Boris Godunov.*

While he was at City College and for a long time after, George was in financial difficulties. After the family arrived in California, his father never worked again. His mother took in sewing and various other jobs to keep them going, and George was forever grateful to her. She told him that she stayed with his father because of him, the son, and thus laid the foundation of what he called "my Jewish guilt feelings," which he carried through life. He had done his bar mitzvah in Hebrew while still living among his more religious relatives in Montreal and would retain, in spite of all events, a solid belief in God and a pride in being Jewish.

Perhaps this had something to do with his absolute dedication to his work from the very beginning. He set out to "make it" against terrible odds: he had to take lessons, had to support his parents from the time he was eighteen, had to get more musical experience and at the same time accept whatever paying job he could get. He never forgot his struggles and later did everything possible to provide help for other young singers.

He resented having so little money most of all because he could not afford dates with girls. He felt awkward, too thin and unattractive, and since he could not take his date to a decent restaurant or pick her up in a car, he felt that he did not have a chance with girls who appealed to him.

He was most self-conscious about his ill-fitting clothes and his somewhat protruding lower teeth and resented his parents' neglect of this problem when he was younger. With his first sizable check he bought a new suit and later had orthodonture as soon as he could afford it.

However, he never wavered in his determination, and after ten years of struggle, in October 1947, he wrote to his parents: "I have something different and unusual to offer as a singing actor. I feel so certain that within a year or two I will be in the Met and in a position to make a real career for myself."

During the ten years between his audition for Strelitzer and the writing of this letter, George developed from an ignorant albeit earnest young man into a knowledgeable, cultured, and accomplished singer. When the opportunity was finally given to him, he was perfectly prepared.

It is not unusual to take this long to become a major artist. To be an important opera star it is necessary to combine so many assets that it takes years to perfect them. Of course, to start with, the voice has to have a specially beautiful timbre, preferably of a velvety or dramatic or bell-like or stirring quality that will distinguish it from all others. The voice has to be uniformly well produced throughout the range, high, middle, and low notes alike. This alone often takes years of study. The singer has to be able to project this voice; he or she has to have a perfect knowledge of the words and music of a number of operatic roles in their original languages. The singer also has to be able to act and to perform these roles in a way that will make a strong emotional impact on the audience. Then there is a physical aspect, a charisma that is inborn, but years of practice and an inner faith in the self will magnify these to such an extent that this singer will project from the stage and reach out to the audience in a powerful way.

Even with God-given gifts, great singers do not happen by chance. George was determined to work to be successful. He did not want a "career," he wanted to be a great singer. But he also wanted to be a great musician, a well-rounded artist. He worked out in gyms to develop his narrow, lanky frame and grew into a powerful six-foot-two young man with a dashing figure. He decided that his name would be an impediment in the world of opera and changed it first to Burnson in October 1942, then to George London on February 21, 1949. The second time was at the advice of Arthur Judson, president of Columbia Artists Management, who thought "Burnson" was not glamorous. The only reason he chose London was because it sounded good and Judson approved.

In order to survive, George took any kind of job. Because he had no money for a car, he would take buses in the early mornings to get to the movie studios in the hope of getting work as an extra. It happened that he was hired for *Casablanca,* and can be seen for a second singing the "Marseillaise" in late, late show replays. He toured for some months in the chorus of the Ice Follies and fell in love with a graceful figure skater. But he became so ill with bronchitis that he had to quit. He performed in a number of musical shows, which he enjoyed and which gave him much-needed stage experience. Ultimately he knew that he had to get to the East Coast. In the 1940s and to this day, New York was the center of classical music. No one could hope to launch a big career without the help of a prominent manager. And prominent managers worked out of New York.

Without money, his only hope to get there was to be a member of the cast of a show that could successfully tour the United States and make it to New York. George's preference went to opera, but he also loved lighter music and admired particularly the American musical theater. In his recitals he often included some Broadway songs, for which he had a special affinity.

George recalled in a speech in 1968:

> I came to New York in 1946 in a touring company of *The Desert Song*. Don't assume that I played the lead, nothing of the kind. I played the second lead, an Arab chief called Ali-Ben-Ali, and I had one song. I did pretty well with it, I got good notices, and when we came into New York I got very good notices though the show itself was not so well received. The headline in *The New York Times* was "Deserted Song." That gives some idea of the production and the condition it was in after six months playing one-night stands. Arthur Judson [the powerful director of Columbia Artists Management] happened to hear me in this performance. God knows whatever took him to the City Center to hear *The Desert Song* but he did and he signed me to a contract with Columbia Artists.

This represented an enormous step forward. George was no longer alone, begging for a possible engagement. He now had his own manager and was backed by a large and well-established organization, working for him.

But at first engagements were slow to come, and his father's brother, Nat Burnstein, lent him some money against future earnings. George told me, "Uncle Nat was the only person who had confidence in my future and the only one willing to help me." No one else ever helped.

Thanks to the loan, he was able to take lessons with the well-known Italian teacher, Enrico Rosati, and get coaching lessons with Peter Adler, another refugee from the Nazis, a conductor with great experience in a wide repertoire.

Little by little, there were some sporadic appearances with orchestras, like a Verdi *Requiem* in Dallas conducted by Antal Dorati on November 25, 1946—George's first important engagement. He received a good review and wrote to his parents, "The review should do me no harm. Columbia should be pleased, since they attached a lot of importance to this appearance. There was a small fire under the stage which the critic mentioned, but I sat through the whole thing without realizing anything was wrong. The other soloists all smelled the smoke. I smelled nothing. I guess I was too absorbed in the music."

Toni Dorati remembers that he had engaged a well-known Hungarian bass to sing the part and took George when the Hungarian could not get his visa in time. He was so impressed and attracted by the young American that he did not have the heart to send him back even after the Hungarian arrived after all. He did not regret it, for the concert was a great success and we have remained close friends to this day.

George also sang a few recitals with the Community Concerts, a part of Columbia Artists that arranged concert series throughout the United States. These concerts were sponsored and financed by local organizations that wanted to increase the musical life in their town on a nonprofit basis. Leading citizens formed an association and raised money by subscription. Then Columbia Concerts came and sold a package or series to the Community Concerts Association in each city. Because most cities did not have very large budgets, Columbia sold them a package of three or four events, including well-known names together with talented newcomers. This was a way to introduce new artists to the concert circuit.

George remembered that before he was given a contract with Columbia Artists, Arthur Judson

> had just signed up a young tenor by the name of Mario Lanza and he didn't know what to do with him at the time. And he also had a young soprano by the name of Frances Yeend from Vancouver, a girl with a glorious voice. Somebody in the corporation got the bright idea to put these three youngsters together, and they dubbed us the Bel Canto Trio. We toured the U.S., Canada, and Mexico for one entire season. I couldn't tell how many concerts we did, I could not believe it possible, but when you are that young and that ambitious, nothing is too difficult. At the end of that tour Mario went into the movies, he was snapped up immediately. Frances went on to other

operatic activities, and I decided that the time had come to get down to serious work on my operatic career because in truth up to this moment I had sung only sporadic performances of opera though I had had quite a good deal of experience on the stage.

The success of these talented young people with exceptionally beautiful voices was extraordinary, and to this day people who heard them cannot forget these concerts.

George had met Mario Lanza at Rosati's studio. They became good friends and remained in touch for many years although their lives took different roads. During the tour with the Bel Canto Trio, George at last made some money, although as the baritone and least known of the three he was also paid the least, two hundred and fifty dollars per performance. The three had great times and much fun together and enjoyed their success, yet all of them knew this was just a first step.

George recounted:

So [in 1948] I sought out a Russian bass-baritone by the name of George Doubrovsky. He was a younger colleague of Chaliapin and he was a product of a school of acting which was typical of the Russian lyric theater and also of the Moscow Art Theater. I went to Doubrovsky and with him I studied *Boris Godunov,* I studied Scarpia in *Tosca* and also Méphistophélès in *Faust* and I worked with him every movement and every gesture. I knew exactly what the people working with me were going to do. I was ready in these parts. I was ready to work the next day if it was necessary.

One of the parts that I studied prior to leaving for Europe was the part of Escamillo in *Carmen,* and this was a less successful venture. I went to a Spanish ballet master to study the toreador. It always struck me that most Escamillos were decidedly un-Spanish in their deportment and I wanted to be authentic. Well, my ballet master got carried away with this; he had never worked with a singer before so he showed me how to walk and to gesture like a Spaniard, like a bullfighter, and this was all to the good. However, he studded the aria with so many leaps, lunges, twists and turns that at the end of each session I was a candidate for an oxygen tent.

When I sang Escamillo for the first time in Vienna, my Carmen was the distinguished Italian-American soprano Dusolina Giannini and she didn't hesitate to tell me, a younger colleague, that I was making my life unnecessarily difficult. She told me to cut out a lot of the business and stand there and sing and think it and not carry on like a crazy man. So I cut out a lot of the calisthenics and as a result my vocal performance improved considerably.

George was well aware that he would get ahead only if he went to Europe and auditioned for opera houses there, primarily in Germany and Austria. In the 1940s, even more than now, opera singers could really get experience in their craft only by being engaged by one of the numerous opera houses in Germany, where a performance is given every night throughout the year. Every large city in Germany has an opera house. Singers have to perform several times a week in a variety of repertoire. Moreover, George was convinced that he would get a good offer for principal parts at the Metropolitan Opera only if he was a success in Europe.

So, once again he borrowed money from Uncle Nat, a thousand dollars, which he added to two thousand dollars that he had saved, and sailed for Europe in June 1949.

He landed in Paris, and as George remembered in a speech to students:

> I called an agent in Vienna who had been recommended to me by his brother, who was an accompanist in the U.S., an agent by the name of Martin Taubman. I called him and I said, "I know you have heard about me from your brother. I am in Paris and I would like to sing for you. Shall I come to Vienna?" He said, "No, stay in Paris, I am going to be there in two days."
>
> So Martin Taubman came to Paris. I auditioned for him and he evidently liked the audition. He said, "The Vienna Opera is doing a series of guest appearances in Brussels currently and I suggest that we get on the train tomorrow and go over. Let's

see if I can arrange an audition for you. I can't promise a thing but I think it is not a big trip and there is not a great risk."

The next day Taubman and I went to Brussels, and we went into the Palais des Beaux Arts where the company was giving the performance and into a rehearsal room where they were rehearsing *The Marriage of Figaro*.

By 1949, many of us had heard about the fabulous Mozart ensemble of the postwar Vienna State Opera. The big opera house had been bombed out in the closing days of the war in 1945. But no sooner had the last shot been fired than the company moved into the small eight-hundred-seat Theater-an-der-Wien, which was famous for the fact that Beethoven's *Fidelio* was first given there, as well as many of the first performances of the famous operettas by Franz Lehár. Because several of the great singers of the eastern countries fled ahead of the Red Army and some Austrian and German singers of the highest quality were in Vienna and couldn't get out, an ensemble was formed at that time, one of the greatest operatic ensembles in the history of Vienna and certainly in the history of the operatic world.

It was a rehearsal of just such an ensemble that I witnessed that June afternoon in 1949, and it was a revelation for me. I couldn't imagine that Mozart could be done that way. I was just bowled over, enchanted, and when the rehearsal was over, Mr. Taubman got up and went over to Karl Böhm, the great conductor, and he said, "I have a young American baritone here, I know you are very tired but could you hear him?" Well, Böhm indeed was tired but he said, "All right, I will hear him."

In the meantime, the artists had left the rehearsal room and I started to sing. The first thing I sang was the Toreador song and I had sung about ten measures of it when the door opened and all of those great singers of the Vienna Opera ensemble came back into the room and stood in a semicircle facing me. When I got through the aria, they all applauded. Taubman said that he was certain that no matter how many years I sang I would never receive a greater compliment, and that was true.

George was asked to perform one aria after another and was feeling rather good but couldn't help noticing that Dr. Franz Salmhofer, the director of the Vienna Opera, who sat next to Karl Böhm, kept shaking his head. He became seriously worried and wondered what could be wrong. "It can't be that bad if the other singers like me," he thought. When the audition was over, he asked Taubman about this and he replied: "Salmhofer was just shaking his head and mumbling, 'What a voice, what a voice,' and they are offering you a contract with the Vienna Opera for four months starting with the opening of their season in September."

George was incredibly excited and wrote to his parents: "This is the first time in Mr. Taubman's memory that an American singer was offered an engagement simply on the basis of one audition. I am the only American singer who will sing with the Vienna Opera in the five years since the war."

As soon as his contract was signed, George went to Vienna and settled down in the cozy Pension Schneider, not far from the Theater-an-der-Wien where he was going to perform. He started intensive coaching of all the roles he was scheduled to sing in the forthcoming season and took a crash course in German, which he did not know at all.

One of his favorite stories of this time was about a short vacation he took in Salzburg some weeks before the Vienna opening. Feeling good about the future he decided to have a few days of rest. With his friend Bobby Halmi, he drove the short distance from Vienna. The two young men were determined to have a good time and went to a well-known nightclub. In no time at all, they made the acquaintance of a pretty blond. To impress the girl, Bobby, who was acting as interpreter, boasted about George's future at the Vienna Opera. When the girl expressed some doubts, Bobby went over to the orchestra and convinced them to play for George. Then George got up and gave a stentorian and impassioned rendition of Tosti's "Mattinata." There was tremendous applause, the girl was overcome with admiration, and the evening was a huge success.

Encouraged by their good fortune, the two young men decided to go back to the same restaurant on the following day. They met another pretty blond and enacted the same scenario. However, when George launched into the first phrases of an equally fervent "Mattinata," he saw to his horror that the girl from the previous night was sitting at another table with a huge grin on her face.

These youthful pranks eased some of the tension that was building up as the date for his debut approached.

In 1968 George remembered in his speech:

> I made my debut at the Vienna State Opera in September 1949, as Amonasro in *Aïda,* a role which I had never sung in my life before, but since my repertoire sounded pretty sparse at the time that they had asked for it, I just mentioned it as a part I knew. And the director said, "Marvelous, we need an Amonasro right at the beginning of the season. It will be your debut role." I had no stage rehearsal, I had one short rehearsal on the rehearsal stage in a room, and here I was making my debut with one of the great opera companies in the world.
>
> Nobody knew the truth except a few close friends that I had made. Well, during the second act, there were some traffic problems, the chorus and I did not have the same idea about where we were going some of the time, but the way I behaved you would have thought that the chorus was wrong.
>
> One of the old-timers of the Vienna Opera, a character singer who had been there many many years, came backstage afterwards, took me aside and said, "You dog, you could only have done that with your American nerves."
>
> But I knew my way around the stage, and the stage experience that I had had in the past, even though it was not in that particular role, came to my assistance.
>
> During that first season in Vienna, I became sort of the darling of the fourth gallery. I sang quite a variety of parts. I sang Méphistophélès and I did the four villains in *The Tales of Hoffmann*. I had a wonderful experience with that. In the Venetian act, I had rehearsed with a simply beautiful and wonderful singer by the name of Sena Jurinac, a distinguished artist, slim and lovely. I rehearsed thoroughly with her and the night of the performance, I sang my aria, then the orchestra comes in with two brisk chords. I turned to my beautiful soprano and in came a small heavy cruiser dressed up like a woman, the

fattest soprano I had ever seen in my life! Nobody had told me about her. Sena had gotten sick and there she was. It really almost threw me.

On the recommendation of Martin Taubman, who became his manager and wanted George to meet some of his compatriots in Vienna, he was invited to dinner by Henry Pleasants and his wife Ginny. Henry was then liaison officer between the U.S. High Commission and the Austrian government and musical correspondent for *The New York Times*. Henry and George discussed singing and opera, and George (who had yet to make his debut) proceeded to talk in detail about his future plans. He spoke of *Don Giovanni, Boris Godunov,* all the parts he was going to sing, and about "the voice" that he had been given. He always spoke of "the voice" in the third person. When he was gone, Henry, irked but impressed, turned to Ginny and said: "The cocky little bastard! You know, he might just do it all."

Through Henry he met other Americans working in Vienna, most of them journalists. George loved to talk politics with them and entertain them with jokes. Henry, Ginny, Simon Bourgin, and Franz Spelman witnessed his amazing success and became close friends. The entire American press corps attended his performances and applauded their young compatriot.

In November 1949 he gave his first recital in Vienna. It was a triumph. He wrote to his parents: "I've never in my life experienced anything like the applause, the shouting and the stamping of feet that I received at the end of my program. I had to take so many bows I lost count of them."

But the success did not corrupt him and never would. Again, he wrote to his parents: "I can't really believe that I deserve that kind of success and ovation. This is not false modesty on my part. It's just that my demands upon myself are even much greater, and I am very, very far from being able to sit back and be satisfied with it all. In any event I am very happy and very fortunate and feel even more the need to work and study and constantly improve." George recalled this period in program notes to the *Boris Godunov* recording that he wrote in 1964:

Everywhere I went my steps were dogged by autograph hunters. I had quickly become somewhat of a sensation. It was this unusual state of affairs which gave me the courage to request a performance of *Boris Godunov*. It was pointed out to me that priority in this opera went to either of two distinguished senior colleagues of the company, Ludwig Weber and Paul Schöffler. I waited patiently, though without much hope, but early in December I was called in by the director and told that on Christmas night I would sing my first Boris.

In those early, critical days I was surely protected by a most indulgent Providence. I sang my first Boris with only one orchestra rehearsal and little help from a stage director whose name I have managed to forget. I was honored at the performance by the presence of the American minister (later ambassador) Walter Donnelly, and his staff, as well as the entire American press corps. Vienna was then still occupied by the Four Powers. Someone quipped that, had the Russians decided that night to take over the city, there would have been no Americans around to report on it. As I made my lengthy entrance in the Coronation Scene, I saw that the two front rows of the Theater-an-der-Wien were filled with Russian officers in white dress uniforms. After the performance, a group of Russian officers and civilians came backstage and congratulated me enthusiastically in Russian. They seemed chagrined when I explained, through an interpreter, that my knowledge of their language was pretty well confined to the Pushkin libretto.

It was after this performance that George decided that someday he would sing *Boris Godunov* in Moscow.

His life in Vienna was not restricted to opera. With success on the stage came also social rewards. At long last he could live comfortably. He rented an apartment in a stately private house, he bought a small car; above all, he could afford to take out girls. Gone were the days when he had trouble finding a date. The Viennese loved the tall dark American, and he certainly returned their feelings. The years of study and yearning gave way to an explosion of joie de vivre. He had an active social life, made many friends, plunged into a number of love affairs. Eventually he settled down with an attractive young soprano from the Vienna Opera with whom he had a long relationship. Very soon he acquired a command of German; he could not only speak with a perfect Austrian accent but could also imitate the Viennese dialect.

But George never forgot his career and made sure that he was always ready and prepared for his performances. He recalled during a master class:

It was during my second season at the Vienna Opera [in 1950] that Rudolf Bing heard me. He heard me in *The Tales of Hoffmann* and in *Boris Godunov*, which I sang on successive nights. It is the kind of thing you do only when you are very young. And he invited me to join the Metropolitan Opera for the opening-night performance of *Aïda* of the season 1951–52. So as it turned out Amonasro was my good-luck role; it was my debut role in Vienna and also at the Metropolitan. The great Italian tenor Mario del Monaco made his debut that same night and the soprano was the incomparable Zinka Milanov.

After his debut, the critic Virgil Thomson hailed George as "the greatest singing actor of our times." He had become an undisputed opera star. He was a little over thirty-one years old.

After two seasons of adulation from the Austrian public, the long-awaited debut at the Metropolitan Opera came almost as an anticlimax. George knew the exhilarating feeling when a house full of people applauds you. He had already enjoyed that extraordinary confirmation of success.

Yet most of all, he needed the approval of his parents, and this performance at the Met provided the occasion. They knew of his triumph in Vienna, and by then he had had his first success in Bayreuth, but those were remote places and vague notions for them. Now he made sure that they would see their son with their own eyes on the stage of the most famous opera house in the United States, and not just in a small part but in one of the principal roles of the opera.

He arranged for his parents' trip to New York for the opening, November 13, 1951, and there is a picture of them with George after the performance. He stands clearly elated towering over the older couple, who are dressed in stylish new clothes. His mother is wearing a corsage of orchids, the final proof of affluence. He is no longer the lanky youth of earlier photos but a well-balanced, broad-chested young man, obviously at ease in his well-cut tuxedo and eager to show his good fortune to the world.

At last he had shown his parents that the long years of work and deprivation were not in vain and that his confidence in his own abilities was more than youthful dreams. It was certainly a special moment of bliss for him.

But this feeling could not last, for he was driven by the same competitive spirit that had gotten him this far. He took a sublet apartment for the duration of his Met engagement, and between performances he proceeded to work to prepare for forthcoming re-citals and for the parts he was to sing in New York the following years: Don Giovanni, Boris Godunov, the Count in *Figaro,* Scarpia in *Tosca*.

At this time George signed his first recording contract with Columbia Records and made his first solo recording, always a great event for a young artist. And he signed an agreement with an artists' public relations management firm, a step considered essential to keep the name of George London in the news as much as possible.

During the next few years he sang all his favorite roles at the Met in New York as well as on the Met tour and became one of the leading bass-baritones of the company.

As one of the Met's regular subscribers, I had several oppor-tunities to hear him again after the first *Don Giovanni*. Each time I was bewitched by the velvet voice with the seemingly boundless power and impressed by the forceful elegant acting.

However, it did not occur to me that I would meet him. In spite of my interest in opera and my close friendship with the Cha-liapins, I did not know any of the current opera stars and was content to admire them from afar.

Years later when I told George that I was sorry we had not met during my trip to California in 1941, he answered, "It would have been meaningless, I was not ready for you."

3

Our Meeting
and Courtship

"La ci darem la mano
La mi dirai di si."
—*Don Giovanni*

We met on Sunday, April 24, 1954. By midday I was still in bed, feeling sorry for myself. Gene as usual was away, and I was determined to spend the day at home with *The New York Times* and my setter Banco at my feet. My mother, who lived just a block away, arrived in a chic black suit and bright blue hat, as always perfectly groomed, and determined to force me to get up.

"How come you're still in bed? You know you're going to Lydia Chaliapin's Easter party with me." When I answered that I did not feel like going, she was upset. "You never want to go anywhere with me, but you always tell me that you like Lydia so much. We never miss her Russian Easter party. She makes beautiful colored eggs and great *kulitsch*. There will be my friends but also all the young students. I understand that Leo Taubman, the accompanist, has promised to bring George London."

It was difficult to resist my mother's arguments. She had an imperial bearing and a matching temperament, and in a clash of our personalities, she almost always won. We were close and I adored her, but I made most major decisions without consulting her because I knew that if she disagreed I would have a terrible time convincing her. She had guessed that my marriage was far from successful and that this was the reason for my gloomy disposition. However, I avoided discussing my problems with her, for I did not want to upset her. In fact, there was nothing she could say to relieve my anguish and so I decided to keep silent. I was not going to fight about an ordinary Sunday afternoon party and, after all, maybe she was right and I should go out and meet new people.

I dressed quickly in an elegant outfit that I had brought back from Paris. All these years later, I remember it exactly: it was a black sheath with a white satin bolero, knotted tight under the chest, which showed off my small waist. It was a beautiful day and we had no trouble getting a taxi, which took us from my Park Avenue apartment to Lydia's at Seventh Avenue and Fifty-fifth Street, very close to Carnegie Hall. At the entrance Lydia greeted me affectionately and said at once: "Norechka, you must meet George London!" She took my arm and directed me toward the dining room.

At the same moment Leo Taubman, who was George's accompanist and Martin Taubman's brother, turned to George, who was eating a succession of caviar sandwiches. "There's a girl, quite a dish, who just arrived," he said. "You have to meet her."

As I walked through the crowded living room, I could see George standing in the next room. His ebullient personality seemed to fill the room. He was wearing a light-gray suit, a blue shirt, and a rather wild tie. His hair was black, very shiny, and slightly wavy. He was smooth-shaven, his skin slightly tanned (he later told me it was from the floodlights). As I entered we stared at each other. I caught a look of admiration in his dark-brown eyes and for a fleeting moment I felt captivated by his radiance.

We were introduced and I remember complimenting him on a wonderful performance of his I had seen recently. He seemed pleased and we exchanged a number of pleasant remarks. I was enchanted by his speaking voice, which did not have the booming low sound typical of bass singers but had more of a caressing baritonal quality, as if each measure invited you to a dance. I tore myself away, thinking that I should not monopolize this important guest, and drifted toward the living room to greet friends. All the young hopeful singers present were dying to speak to the successful star; perhaps some advice, some special touch would rub off.

I noticed that George spoke very kindly to everyone, but within minutes he was again at my side and did not leave me for the rest of his stay at the party. He sat next to me while we were eating, both of us having piled our plates full from the lavish buffet. I don't remember what we talked about. In the end he told me that, unfortunately, he had to leave early because he was going to join the Met tour and perform Don Giovanni the next night. But he hoped to see me again upon his return to New York.

After his departure, Lydia told me that everyone had noticed that George was attracted to me. I, too, had noticed and felt very flattered, but I dismissed any expectations, thinking that such a handsome man was bound to be a flirt and nothing more would happen, even though, in my anger with Gene, I was ready for an adventure. Two days later our maid announced that I had a call from Atlanta. I said, "I don't know anybody in Atlanta," but she said the party at the other end insisted on speaking to me. It was George. He said he wanted to see me, he would be in New York that weekend, could I have dinner with him? I agreed and on Friday I was waiting for him to pick me up, getting quite excited at the prospect of our date.

When I opened the door to him, he looked at me with delight. I was wearing high heels but from my five feet five inches I had to look up into his shining eyes. We decided to have dinner at Quo Vadis on East Sixty-third Street. For years afterward we went back there to celebrate the anniversaries of our first evening together.

It was a comfortable, very good restaurant with red-covered banquettes around the main room. We were seated at the right of the entrance and ordered our meal and some red wine. And after that I don't remember anything except that George, looking straight into my eyes with great intensity, spoke on and on. He talked about himself, how he had now reached a comfortable stage in his career but he did not feel happy alone. He was ready to make a permanent commitment. The woman he would marry would have to be attractive, she would have to be a lady and know how to get along in the world, she would have to love and understand music and opera, she would have to love children. In return he would love and worship her and give her everything he possibly could every day of his life.

I thought that either he was the greatest master at courting since Casanova, or perhaps, just perhaps, the most extraordinary person I had ever met. My experience with postwar society, to say nothing of Gene, made me skeptical, and I laughed when he told me he had thought of me constantly since our meeting that Sunday.

I was quite ready to consent to a flirtation but I certainly had not thought of anything more serious. Here was this man, immensely attractive and persuasive, who was practically proposing to spend the rest of his life with me. I felt as if I had had too much to drink.

Still, we enjoyed each other's company so much that we did not feel like going home after dinner. He suggested we go to Upstairs at the Downstairs, a nightclub in fashion at the time. This turned out to be the only time we ever went to a nightclub together in our life. We sat in a crowded room in total darkness, listening to performers singing love songs or reciting poetry. George took my hand and, at the touch of his incredibly soft skin, I was lost. We held hands for a long, long time.

Still we could not part. He took me home to my Park Avenue apartment and I proposed he wait for me. I would get my setter and we could walk the dog together. We walked around the block again and again. It was my turn to talk. He knew from Leo Taubman that I was married. I told him about my life and my two precious little boys. He was a good, supportive listener. Suddenly it was nearly three o'clock, and reluctantly we said good-bye in front of the apartment house.

I got back home in a daze. What had happened to the down-to-earth unemotional person I had been just the day before? I was bewitched. In one evening George had unlocked a flow of emotions that I had carefully buried in my subconscious. Although I was profoundly moved, I thought it was still time to push these feelings back where they belonged and prevent my life from becoming incredibly complicated.

After that evening George confided to a friend that he was crazy about a girl he had just met, that he was possessed and dreamed about her all the time. He was desperate, for he was traveling all the time and was about to leave for Vienna, where he had many engagements. He had to see me once more before leaving and called me from Boston. "My last performance is *Tosca*," he told me. "This is a great opera for me, Scarpia is a wonderful role, and he dies at the end of the second act, so I'll be free early. It's our only chance to see each other again. The next day I have to leave for Europe." In spite of my misgivings, I did not seriously hesitate to meet him. I was starved for attention, flattered by the urgency in his voice. After all, I reasoned, nothing had happened; furthermore, he was leaving, so that would be the end of it.

It was a short date but long enough for us to find out how much we meant to each other after only two evenings together. In spite of the explosive character of our first date, I had concluded that it might have been a one-time event. I had little confidence in men's sincerity. I was not prepared for the wave of passionate feelings that engulfed both of us when we met after *Tosca*. We promised to write and hoped to meet in Europe, for I was going to France in June, first to Paris and then to a rented villa in Deauville for the summer. We parted with a passionate kiss full of promises and many questions.

We started a correspondence. He wrote beautifully, in a large artistic handwriting with every letter well formed, typical of his outgoing and generous nature. His letters told about his performances, his life in Vienna, his friends over there, and his desire to show all of this to me. I had to tear the letters up, for I did not want to leave them around although, as usual, Gene was mostly absent and seemed to be relieved whenever I was busy. Otherwise I did not yet feel particularly guilty about my romance. Rather I felt somewhat proud that I had a distant admirer and was carrying on an illicit correspondence with him.

In June, as usual, the household left for Paris; the boys were now nine and seven, and we had to wait for the end of the school year. We had rented a summer house in Deauvville and after two weeks in Paris, we moved in with Sasha, our maid, and the faithful Banco. Gene made a brief appearance in Paris, but did not get involved in the tedious transportation of the family to the seashore. He had "urgent business" in New York.

I received George's letters *poste restante* at the post office. He wrote that he would have some free time in August and wanted to visit me. I answered that it would be fine as Gene was away, but that I could not meet him in Deauville where I knew too many people. However, there was an adjoining resort on the Normandy coast called Trouville-sur-Mer where I could reserve a room for him in a nice hotel. He agreed with my suggestion—we were going to see each other again after three months of separation.

I became very agitated at the idea of seeing him again. How would it be, how would I feel?

In New York we were clearly infatuated with each other. I wondered if it was love or just a passing romance, and if it would deepen when we met in France. Perhaps we would wonder why we had been attracted to each other. Three months is a long time, and in the interim we had each gone about our lives as if nothing had happened. The letters had woven a tenuous thread between us.

So I drove to Trouville full of apprehension. He had come all the way from Austria to see me. Would the passion be there? Would he still like me? As I walked into the hotel lobby he looked at me. The piercing black eyes became soft light brown, and joy was dancing in them. I knew that he was thrilled to see me and for him at that moment, I was the most beautiful woman in the world. He had the ability to make me feel that way all the years we were together.

I was smitten all over again, and each day I waited impatiently for the time when I could be with him. We went to many restaurants along the coast and walked along the old port of Honfleur at sunset, which so many French painters have painted. Every hour we spent together seemed enchanted to both of us. But each time I had to go back to my household and the children and was unable to spend as much time with him as he wanted. He begged me to come to Switzerland and spend a week with him in a resort called Arosa at the end of August.

I was terribly tempted, but hesitated. First, it was difficult for me to get away without telling anyone; but above all, I was afraid. Obviously I was in love with him, but I felt this was still just an affair that I could forget someday. If I took this trip and lived with him, there might be no way back. I knew that I was not an adventuress looking for cheap thrills to spite my husband. My love for George was already much more than a mutual sexual attraction. I admired his generous spirit, his zest for life, his strength mixed with gentleness, and I was in awe of his single-minded drive for perfection in his art. It was clear to me that with such a man one did not have a "fling"; but I also wondered if I was ready to take the risks and make the sacrifices that a commitment would require.

Before George left Trouville, I told him I would try to come three weeks later. The arrangements were complicated. I told the maid that I was going to see a friend in the South of France and booked a plane flight to Zurich. Twice every day I changed my mind about going or not going and wrote wavering letters to George. Finally the day came, and of course I went. This was the first time in my life that I had ever taken a trip in hiding. I was extremely nervous and yet full of wild anticipation.

The plane landed in Zurich after a short, uneventful flight. Zurich is a busy airport. The passengers are herded into a huge baggage claim area, which is separated from the public room where friends and relatives await them by a large glass wall. As I was waiting for my suitcase, I could see a very tall, dark-haired man, in a navy trench coat with epaulettes on his broad shoulders, pacing back and forth in frenzied agitation. Apparently George was not sure I would come and was so worried that at first he did not see me. I waved and waved and finally he recognized me. A huge smile transformed his brooding face. Again the black eyes turned light brown. He greeted me with delight.

He took my luggage and escorted me to his sports car, an Austin-Healey convertible, which fortunately had the top up. It was pouring rain and I looked in vain for windows to roll up. This particular model had plastic windows that could be attached in case of need, but George did not think the weather warranted being closed in. I settled down in the seat next to him and we left for the hour-long drive up the mountains to Arosa. He drove like a lunatic, and I was speechless with fear at every curve. He turned to me and said: "You like *Boris Godunov,* don't you? I will sing the part of Boris for you," and proceeded to do so.

There I was being driven at one hundred miles an hour, in a downpour, getting wet and cold and being serenaded with an entire opera by a world-renowned singer who was probably catching pneumonia along with me.

I thought I must have been crazy to come. I was tempted to

jump out at the next stop sign, but he never slowed down. At last we were in Arosa and soon arrived at the hotel, where I warmed up and where a delicious meal lifted my spirits.

Since late August was the end of the season, we were almost alone in the hotel and I did not feel too conspicuous. After the initial uneasiness, our week together was a time of bliss. George loved me passionately and with gentleness and consideration. I discovered the meaning of love and affection and trust. I began to appreciate even more the many qualities of George's character, his generosity, his absolute honesty, his sensitivity, his sense of humor, and his extraordinary vitality, which he injected into everything around him.

We took long walks in the mountains, and the breathtaking sights seemed in harmony with our happiness. We talked about his life and his plans for the future. I discovered that everything he told me that first evening at Quo Vadis was true. George could never make small talk; rather, he spoke about feelings, about convictions, about disappointments. He believed in what he said and was prepared to go to great lengths if necessary to support his beliefs.

I became acquainted with his extraordinary self-discipline. Every day he set aside several hours to study his role in *Arabella* by Richard Strauss, which he was due to sing at the Metropolitan the following February and record in Vienna. He was to be the male protagonist, Mandryka, a rural nobleman who falls in love with the heroine. It is musically very difficult, and he repeated one particularly difficult phrase endlessly. "Every word, every note has to be second nature to me before I can think of going on the stage in a new part," he told me. Years later, at the yearly opening ceremonies of the Moscow Conservatory, I understood so well when the director told the new students: "Starting a career as a singer is like entering into religion."

As our euphoric week in Arosa drew to its end, George began to tell me about the torments that assailed him. He seemed so sure of himself but inside there were always doubts about the next role, worries about "the voice" although he felt sure of his technique; and there was the self-inflicted torture from his quest for perfection. I discovered his addiction for late-night discourses about everything that was wrong in the world, which he would forget completely the next morning when I got up greatly concerned about what he had said. I found that he wanted my complete approval, even my enthusiasm for the choice of his ties as well as for anything big or small that he bought for me. He was convinced that if he liked something I would like it, too, as a matter of course.

During that week he proposed to me and brushed aside my arguments about difficulties, about the children. Knowing the facts, he did not feel any guilt about taking me away from my husband and he was sure that he would love my boys because they were mine.

As for me, I had no feeling of remorse about terminating a failed marriage but I knew the divorce would be difficult and complicated, and I worried a great deal about the welfare and happiness of my sons.

George told me over and over that I would be the perfect wife for him, both physically and intellectually. I warned him against idealizing me and feared I could not measure up to his expectations, but he reassured me constantly. We talked about music and art, literature and politics, and found that we were stimulated by our conversations, but we could also sit together in silence enjoying each other's presence. He opened for me a world of emotions and understanding. I was engulfed in a maelstrom of passions and feelings that made clear thinking very difficult. But I realized that, because he expected it, he brought out the best in me. How could I not rise to the challenge of a man who treated me with such adoration and respect?

Life with him might not always be simple. Perhaps his dedication to opera would be greater still than his love for me, but I could not refuse this extraordinary offering of living with a man of such caliber. When George asked me to become his wife, I answered, "Yes I will with heart and soul." I could no longer conceive of life without him.

4

The Divorce

The week in the mountains remains to this day in my memory like a luminous dream. But when you wake up you find yourself face to face with reality. And so it was that on the plane while I returned to Paris I began to ask myself questions. How would I tell my boys, how would I explain to my mother, above all how would I tell Gene? I had promised George to become his wife; now I realized that it would not be an easy promise to keep.

I would have to ask for a divorce, and I had no idea how Gene would react. I wanted to shield my two little boys from any harm at all costs. Andy and Philip were old enough to understand a good deal of what was happening. I was anxious to protect them from possible trauma. I never wanted to hurt them. More than anything I wanted them to have a happy and secure childhood, and now I might endanger this precious gift. But if I stayed with Gene, I would become increasingly sad and depressed; what good would that be? Their father did not spend much time with them anyway. He did not really care for children.

Even if I had not met George, I reasoned, I could not stay married to Gene. How could I lock the door to life at thirty? If my sons were grown they would not ask for this sacrifice, and no doubt if I was happy and joyous I could also give them a better quality of life.

I was still dizzy from the perfect days with George, but once in Paris I began to wonder when the opportunity to talk with Gene would present itself. George had pressed me to talk to him as quickly as possible but it was not so easy, for Gene was in New York at that time. It would have to wait until I returned there.

As long as I was in Paris, George could call me from Vienna where he was performing. He sensed my torments and gave me renewed assurance of his love and concern. He bolstered my courage and helped me through the weeks of waiting for the meeting with Gene. Once I was in New York, I could not communicate with him any more and we decided he should not write to me directly.

The first confrontation with Gene would be the most difficult, I knew. I had never before held my own against him. He was domineering, unbending, and much older; he always made me feel inconsequential. It was mid-September, and I was extremely nervous when he arrived. Because we no longer lived together, he came to see me in our apartment. We sat stiffly at opposite ends of the beige sofa in our huge living room. We talked briefly about my trip and various family members but he knew that I wanted to speak about something important. The time had come; I told him that I no longer wanted to be married to him.

If he was shocked, he did not show it; he remained cool. He looked around the elegant room. "Don't you have everything you need?" he asked. I answered that he could not give me what I needed most, love and tenderness. He may have heard something about my relationship with George, for he told me that he did not mind if I had an affair if that was what I wanted. I denied it and said that this was not my reason for leaving him.

I made it clear to him that this permissive attitude was the basis of a kind of marriage I could not tolerate. I said that I knew of his numerous affairs and that I could no longer stand his high-handed and disrespectful manner toward me. On the other hand, I was not made for this kind of free life. I was not content with being a decorative nonentity, like a piece of furniture. I wanted a real involvement and devotion in marriage, and if I could not have that, I wanted a divorce.

He realized my determination, understood that at last something had broken between us that he could not repair in spite of all his suave urbanity. Now he became cold and matter-of-fact. He told me I had to consult a lawyer and gave me the name of someone he knew. I followed his advice and went to this man, but because he was a friend of Gene I don't think his advice was really impartial, and I know now that the settlement should have been more favorable for me.

There were many more conversations about my decision to divorce. Members from both sides of the family tried to convince me to change my mind. My mother told me that I was crazy to give up security and a good life for adventure and inevitable solitude. I never mentioned my love for George, although many people suspected I was involved with someone.

Once I had taken the first step, nothing was going to make me return to the meek attitude that had been mine for so many years. Still, it is not without great turmoil that you terminate a relationship that has lasted for over ten years. In order to protect the children and avoid any fights at that time and in the future that might affect them, I agreed to Gene's financial conditions. I did not want anything for myself, only support and schooling for the boys and a lump sum for each of them when they grew up. I agreed not to make use of the many proofs of his infidelities that I had accumulated. However, he took the blame in the separation agreement. It was decided that I would have to go to Las Vegas for the required six weeks to obtain a Nevada divorce, and Gene settled for the ridiculously low sum of forty dollars per day as my allowance during that time.

In retrospect, I think that I was foolish to agree to all of Gene's demands. As the years went by, I realized that I should have asked for greater financial security for me and particularly for the children. At that time, Gene had a sizable fortune, which he squandered over the years. Ultimately he did not give the promised sum to Andy and Philip when they grew up. Looking back, I think he did love me in his fashion but he was not made for marriage, at least not the way I understood it.

In 1954, though, I was glad that we parted on fairly friendly terms. And some years later we were able to resume a rather pleasant rapport. He came to like George and was even fond of my younger children. He could be a good friend even if he made a rotten husband.

But a divorce is a terribly traumatic period. I was beset by guilt feelings, fear of the future, and worry about my children. I felt terribly alone, for I was afraid to communicate too often with George and even when I did, he could not really understand my torments. He was very much in love and impatient to have me with him all the time. He considered the divorce as a step to this end and particularly at first did not comprehend all the ramifications.

For his part, he spoke to me at great length about his mother. He told me that she was a wonderful woman, that she had always encouraged him, and that she would surely approve his choice of me.

I begged him not to say anything to anyone. My first reason was that if Gene knew of our intentions, it would make the divorce more difficult. I told him that we did not know how long all these legal matters would take. Perhaps a year would go by, and it was too early to discuss our hopes and our dreams with anyone. I was afraid of his mother's reaction. Perhaps she would not be as enchanted with George's ideas as he believed. In New York I had met a friend who told me, without knowing the extent of my involvement, that she had heard that George London had a mother problem, that she consistently interfered with his private life and his career to his detriment. Of course I made believe that I was not very interested, but obviously my friend had heard some rumors. I tried to shake off the fear, yet hoped George would keep our secret.

But, as I found out in later years, George simply could not keep good news to himself. He could not imagine that his mother would disagree with him when he described all my virtues to her, and so he told her all about me.

She was violently opposed to our marriage. All she could see was the fact that I was married with two children whom one day he might have to support, and on top of all, she thought I was not even Jewish.

He could set her right about the last objection, but he was dumbfounded by her reaction. He was convinced that when he came to her with news of his great love she would be delighted. If he remembered her opposition to his former relationships, he dismissed it, thinking that they had not been serious and that perhaps she had sensed that fact.

During that autumn I saw George only a few times. He was on a concert tour in and out of New York. Whenever he came to town he stayed in the same suite at the Alden Hotel on Central Park West. I looked forward to our meetings with tremendous anticipation. We would fall into each other's arms with renewed passion, and yet we could not recapture the perfect harmony we had felt in Arosa. I tried to tell him about the tribulations of my divorce. He told me that he was shattered by his mother's opposition to our marriage. He said he had always thought so highly of her, of her sacrifices for him during his adolescence, and he had always been sure that when he finally chose a wife she would approve his decision without reservation.

I replied that I could understand her objections; after all, it would be normal for her to have preferred a young girl without children for her precious only son. His attitude toward me seemed to change. We could not spend much time together to talk and straighten things out between us, for he was always leaving for another recital. Knowing that it was difficult for him to function in an atmosphere of strife, I tried not to upset him even more. I did not press him for decisive statements and promises. He told me how much he loved me but I wondered how strong his mother's influence would be.

George hoped to improve the situation by arranging a meeting between his mother and me. He thought she would be won over by my personality. He was scheduled to sing a performance of *Aïda* and his mother and I were to sit together in the orchestra. We met at the stage door. George introduced us and she greeted me pleasantly. She was barely five feet two inches, very slender with a good figure and shapely legs. She had dark hair and brown eyes and in spite of her youthful figure seemed older than her sixty-four years. There was clearly a family resemblance between her and George except that it was hard to believe that he could be the son of such a small woman.

We went into the auditorium. To my relief, the opera started almost immediately so there was little time for small talk. George was superb in the role of Amonasro; I was totally engrossed in his performance, his velvet voice and perfect phrasing. But his mother looked at her watch to see how soon the opera would be over. I thought, "How can I ever get along with her?" Obviously this feeling was mutual and I certainly did not charm her in the least. We had little to say to each other during the intermissions and parted politely without much warmth on either side.

George was terribly torn and depressed. I was becoming more and more doubtful about our future. Nevertheless, I wanted to go through with the divorce. I was glad to have gotten the courage to break away and leave a useless, stagnating life. By the end of November, I left for Las Vegas, Nevada.

I did not want to be away from my children at Christmas and so I obtained a special dispensation from the court: I could go back to New York for a week but then would have to stay an extra week to make it the total six weeks.

I took a room with kitchenette in a motor inn just outside town. It was cheap—which was important as I did not have much money except the forty-dollar daily allowance—but at least I could take long rides in the desert behind my bungalow. At that time Las Vegas was nothing like the amusement town it is now. There were some casinos where you could gamble, which I did not do, and get a very lavish and cheap buffet lunch, which I did. I economized on everything, including meals, to bring back Christmas presents for everyone. Besides riding, there was nothing to do. There was no television then and I could not get any classical music on the radio, only country music, which I detested. I was terribly lonely and missed Andy and Philip acutely. I had never been separated from them for such a long time.

I spent hours exploring the shops in Las Vegas to find gifts for George and for the children. There was little choice, and my budget was limited. I had to settle for identical toy cars in different colors for the boys and a special tie case for George. I thought it was rather appropriate as he had such a weakness for pretty ties and traveled so much. I wished I could give him a more important present, but I simply did not have the means.

The days seemed endless until December 23 finally arrived and the plane took me back to New York and everything I loved. Christmas with the children was wonderful. Gene was skiing in Switzerland for the holidays and would not interfere. They were delighted with their toys and many others they received from my mother and other members of the family. As usual we had a beautiful tree and spent a cozy evening with much hugging, happy to be together.

On Christmas Day I met George. He had called me often while I was away and we had many good conversations. We were very excited to see each other after being apart for so long.

Years later, after twenty years of marriage, I still felt that extraordinary anticipation whenever I was to meet him after a separation. He would stride toward me on his long legs with an expression of love and admiration on his face that always made my heart beat faster.

That Christmas Day he was obviously delighted to see me and immediately handed me a little box. It contained a blue enamel locket on a chain, which he declared fitted me perfectly. He seemed very pleased in turn with my gift. We had a short but harmonious visit and we promised to see each other at length the next day.

When I met him the following evening, I sensed at once that there was something wrong. He was unhappy and distant. I questioned him repeatedly until he finally admitted that he had had another discussion with his mother, that she thought our relationship had no future, that I obviously did not truly care for him, that the present I had given him was unworthy and too cheap from someone as wealthy as I was.

At the mention of my wealth I became furious. I was overcome by the injustice of the accusations and was seized with an uncontrollable rage, one that devours me very rarely but takes frightening proportions. I screamed at him that he was insensitive, that he had no idea what I had been through, that I had not told him but Gene was giving me a very small daily allowance and I had no access to other money at this time, that I could see that he was incapable of making his own judgments. And in a fit of anger I took an ashtray and threw it at him.

At that he suddenly burst out laughing, the sound filling the room with music and covering my high-pitched voice. He laughed and laughed. "You're even more beautiful," he told me, "and I love you still more knowing you're no pushover. From now on I'll be careful so you won't hit me." Then I laughed too and calmed down. We made up and we were sure of each other once again. Never again would we doubt the sincerity of our feelings toward each other. We put aside the heavy decision about marriage for a time and proceeded to enjoy the happiness we felt in each other's company. For years afterward George teased me about my temper and joked that he could not contradict me because "You'll start to throw the china at me."

After this meeting, George decided that I had to meet Paola Novikova. She had been George's singing teacher for the past four years and would remain his teacher for the rest of his career. The relationship between a voice teacher and his or her pupil is often very close. Singers feel a greater dependency than do instrumentalists, because a singer carries his instrument within himself. He cannot hear himself objectively and depends on someone else's advice more than any other musician. Also, the voice changes as it develops and as the singer grows older. Therefore, most opera singers continue to take lessons throughout their careers, even when they are already well known. The voice teacher develops a strong bond with the pupil, a bond that often becomes very personal.

Paola was informed of all the offers for new roles that George received. He was expected to discuss with her if the role was suitable for his voice and if she thought it was right for him at the current stage of his career. As he would be studying the music with her, her approval was essential. George told me that if she did not approve she could undermine the learning process and make it virtually impossible for him to give a good vocal rendition of the part.

With this kind of control over the career of their pupils, many teachers, including Paola, are tempted to assume control over their pupils' private lives. They reason that the singers' activities besides lessons and performances will influence the quality of their work. Paola was certainly most critical about George's female interests, which she felt had to be on a special level worthy of her star pupil.

Therefore, George introduced me to her with some trepidation. During the week after Christmas he took me along to one of his lessons. He had told Paola all about me and I knew pretty much what to expect. She was Russian, a roly-poly person with dyed red hair, white skin, and big brown eyes. She had a regal air in spite of her short size, for she had been a performer when she was young. She had a tremendous musical knowledge and was without doubt one of the best teachers around.

She adored George, admired his talent, and wanted the best for him. This was so evident that I immediately liked her in spite of her theatrical greetings. Soon we chatted away in Russian. Then I sat down silently while he vocalized and she made comments. I admired her perfect ear and her suggestions and his uncanny ability to implement immediately what she indicated.

From time to time she turned to me before playing the next exercise on the piano and said with finality in Russian, "George is a genius." I nodded my approval and smiled. When we left she kissed me affectionately and I knew she approved of me: I was the right one for him.

I was much relieved. I don't think I could have maintained a relationship with George if Paola too had been against me. George was delighted. There would be no jarring criticism from her. In fact, we were both invited to her New Year's party.

We were in a great mood during that evening. We made a handsome couple, dark and fair. I was thrilled to hold his arm as we entered Paola's apartment. Evidently we were expected with a good deal of curiosity. Everyone wondered "who was the girl whom George London was bringing into the inner sanctum?"

It was an international crowd, about thirty people, including several well-known singers, musicians, and accompanists, Werner Singer, Paola's husband, being one. The talk was mostly about music and opera; who was singing which role during the Met season. I was well informed about those subjects and managed to talk with different groups sometimes in Russian, or French when necessary. Everyone treated me with kindness and seemed to like me.

George was radiant; he felt confirmed in his conviction that I was right for him. But we did not talk about the future; we were basking in our love for each other. When midnight came we embraced passionately, and it seemed our love would never end.

I could not help wondering what the year 1955 would bring. The next day I returned to my exile in Las Vegas in much better spirits than when I had left. Another four weeks lay ahead of me, and the time went by slowly. Finally the day came. I went to court and the divorce decree was issued. It took a little over ten minutes to erase eleven years of my life. I was free.

5

Marriage

One must, in this world, love many things
To know finally what one loves best.
                                    —ISAK DINESEN

I never thought much about personal freedom. I have always felt free and independent within myself, but I have also felt totally committed and bound to the ones I love. Naturally I am happiest when I can devote myself to those closest to me.

Flying back from Las Vegas, I realized that I wanted to make up to my sons the time that I had been away as well as the relative neglect of the last few months. We would be together. I would love them better than ever. I had to face the fact that we had to leave the ten-room Park Avenue apartment and give notice to the governess; I could afford neither. I was fortunate to find an apartment just two blocks away on Eighty-fourth Street, between Park and Lexington avenues. It was far different from what I had before, three tiny bedrooms and a large living-dining room, but it was in the same neighborhood, important because the boys would not have to change schools. I was delighted with our new quarters, although friends and family could not understand that I was satisfied with such a come-down in my standard of living.

Now that I was divorced I wanted to be settled with the children in my own place and not give George the feeling of being pressured into marriage. In fact, even if it had been possible, I did not think it wise to marry again immediately. After all the turmoil of the past year, I needed some time to myself to reorganize my life, and I thought that too many sudden changes would be overly stressful for Andy and Philip.

For the present I was content with loving George and being able to go out with him openly. After my return from Las Vegas, he had a very busy schedule at the Metropolitan and we could not be together as much as we wanted. I was busy with moving and spending more time with the children.

Unknown to me, while I was in Las Vegas, George, too, had his share of aggravation. In November 1954 he wrote to his parents and specifically to his father, for his mother knew already, "about my big and serious romance . . . Nora and I were drawn to each other enormously from the moment we first met. . . ." He explained that I was about to divorce and that he had seen me over the past year. He continued:

> The time we spent together proved to me that I had met the woman whom I felt as destined to be my wife. As mother will confirm, she is very attractive, fairly tall, slim, with beautiful green eyes, a wonderful smile and a luxuriant crop of dark blonde hair. She is of Russian-Jewish stock. Mother thought she was White Russian (she looks like it) but both her parents were Jewish. . . . She has had a wonderful education and a wonderful up-bringing. Yet there is absolutely nothing snobbish about her. She is completely natural and unspoiled and completely sincere. She is warm and kind and has the most serene disposition I have ever encountered. She is highly intelligent. She is tender and understanding. And in a crisis has character and strength. Above all, she loves me with all her heart and wants to be for me a help and a support, a source of inspiration and strength, a refuge of tranquility and peace and, indeed, she is all of these.

He added,

I know that you will find it an objection that she has two children. Indeed, I admit it would be more ideal if she did not, although her boys are adorable, charming and affectionate. But you see, I love Nora, and she is the woman I have been waiting for all my life, though I confess I never expected ever to meet anyone as wonderful as she.

I read this letter for the first time over thirty years later.

In the last paragraph he said, "I want my dear parents' understanding and love and support in what I am planning. . . ."

Evidently, even though he pleaded his case so eloquently, he did not get a favorable response, for in another letter some weeks later, he tried again: "Right now she is the woman I love, the inspiration I have been so sorely needing, and I feel she is indispensable to my future happiness. If we are worthy of it, God will bless our union. . . ."

But it seems that nothing he said could convince his parents. When I saw him again, he was in a somber mood and soon he told me that he was terribly tormented. His mother, whom he had always worshiped, was constantly talking against me and opposed his marriage vehemently. He could not sleep and it was affecting his work. His mother had come to New York from their home in California and was staying at the same hotel where he was living. She would visit him in the morning at breakfast and upset him for the rest of the day with her negative attitude.

He begged me to talk to her, hoping I could change her mind about me. At first I refused, but he seemed so dejected that I agreed. I could not bear to see him so unhappy.

It was a most awkward meeting. I had not seen her since the night of *Aïda*, before my divorce. Evidently I was more threatening than ever, as I was a free woman now. Our conversation was labored. When she objected to the fact that I had children, I replied that I could understand her feelings but that if George and I married they would not be a financial burden to George for they were well provided for. I told her that, furthermore, we had not set any time for a marriage and that there were still a number of obstacles. Nothing I said seemed to have any impact on her. Finally she said, "When you marry George you will possess him." I answered: "No one possesses another human being, I could never feel that way, and I certainly would never interfere with George's career." She remained unconvinced and I left, feeling that my visit had been futile.

On my way home I felt sorry for her in spite of my anger. There she was, sure that she was losing her only son, her famous son, because of me. She did not realize that he had grown away from her *because* of his fame, his talent, his travels, his taste for culture and beauty. He had changed and she could no longer understand him even though George took great pains to appear steadfast in his feelings toward her. In spite of everything, he remained attached to her and continued to write to her every week until his last illness.

I wondered if his father was as difficult as George had warned me. I did not meet him until the following winter and eventually got along quite well with him. In spite of himself, he rather liked me and enjoyed talking with me, although our conversations were laborious because he was somewhat deaf and refused to wear a hearing aid. With George's mother, I eventually achieved an uneasy peace. I resented her behavior most of all because she crucified George and tormented him constantly instead of enjoying his success and being grateful for such a devoted and supportive son.

I told George about the failure of my meeting with his mother. He was dejected; his hope of getting his parents' approval, which he had wanted so much, had faded. Some weeks later his mother returned to California and I could tell that he would make his decision without her.

By now the major obstacle to our wedding plans was the fact that George and the children did not know each other. Once, when I first met him, he saw the boys from a distance in the park. They were wearing identical gray flannel pants and "looking very French," as he said.

During the many months of our courtship I had purposely avoided any meetings between George and the children. As long as this was just an affair, no matter how serious, I felt that it was not proper to expose the children to it.

It was spring, and George was about to leave for Vienna once again. He had made up his mind to marry me and was pressing me to set a date for our wedding. Now I was wavering, and although

I loved him as much as ever, I told him that I could not marry him unless I was sure that he and the boys would like each other. If there was too much friction between George and the children life together would be impossible.

The summer provided a perfect time for a meeting. As soon as school was over, I went to Europe with the boys as usual and spent a few weeks at my mother's house in Paris. Then George and I both made reservations at the Hotel du Lac in Brissago on Lake Maggiore in Switzerland. I traveled by train with Andy and Philip and we arrived first. The hotel was beautifully located and from the balcony of my comfortable room I looked at the glistening lake and the breathtaking landscape beyond. I was nervous; another very important step in our lives was about to take place. The perfect atmosphere of the hotel and the beauty of the site seemed to be a good omen.

George arrived by car some hours later. Our reunion was wonderful. There was no discord between us and we felt immediately totally in tune with each other. He felt supremely confident and I felt optimistic. He met Andy and Philip in the garden of the hotel and set out to charm them. He did not even have to make an effort for he truly loved children and naturally appealed to young people, but most of all he was everything they wanted and they were ready for him.

Here were two boys in need of fathering, two little New Yorkers surrounded by a European family. As they told me years later, "He was filling a gap in a welcome way. We thought he was very American, that was very exciting. He talked about baseball, he understood us, that was great stuff, we liked that and we called him Tex!" I need not have worried. I watched with deep pleasure as they built up an easy friendship that would grow into lifelong ties.

One day George sat patiently on the pier with Andy, who was an ardent fisherman; another day he persuaded Philip, who was rather shy, to go into the water and try swimming. We went on excursions around the lake and visited my uncle Senia who was vacationing in nearby Locarno. We had remained very close since we left France together in 1940 and I was devoted to him. He liked George, understood immediately what he meant to me, and gave us his blessing.

Soon our two weeks were up. Our stay was a complete success, and I knew George would be the kind of father I wished for my children, these two and any others to come.

Now it was only a question of deciding where we would get married. George had taken the summer off but he needed to do some work with a coach in Salzburg, so we thought that would be the perfect place. He went ahead to prepare matters.

I brought the boys to Geneva where they met their father with whom they spent a week before going to summer camp in Villars, Switzerland. It was the first time I had met Gene since our divorce and I felt rather apprehensive. He looked tanned, well rested, and was quite pleasant. I decided to tell him that I was going to marry George in a few weeks. I told him that neither George's parents who lived in California nor my family vacationing all over Europe knew about it, but that I did not want him to find out from someone else. He said that he was not surprised, for he knew about my involvement, but he was flattered by my confidence and he wished me well with sincerity. I asked him to keep the news to himself, which he promised, and we parted in a friendly manner.

I was greatly relieved that our meeting was over and had gone well. It seemed now that the last hurdle had been passed. I said good-bye to my sons with special tenderness, knowing that our life would change again and that it would be a happy change for them, as well.

George met me at the airport in Munich and surprised me with a brand-new Mercedes sports car, white with beige leather seats. He was immensely proud of his purchase and I admired it enthusiastically. He drove, faster than ever, the short distance to Salzburg. We stayed at the Hotel Zistelalm, which is just outside of the town, up on a mountain with a beautiful view.

The location was idyllic, we thought, perfect for a wedding, but now we encountered unexpected difficulties. An Austrian law required a period of ten months between a person's divorce and remarriage. So in my case we had to apply for a special dispensation, and we were not sure when this would come through.

George was getting nervous, for he would have to leave for Vienna soon and we much preferred getting married in the intimacy of a small town where we could avoid the press. The Salzburg festival was over and there were not many tourists. I met an acquaintance on the street who tried to pry some news from me, mentioning that he had heard rumors about my marriage. I denied flatly anything of the kind.

Because neither of our families were present, we wanted the event to be kept private and in fact we did not know ourselves when it could take place.

George wrote to his parents later: "On the morning of the 30th of August, 1955 I received a call to the effect that everything was in order but that I had to go to Linz, 75 miles away, where the courthouse for that district is, in order to get an official seal. I was back from Linz at three and at five we were all in one of the beautiful rooms of the Mirabell Palace, which must certainly be the most beautiful setting for a civil ceremony in the world."

We met George's friends Henry and Ginny Pleasants, then at the American Embassy in Bern; Franz Spelman, music correspondent for *Newsweek;* and Erik Werba, George's accompanist, in front of Salzburg's City Hall, located in the Mirabell Palace, once the sumptuous residence of Salzburg's mighty cardinal-archbishop.

George had been in such a rush that he had to ask Henry Pleasants and Franz Spelman to get flowers on the way. He gave me the bouquet of sweet tea roses. I was wearing a white linen suit, and George wore a gray suit with silk shirt and pale-blue tie, unusually conservative and solemn looking.

We climbed the majestic marble stairs to the first floor inside the palace and our small party was directed to one of the main halls. Evidently, in spite of the sudden decision, the authorities had been warned in advance and wanted to do things right for the wedding of George London.

We entered a huge room with marble floors and pink marble columns, which must have been the cardinal-archbishop's reception room once upon a time. The room was almost empty except for a long table covered with green cloth in the center where the *Standesbeamter,* the Austrian justice of the peace, was sitting flanked by a clerk and a secretary. He looked solemn, and we took our assigned places silently. Henry and Ginny, Franz and Erik sat together on a bench, George and I stood in front of the table.

A flood of sunlight coming through the tall windows illuminated our group and I glanced outside for a second at the glorious French garden bursting with flowers in bloom, all in my honor. George and I were holding hands, pressing so hard I thought mine would break. We were profoundly moved and I was afraid I would start crying.

The judge got up and the tension was broken. He spoke in such a strange Austrian dialect that we could barely understand his little speech and suddenly we both could hardly refrain from laughing.

The judge called the witnesses, Franz Spelman and Erik Werba, and we composed ourselves. Behind us, Ginny was crying and we were overcome by emotion. George put the ring on my finger and we took our vows with great solemnity.

Suddenly, after we were pronounced man and wife, a little old man hobbled in and sat at an organ on the far side of the hall. He proceeded to play with great fervor, ending with Mendelssohn's wedding march. The music resounded in the great empty hall, and we all had tears in our eyes. George kissed me and held me tight in his arms for a long time. I felt intense happiness, and I swore to myself that I would do everything in my power to bring happiness to the man I had just married.

George, too, was overwhelmed with emotion. We walked out dreamily to have pictures taken in the palace garden. For years afterward George regretted that, owing to his excitement, he did not give a good tip to the musician who had given us such a unique pleasure.

In the evening we had a small candlelight dinner party at our hotel, the Zistelalm for the few people who had been at the wedding. We were glad that these devoted friends sensed our feelings and left shortly after the meal. We felt so intensely our tremendous dedication to each other that we wanted to be alone to start our new life.

6

Return to the Sickroom

That was thirty years ago. The image of two radiant young people full of promise lingered in my mind as I sat day after day next to his chair holding hands with my fallen hero.

He loved me passionately all these years. Every day he found time to tell me how beautiful I was. He had so many gifts, he gave so generously of himself to his public, to his friends, to anyone who needed him. He was loved by so many yet never took anything for granted.

Thinking back, I am in awe of his achievements and his humanity. Was I good enough for him? Did I do everything possible to give him joy and support? Did I make him happy? Did I love him enough?

For eight years I asked him these questions and told him over and over that *he* had given me perfect happiness.

I know that he will never talk to me again and for my answers I will have to be content with a few lines George wrote to me for our anniversary on August 30, 1975:

My darling,—I thank you with all my heart for all the Happiness you have given me these past twenty years. And I am so grateful for the boundless and unfailing support you have given me through good times and less good ones.

You're the best woman I've ever known, and I love you very dearly.

Your George

7

Vienna

Three days after the wedding, on September 2, George sang in *The Tales of Hoffmann*. We had piled our luggage into the trunk of the white Mercedes and driven to Vienna. George had rented a furnished apartment in a handsome old building at Schubertring 4. It was within walking distance of the opera, near the concert hall, and came complete with a maid named Gretl, who had blond hair and a white apron and cap, as in a Viennese operetta.

She opened the door, curtsied, congratulated us, and we entered a room filled with flowers. The news of our marriage had spread quickly. The wire services had picked up the story and there had been a mention in papers not just in Austria but all over the world. George had sent a telegram to his parents, but the notice appeared in the *Los Angeles Times* before they received it. A friend had called his mother and broken the news to her. It was a shock, really not what George had planned, and did not make things easier for our future relationship.

I had the good fortune to reach my mother by phone in Montecatini, where she was taking the waters. After my announcement to her, there was a moment of silence and I said, "Maman, aren't you going to say something?" "Yes, yes, I wish you great happiness," she squeezed out at last. Later she came to love and admire George and once remarked to me, "George is the favorite of my four sons-in-law" (my sister having married for a second time as well).

These shaky beginnings in our family relations no longer affected us. We adapted to our married life without any effort, as if we had always lived together. The apartment was very comfortable. It had a large living room, with dining area and a balcony and a handsome bedroom with a beautiful porcelain chimney. Oddly the bathroom was at the end of a long hall, unheated in the winter, and when the weather was cold, we had to sprint from bed to bath if we wanted to avoid freezing on the way.

I was thrilled to be with George. There seemed to be a shining light around him and I was now a part of his luminous orbit. I adapted carefully to his ways for I knew how important it was for his work.

The Tales of Hoffmann was given at the Theater-an-der-Wien. By now George had become a seasoned member of the famous Vienna ensemble. The performers were mostly attractive, talented, dedicated, and with beautiful voices. The sets were often quite simple but the artistic level was always high. The same singers performed together again and again; they enjoyed their work. No one was in a hurry to take the next plane to another opera house at that time.

George had been accepted by the close-knit ensemble as one of their own, and he loved to sing in Vienna. He told me later that in those days performing several times a week with the same colleagues was such a joy he would have done it for nothing. He was proud to be part of this famous group and at the same time enjoyed his personal popularity. He spent long periods of time in Vienna and sang a total of one hundred forty performances between 1949 and 1955 at the Theater-an-der-Wien. He sang *Don Giovanni,* thirty times; the four villains in *The Tales of Hoffmann,* nineteen times; *Eugene Onegin,* thirteen times; the Speaker in *The Magic Flute,* which is a cameo part usually given to an important star, thirteen times. In this role he was part of the cast of the last performance of the Vienna State Opera at the Theater-an-der-Wien on October 2, 1955.

The Viennese public was knowledgeable and rewarded the artists with enthusiastic applause and the kind of adoration reserved for pop singers in the United States. The fans loved the young American baritone with the dashing figure and romantic dark looks.

After the *Hoffmann* performance, I was introduced to the fan phenomenon. As George emerged from the stage door he was besieged by hundreds of ardent admirers, mostly young females begging for autographs. This scene was repeated after every performance, and it took George an hour of signing and answering questions before he could leave the theater. Some who came backstage, of course, were true friends, and I liked them at once and they in turn approved of me.

It must have been difficult for those of his friends who had in a way appropriated him as "their" star to accept that he now had a permanent mate. Edith and Gottfried Kraus, two of George's best friends, were present after each performance, and they propelled me through the crowd and kept me company for as long as it took George to get out. They obviously adored George in a knowing and perceptive way, and their friendship helped me to endure the waits. I was never jealous of the fans; that was part of his life. I accepted the adulation like everything else, but it would have been difficult standing there all alone next to a crowd that ignored me.

Before our marriage, George had become known as a ladies' man in Vienna, where he drove around in a succession of sports cars. As Joseph Wechsberg wrote in his *New Yorker* profile of him in 1957:

> . . . somehow an alluring young lady seemed to be a built-in accessory of each of these cars; at least, the idea was current in Vienna that when London traded in a car the young lady went with it and he got another with the new one. . . . When he was billed at the Theater an der Wien, a special "London audience" would show up, consisting of attractive postgraduate bobby soxers. But women of all ages were drawn to him, and while the younger ones carried on about "Georgie," the older ones sent him yards of still warm Apfelstrudel, a delicacy that, in a thoughtless moment, he had publicly announced he was fond of.

After our marriage, prophets predicted that the fans would abandon their idol. But it made no difference to them. They were there in growing numbers, as we were able to see after the first *Tales of Hoffmann*. They just made believe that I did not exist. When George sang at the big opera house they migrated there and, taking the cue, I would wait with our friends across the street, as inconspicuous as possible until he was free and could join us for supper.

I understood very soon that this adulation, this signing of autographs was part of the performance for George and the other artists. The approval of public and fans is essential to the singer who puts his artistry up for examination at each performance. In fact, is there ever enough applause to compensate for such a trial?

On October 2, with *The Magic Flute*, the Theater-an-der-Wien closed. The entire company was preparing for the move back to the rebuilt Staatsoper. For a month, George's time was spent in rehearsals and preparations for the opening. On November 6, he was to sing the title role in *Don Giovanni* and on November 11, Amonasro in *Aïda*.

George told me that "the four months I'm giving the Vienna Opera this fall is a *must*. It is the climax of my career here, where my important career started."

I understood perfectly what this meant to him. I also knew well before our marriage that there was a good deal more to him than the dashing, gregarious façade. He was a true Gemini, endowed with a dual personality. For every joke that he told with such mastery there was doubt and torment about the next performance, the next concert, the next note, and there was a supersensitive ego wounded at the slightest provocation.

George discussed everything with me. He never went out on the evening before a performance and we spent much time together. It was again like being in Arosa. I served somehow like a captive but sympathetic audience to whom he could externalize his constant worries about his interpretations, his career, his next engagement, his finances, his rapport or lack thereof with his friends, colleagues, conductors. Often he was theatrical, sometimes repetitive, but always sincere. I sensed that he needed to expurgate these self-doubts to be able to present the assured extroverted persona to the outside world.

If he tried my patience, he sensed it and would make up for it a hundred times by his constant proof of love and affection. In his effort to make me understand and share his love for Shakespeare,

Shaw, and Sean O'Casey, he would read to me, in bed, long passages from their works. With his voice and sensuous accent, everything became clear and miraculous for me and he was childishly pleased with my approval.

Best of all, he delighted in my happy disposition, particularly in the morning. He had a terrible time waking up and couldn't get over my energy and cheerfulness as soon as I arose. Actually he seemed enchanted by everything I was doing except that he soon discovered that I was no great financial genius: one or more zeros did not make too much difference for me. He lamented that both of us were "hopeless" in finances, which in fact was not true, for he had a great aptitude for numbers and could perform very complicated calculations in his head. He was quite capable of managing his affairs except for occasional shopping sprees, which usually included some extravagant present for me. He loved jewelry particularly, and was delighted if he could give me something unusual.

I was living in a state of bliss and was more determined than ever to make his life as easy and harmonious as possible. It seems that I succeeded, since he wrote to his parents in December: "Nora's never-failing good humor provides an ideal atmosphere of tranquility for me which I need for the rigors of work and contact with the evil world. She is a wife and companion in the truest sense of the words."

The apartment was very cozy. Gretl curtsied whenever I spoke to her, and in spite of her Viennese dialect I soon managed to understand her. I had a good deal of housekeeping experience, I enjoyed the marketing in the open-air stands, and, thanks to Gretl's cooking, provided pleasant meals for us. We settled into a happy domestic routine, which we unwisely disturbed by acquiring a wire-haired dachshund called Daisy, one in a series of dachshunds, of which I have two to this day.

I took Daisy with me everywhere. This is possible in Austria, where dogs are allowed even in restaurants. On days when he was not singing, George and I took Daisy for a walk, which invariably led to Demel. George loved sweets, and in the 1950s Demel was the most famous pastry shop in Vienna. The waitresses were draconic old maids who melted with love when George appeared. They couldn't do enough to please him, and he had barely sat down at his favorite table when a piece of fresh apple strudel was put in front of him.

Then there was a serious discussion about the best dessert of the day and then, almost as an afterthought, I was allowed to order, too. The preferential treatment George was given by the waitresses was so obvious that George and I laughed about it, and I admitted magnanimously that he was surely their best customer.

Immediately after his last performance at the Theater-an-der-Wien, George started rehearsing at the big opera house. The inside was not completely finished, there were workmen everywhere, carpeting the stairs, painting the ceilings. It was chaotic but rehearsals had to go on. Under the circumstances, I thought I could take my dog to a rehearsal, so I sneaked Daisy into the theater. She liked music, I guess, and stayed quietly under the seat where no one could see her. But when I walked through the foyer one of the workmen exclaimed in horror, "What, a dog in the emperor's opera house!" I felt terribly guilty until a few days later I met a famous tenor backstage with his huge German shepherd.

After rehearsal, George often went to the workshop of the opera for fittings, and he insisted that I come with him, which I was only too happy to do, for this was a new and interesting experience for me.

The head of the costume department and his staff hovered around George and did their utmost to satisfy him. They kept addressing him with his title, "Herr Kammersänger" (court singer), which in 1954 the Austrian government had bestowed on him. He was the first American to receive the honor. In an excess of zeal, they even addressed me as Frau Kammersängerin, for in Austria everyone must have a title. The first time this happened I turned around to find out to whom they were speaking.

George was very demanding and wanted everything to be perfect. For *Don Giovanni* the costumes were made of the finest silks and softest leathers. In the first act, he wore a trim red suede jacket, very flattering for his slim waist. For the famous Champagne Aria, the traditional white silk costume had to have very big puffed sleeves and the breeches were to be as short as possible to show off his graceful long legs. In spite of everyone's efforts, it seemed impossible to find a pair of white tights long enough to accommodate those legs. This created a crisis; the head of the department was summoned and swore that there would be tights for the general rehearsal.

There was a similar costume in black for the second act, thus another problem finding the correct black tights. Each time George wanted to know what I thought and listened carefully to my advice, which I gave as if I had done it all my life; and, in fact, choosing for him was not that different from choosing the clothes I used to order for myself in France.

When the tailor was finished, George had to try the shoes, white pumps with a large buckle for the white costume, the same in black, and high gray suede boots for the first scene. There was a new crisis, for nothing fit even though the shoes were made to order. Only Americans could have such long narrow feet!

Again there were many "Herr Kammersängers" and promises that all would be well before the general rehearsal, which no one, including George, believed for a moment. We came back often to make sure that everything would actually be ready in time. Eventually the costumes turned out beautifully and enhanced George's performance.

Although George was working, these first weeks in Vienna were our honeymoon. We were together constantly and yet we never got tired of each other. We always had so much to talk about, music, arts, politics. Sometimes we went to museums where George wanted to show me his favorites, Brueghel and Dürer, or we just walked through the winding streets or window-shopped at night in the Kärntnerstrasse, a favorite occupation for George, who did not like to go to bed right after dinner.

But I had to interrupt my stay in Vienna to take Andy and Philip back to the States to go to school, at ten and eight they could no longer miss too much school. I picked them up at the pension in Villars and we flew from Geneva to New York. They had had a wonderful time in the mountains and looked suntanned and healthy. We had a huge lunch in Geneva in their favorite restaurant, the Mövenpick, where they ordered elaborate ice-cream concoctions. I told them that George and I had been married in Salzburg. They were delighted and kissed me joyously, perhaps sensing my own happiness.

I had to explain that I would go back to Vienna once more to be with George for the opening of the opera, but that we would all be together at Christmas. They accepted this easily because I had persuaded Miss Buchler, our nanny, to come back and stay with them. They loved her dearly, and this way they would not miss me so much.

There was an ulterior motive to Nanny's return. George and I wished for a child as soon as we were married and I was thrilled when I found out that I was pregnant. In New York my doctor confirmed the news, and I was able to tell Nanny that she would have a new baby of mine to take care of next spring. Under these conditions she was glad to take care of the older boys in the meantime.

George was elated. He wanted a family of his own and welcomed the new responsibilities he would have to face. He felt earnestly that it would give a new meaning to his work.

During my absence, George wrote me almost every day. He missed me acutely and complained about Daisy. "This dog roams around so sadly, looks for you everywhere—it is so depressing that I am ready to give her away if you don't come back soon." I answered in jest, "If Daisy is gone, I won't come back." But I realized how much my presence meant to him after such a short time, and knowing that Andy and Philip were in good hands, I hurried back to Vienna.

I knew there was more to his distress than the dog's behavior. Long before we had planned our wedding, George had invited his mother to come to Vienna for the reopening of the opera house. His father was too frail and not interested, but his mother had been eager to go to Europe for years. He wanted her to have this long-awaited trip and even though he was afraid of the tensions it would provoke now that we were married, he did not have the heart to cancel it. She arrived while I was in New York and George installed her in the Pension Schneider where he had often stayed. Everybody knew him there and promised to take good care of his mother, as she did not understand German. George also mobilized our English-speaking Viennese friends to entertain her, as he was increasingly busy with preparations at the opera house. She was delighted with Vienna and duly impressed by her son's popularity. There were many articles in the papers and his picture was prominently exhibited in the record shops all over town.

George was waiting for me at the airport when I returned, and we embraced lovingly. Although we had lived together only a short time, we had grown much closer and we felt an intense joy at being together again. During the drive home, however, I felt that he was nervous and I asked him why. He told me that his mother's presence made him anxious and he was worried that the atmosphere between his mother and me would breed tensions. Such tensions always made it impossible for him to function and perform, he said.

I was deeply troubled by his distress and I promised him that if I could, I would become the best of friends with his mother. I knew this would not be an easy promise to keep, but I loved him so much I had to be prepared to make things easier for him.

I greeted Bertha as warmly as possible, commented on our pleasure about her visit, and made a date for the next day to shop with her for an evening gown. I think our relationship was greatly facilitated by her genuine happiness on learning that I was expecting a child. Also she could not fail to see George's joy at this prospect, and this helped, too.

Our first evening together went extremely well, and George went to bed in a great mood. But in the morning I was dismayed when she came at ten-thirty, a visit timed to coincide with his breakfast. While he was eating, she started telling him unpleasant news about people back home in California, about her fights with his father, about their financial difficulties.

She went on and on with her depressing litany and I could see that he was getting nervous and angry. Eventually he could no longer eat and lost his temper, telling her to leave him alone. The day was ruined for him and he was able to work only with great difficulty.

He told me that she had been coming over almost every morning, making him miserable. I realized that I would have to interfere at the risk of spoiling our newfound friendly relations if George was to be in good shape for the taxing schedule of the opening performances. I decided there could be no more morning visits and no visits on the day of a performance or an important rehearsal.

I proceeded to tell Bertha this during our afternoon shopping. I explained as best I could that George needed a lot of rest, that this engagement was terribly important for his career, that he was even more concerned to give his best in Vienna, where he was so popular, and so on. I don't know if she accepted my explanations or simply thought that I did not want her there, but she did not come uninvited anymore.

I went shopping many times with George's mother and took her to the museums and parks that I had visited previously with George. Our feelings toward each other were never terribly affectionate but they were at least friendly and there was no tension. Later she dearly loved her grandchildren and she was grateful to me for giving George such a good family life.

Once peace was established, George was able to resume work with renewed enthusiasm. He was delighted to learn that his picture would be on the cover of *Newsweek* on October 31, with a story about him and the opening of the Vienna State Opera written by his friend Franz Spelman. *Newsweek* printed a handsome picture of George as Don Giovanni, holding the curtain of the rebuilt opera house and the caption "Baritone George London—Rebirth of Vienna State Opera." He was very pleased, for it was the first time he received such important publicity in the States.

Don Giovanni and *Aïda* were to be given five days apart in the gala premiere week, both with completely new sets and stagings, so George was involved in numerous rehearsals. I went with him most of the time, and he introduced me with pride to his colleagues, the conductor, his dresser, all the people backstage. George was convinced that my presence was necessary to his well-being and that I was the right person in the right place; I, in turn, felt perfectly at ease, as if I had been attending his rehearsals all my life. He had the ability to make me feel that I belonged. Little by little I ceased to be the shy young girl and became the serene and secure woman he needed. I never thought about this; it just happened.

When I was not at rehearsals with George, I did the errands for the household. I returned to the open-air markets where I enjoyed walking between the stands choosing cauliflower in one, salad and carrots in another. I always went to the same butcher near our house who gave me the kind of steaks we liked, somewhat different from the Austrian taste. The butcher knew my name and we exchanged brief greetings at each visit. But on the day of the *Don Giovanni* performance, as soon as he saw me among the crowd of customers he yelled to his aide: "And the best steak in the house for Kammersänger George London who will sing *Don Giovanni* for us tonight."

Every Viennese felt a real involvement in these performances. If they could not be inside the house, they would still listen to every note broadcast by loudspeakers in the square in front of the opera.

Finally it was the night of the dress rehearsal. The theater was filled with an audience of state officials and invited guests. Sometimes, when the show is not ready, dress rehearsals are still tentative, and the rehearsal is closed with no spectators allowed. Then the singers will just mark some arias by singing half-voice to preserve their voices. But this one was just like a performance and it went splendidly. The audience was enthusiastic; George was pleased. "If I sing as well at the performance, I'll be satisfied," he said.

On November 6, George followed his established routine for performance days. I kept out of his way, for I knew that he did not want to talk much. I answered the phone for him and transmitted nothing but good wishes and good news, establishing a peaceful atmosphere around him. He went over the entire score once more, looking specifically at new staging instructions. As it was rather cold he decided against a walk and did his usual exercise program in the bedroom. At 5:00 P.M., he went to the opera house. This routine seemed to soothe his nerves and prepared him so well that he felt perfectly calm and secure when the performance started.

I followed him backstage an hour later, and walked into his dressing room in my new dress looking as good as possible in my pregnant condition. George, who was sitting in front of the mirror, interrupted his makeup and complimented me on the dress and my hairdo. Then he went back to his task, applying the moustache and pointed beard, which he trimmed carefully. Slowly he *became* Don Giovanni. He was already in costume and stood up to vocalize. I could tell that he was in great voice and told him so. He cleared his throat several times and sang another arpeggio. Then, evidently satisfied with my verdict and pleased as well, he smiled and joked that I'd better go in if I didn't want to miss the first act. I wished him the customary *merde* and left. His mother and Paola Novikova, who had come to Vienna for these special performances, had visited him earlier, just for a few minutes. I was the last to go; he was in a good mood, relaxed and confident in his own ability.

I sat down in the red velvet seat, way in front toward the right. There was a hush, the lights went out. Karl Böhm, the conductor, started the overture. I was breathless and prayed that George would be in great form. I knew that he was secure both vocally and dramatically. He had performed this part many times around the world and polished every note, every gesture. On this evening, all of his experience came together for a unique performance. It was the same for the other artists, his friends who had sung with him so often at the Theater-an-der-Wien. There was Irmgard Seefried, an unforgettable Zerlina; Lisa Della Casa, a strikingly beautiful Donna Anna; Sena Jurinac, the perfect Donna Elvira; Anton Dermota, a stylish Don Ottavio; and Erich Kunz, a typically Viennese Leporello. In their new sumptuous costumes, they all looked attractive, acted with flair, and brought to life the perfection of Mozart's masterpiece.

I was carried away into a world where voices, music, and theater merged to enchant the senses. I was transplanted into the eighteenth century, where beautiful people, dressed in shimmering silks, moved with elegance, where passion and humor were intertwined in an eternally stimulating plot, where the music was enthralling and deeply moving in a perfect combination of voice and orchestra.

After the Champagne Aria, George's showpiece, which he sang at great speed, the audience went wild. The bobby soxers in the gallery and the standees screamed and stamped their feet, asking for at least a bow; but Don Giovanni runs out at the end of his aria and the conductor went on as required. At the end of the opera the applause was tremendous and the public stood up in an ovation for the singers, the conductor, the orchestra, the staging, and no doubt the genius of Mozart.

I was especially happy for George. This particular evening was the crowning of his Vienna years, and it was especially important for him to give his best to the knowing public that had made him a star.

The critic Karl Löbl wrote: "The tall, slender, dazzling-looking and utterly charming London has no competitors in this difficult role. His Don Giovanni is in Mozart's spirit. He succeeds in making the difficult transition from the subtly humorous and delicately erotic to the demonic personality driven by destiny."

(Thirty years later I heard, for the first time, a tape of this performance. I listened with some trepidation. Was it going to be as good as I remembered, or had I been intoxicated by the excitement and prejudiced by my love for George? It was great, it was wonderful, even better than I remembered. It filled me with extraordinary emotion to hear his familiar voice preserved here, again young, virile, healthy.)

That night in November 1955 when I went backstage after the performance George was radiant. Still in costume and makeup, his eyes sparkling, almost out of breath with exultation, he was devastatingly handsome. He kissed me lightly, to prevent his makeup from soiling me, and I thought how fortunate I was to be loved by this man.

The dressing room was full of flowers (in Austria and Germany it is customary to give flowers to male as well as female singers). Everywhere there were telegrams of congratulations, chocolates— and the inevitable apple strudels. Our friends helped to carry most of this back to our house while I waited patiently across the street from the artists' entrance in front of the Hotel Sacher.

Finally George appeared, smiling, holding more flowers. He was mobbed by his admirers, signed autographs, and found a kind word for many whom he recognized. At last they let him go, and we met his mother, Paola, and some friends at the Sacher, where a table was reserved for us.

Other members of the cast also went there for supper. The food was excellent; it was the place to go after the opera. The restaurant was crowded, and as each singer arrived the diners applauded. The management shrewdly gave prominent tables to the biggest stars. George was still under the spell of his performance and for a few hours he ate and drank and joked with his friends.

When we got home at last, he kissed me tenderly. "I'm so happy you could be with me on this special evening," he said, "I'm very grateful. Yet we mustn't take anything for granted." He often repeated this phrase with real sincerity. I think it was this side of his character that prevented him from becoming arrogant in the face of his enormous success.

During the opening week, on the nights when he was not singing, we went to the opera to hear *Der Rosenkavalier* and *Die Frau ohne Schatten,* both Richard Strauss operas that George loved. Although he could be terribly critical when the singing was bad, he enjoyed these performances and admired his colleagues.

Five days after *Don Giovanni,* he sang Amonasro. He had a special love for the part, and sang it often in Vienna and at the Metropolitan in New York. He always enjoyed transforming himself into a wild-looking, bellicose, patriotic African king. It is a relatively short part, requiring little more than twenty minutes of singing, but again his success was tremendous.

By contrast, recitals require nearly two hours of uninterrupted singing with only piano accompaniment and no costumes or theatrical effects to help the artist. George, however, loved giving recitals, and I was to experience his unique rapport with a recital audience for the first time in Vienna in the beginning of December.

The recital took place in the big Musikverein Hall, which has beautiful wood carvings and fabulous acoustics. The hall was packed, the public attentive. George sang a varied program with groups of Handel arias, Schubert Lieder, one or two opera arias, and some Negro spirituals, which were loved in Vienna. I watched how his humanity and generous spirit was communicated to each member of the audience through voice and artistry. He told me: "You see, they spend their hard-earned money to hear me and I have to give them the best of me."

The people felt his dedication and gave him an ovation at the end. He was glowing with their love and the feeling of great accomplishment in his art. I like to think of him the way he was during his singing years, joyous, smiling, almost intoxicated with his success, and yet affectionate and loving with me.

Soon after this concert I left Vienna and went back to New York to prepare for Christmas. George came a few weeks later and we had our first family reunion. Then he had a series of performances at the Met followed by a concert tour in the spring.

In May George returned alone to Vienna for the *Festwochen,* or festival weeks, which lasted through June. Because of the children, I could not go with him. We had given up our apartment in Vienna and George decided to go to the Imperial Hotel, which was also close to the opera house and the concert hall.

He was given a huge room facing the front on the second floor. In the morning an old waiter brought his breakfast and asked, "Did Herr Kammersänger sleep well?" Upon George's affirmative answer, he added, "Yes, this is the room where der Führer always slept." Upon which George jumped out of bed and asked to change rooms.

George returned faithfully to Vienna every year. He sang all his repertoire at the Staatsoper and I went with him whenever I could. In the late 1950s the Theater-an-der-Wien was renovated and George returned to the hall of his first success. This house seats only about eight hundred, and the rapport between the singer and the audience is very close. During this concert, George sang Brahms's *Four Serious Songs*. The public was absolutely still. At the end there was a moment of silence full of emotion, then a tremendous burst of applause. They understood the message of the composer and the accomplishment of the artist. George gave his best to the Viennese who loved him so, and they gave him some of the happiest moments of his career.

8

New York and
the Metropolitan Opera

In the fall of 1955 when I visited New York, I looked at our little apartment on Eighty-fourth Street and realized that there was not enough room for George in it. True, he would spend only a few months in the city that winter, as he had a long concert tour in the spring, but he needed comfort and quiet and that was impossible in five small rooms already inhabited by two growing boys and a dog, and about to be joined by a baby.

Then as now it was most difficult to locate apartments in Manhattan, although the prices were not comparable. There was no chance of finding a new place and getting settled, as I was returning to Vienna in a few weeks and would come back before Christmas, just ahead of George. So I rented a furnished studio apartment nearby, which would be like an annex to my apartment. When George arrived, I met him at the airport and took him directly to our little studio. He laughed when he saw it, pronounced it "a bachelor flat," but was, in fact, quite pleased. I felt that it provided a good transition from his carefree bachelor life to the time when he would live with three children. It gave us more time to be alone with each other before facing all the complications of family life.

During the day I took care of the larger apartment, the boys, and the dog, and George came for dinner when he was not singing. While in New York he went for lessons with Paola every day and met with his manager, who was Bill Judd in the Arthur Judson division of Columbia Artists Management at that time. He also took advantage of his free time to learn new music and rehearse his concert material with one of his accompanists, Leo Taubman or Werner Singer, Paola's husband.

I went with him as much as possible because I enjoyed listening to him practice and wanted to learn everything about his work. But I had quite a lot to do, one being the duty of all housewives, namely grocery shopping. My favorite market was D'Agostino's on Eighty-fifth Street where most of my friends also shopped, so it was a social meeting place, as well. One day as I was pushing my cart piled high with food for my hungry men, I was accosted by an acquaintance I had not seen in some years who said, "Well, how does it feel to be the wife of Boris Godunov?" Surprised, I mumbled something, smiled, and pushed on.

But as I walked home it struck me that her question was not so silly. She was right. By day I was the wife of George London, but at night, riveted to my seat in the theater, I watched with total concentration as he became Boris Godunov, Don Giovanni, Scarpia, Count Almaviva, or Mandryka. Each time I became so fascinated with his interpretations that I felt as much a part of his stage persona as of his private life.

Perhaps this was the reason why I understood his needs from the very beginning. On the day of a performance it was essential for him to have pleasant and quiet surroundings so that he could harness all his resources for the evening. Our peculiar setup that first winter suited him, even though he had entered marriage with full intention of sharing all my life.

On January 6, 1956, he wrote to his parents; "I am surrounded by much real affection from Nora's people and her boys who are very attached to me, not to speak of Nora's love, her unfailing cheerfulness and utter devotion. I never believed that my marriage could bring me so much happiness and contentment."

George started his Met appearances for 1956 with Count Almaviva in *The Marriage of Figaro,* in a new staging for Mozart's bicentennial.

After the excitement and adulation of Vienna, the atmosphere of New York was a letdown. The Metropolitan does not occupy in New York the importance that the Staatsoper holds in Vienna. At the Metropolitan, even though a star, George did not receive the same kind of adoration; it simply did not exist. He was greatly appreciated and respected, he had a fan club and a large and devoted following, and he enjoyed singing in the old opera house at Broadway and Fortieth Street, which, he said, had wonderful acoustics. It was a thrill for him to stand on that stage and look out into the Golden Horseshoe, the row of boxes that had been occupied by America's most prominent families. George was a patriotic American and he was proud to be on the stage of his country's foremost theater. In the 1950s and 1960s the Metropolitan was the most famous opera house in the world, and he felt privileged to be part of it. Yet it all did not add up to the exultation of Vienna.

Since his first appearance in *Aïda*, he had sung many roles at the Met, his greatest success having been *Boris Godunov*, which was given in English in a new translation. He also sang in *Faust, Tosca, Tannhäuser, The Marriage of Figaro, Carmen,* and *Parsifal*. In February 1955 I had returned from Las Vegas, just in time to be at the last rehearsals of *Arabella*, which George had been studying so hard while we were in Arosa.

This was a new staging of the opera starring Lisa della Casa in the title role and George as Mandryka, her suitor. Both were perfect in their parts, and for the first time in the Met's history this opera became a success. For me, it was the first time that I witnessed George's progress from learning the first pages of text to the incarnation of a provincial nobleman arriving in Vienna in search of a wife. It was a painstaking process that had taken over six months. In Vienna he had worked with Alfred Jerger, who had created the part under Strauss's own direction. I was present at the general rehearsal at the Met and admired the result of all these efforts. I was sitting near Lisa's husband, Dragan Debeljevic, who had come with their little girl, Vesna. George and Lisa made an extremely handsome couple, both singing and acting so perfectly that it all seemed real.

At the end of the opera when George-Mandryka was about to kiss Lisa-Arabella, little Vesna ran toward the stage and screamed, "I don't want this man to kiss my mummy." I guess that I probably wasn't that keen on him kissing this gorgeous girl, either, but that was part of the theater and I had to get used to it. Dragan was a most handsome man and because George and Lisa sang often together, we four became great friends after this.

George had a special success in *Arabella,* which he considered musically one of the most difficult in his repertoire, for its entire tessitura is high and it starts off with a long aria at Mandryka's entrance. Erich Leinsdorf, who conducted the opera at the time and with whom George enjoyed working for many years, recalled recently, "When George made his entrance in the first act wearing a brown suit and matching fur coat, he looked so fabulous that he had conquered the audience before opening his mouth."

George wanted his return as Almaviva in *Figaro* in 1956 to be special. Although he had sung the role many times before, he gave it special care for this new staging. During the preceding autumn we made a short trip to Paris to catch a performance of *Le Mariage de Figaro* at the Comédie Française. As George recalled, twenty years later in a speech to students:

I was particularly interested in the part of the Count which I was preparing for a new production at the Metropolitan. The cast included two of the most distinguished actors in France, Julien Berteau who played the Count and Robert Hirsch as Figaro.

These two provided an exquisite intellectual duo armed by the mordant words of Beaumarchais. I watched Berteau like a hawk and was busy taking notes during the entire performance. I sketched his costume and paid special attention to his stunning white wig and his beautiful high buckled boots. I was impressed by the economy and the elegance of his gestures and his attitude. The Count is often portrayed as a blustering boor, a sort of addled aristocrat. But Berteau obviously had quite different ideas and played him as a vital, intelligent and dangerous opponent. The struggle between the two men was not merely one of who should get Susanna first, but was rather an ideological confrontation between established authority and the aggressiveness of the rising bourgeoisie which presaged the French Revolution.

When I soon afterwards played the Count I did not slav-
ishly imitate Berteau who was a much smaller man with quite
a different personality, but I implemented many aspects of his
characterization and I did shamelessly copy that wonderful wig
and those marvelous boots; as a matter of fact, I went the very
next day to the Comédie Française and persuaded them to
execute these for me.

Certainly the characterization, the wig, the boots, and for a
good measure the perfect Mozart style he had acquired in Vienna
all contributed to George's success in the new production of 1956.
He tossed off the fiendishly difficult music of the Count's great aria
"Vedrò mentr'io sospiro" without effort. George sang this role many
times at the Met as well as on the tour, mostly with Lisa della Casa,
who was an enchanting Countess; with Cesare Siepi, a superb Figaro;
and with Erich Leinsdorf as conductor.

The Marriage of Figaro, one of the greatest operas ever composed, has always been one of my favorites. It is also one of the
longest, and George is in it to the very end. Until we got to bed
after unwinding and supper, it was close to two o'clock. After the
performance on the evening of March 30, we had supper at home
with an old friend of George from California days, Max Lipin. The
two men kept telling jokes to each other and I laughed heartily.
Finally we separated when it was nearly three o'clock.

At six in the morning, I woke George to tell him that it was
time to go to the hospital. The labor pains had started. Disbelieving,
he mumbled that he had just gone to sleep and could not possibly
get up.

Even though we had been married for less than a year, I was well
aware of George's inability to rise early. Although he clearly took
command of our menage's outside contacts, he let me control the
comings and goings at home. He became very quickly another child
to protect. One of my sacred duties was to guard his rest, above all
his morning sleep time.

He had constant arguments with conductors who wanted to
rehearse at nine o'clock in the morning. George asserted that he
could not possibly sing a note before noon. The conductors liked

his musicianship and total dedication and usually compromised to eleven o'clock. Even that time was a hardship for him; in order to get his voice going he had to get up three hours earlier. He used to say that when he got out of bed he sounded like a cracked basso. He admired Birgit Nilsson even more when he discovered that she could get up and sing Brünnhilde's taxing solos before breakfast, as she proved in London during the *Walküre* recordings. He even had trouble coping with life's ordinary chores early in the morning. If he had to take a plane at 9:00 A.M., he would talk about it for days in advance, then set his alarm for 7:00 and tell everybody in the family to make sure that he was awake. I was well aware of all this, but this once I could not spare him.

There was no doubt that the contractions were coming at regular intervals. I had already called the doctor who told me to go to the hospital. I decided to fortify George with some coffee and toast. Suddenly he was wide awake and got dressed in no time. Now he behaved like any other father-to-be: he was a nervous wreck, much more agitated than I; *it* was his first child, while I had been through all this twice before. When we got to the hospital, last night's aristocratic Count could not find his insurance card and could barely remember his name. It took such a long time to do the paperwork that our daughter was nearly born in the entrance hall of Mount Sinai Hospital.

But all went well, and once again I experienced the incredible elation of giving birth, a joy that was increased a thousandfold by sharing my profound happiness with my husband. We were both enchanted with our little girl and called her Marina, after the Polish princess in *Boris Godunov*.

The hospital room was bursting with flowers, which overflowed into the hall already lined with flowers from an adjoining room where Paul Newman and Joanne Woodward had a baby the same week. The two fathers admired their respective newborns through the glass window like all the fathers in the world. George's happiness was touching. I was very pleased to have a girl now after two boys. George did not care about the sex; he felt a religious awe and love for this tiny human being for which he was responsible.

"My life has now taken on even more meaning," he wrote to his parents, "and I feel that a solid foundation has been built where my life and my career can grow towards heights that I fancied I might one day achieve. God has been very good to me, and I am not too proud to humbly acknowledge how very grateful I am for all of the blessings which have been bestowed upon me."

From the sublime to the ridiculous, on the evening following Marina's birth, Daisy, probably looking for attention, proceeded to have an attack of epilepsy. Poor George, up since dawn, with the help of my nephew thirteen-year-old Patrick, spent the evening in search of a veterinarian working on a Saturday night. The following day he was afraid to tell me that the dog was sick. I was irritated because he yawned constantly, and I kept asking him what he had done the preceding night. He answered that he went to a movie but he was such a poor liar that I did not believe him for a second and wormed the truth out of him. Daisy recovered and never had another attack. I guess she felt that she had made her point.

Shortly after my return from the hospital, George had to leave for a long concert tour. The parting was difficult for him. Like all his emotions, his paternal feelings were extremely strong from the first day and grew even deeper with time. From then on the separations, which were a way of life for him, became more and more difficult. But there was no other way; the career for which he had made so many sacrifices demanded yet more of him. In the end, it mattered more even than his family.

In the course of the trip, he wrote with satisfaction to his parents on April 7: "I am in wonderful condition. I am singing better than ever. I have developed a security and an assurance which I never knew before and am thus able to maintain a consistently high standard."

While he was gone, I moved back into the apartment, which was very crowded now with the boys, the new baby, and Nanny Buchler. Andy and Philip were thrilled with their new sister and kept going into her room to look at her. Although I had told them that I was expecting long in advance, they had not been interested until it actually happened. For them, I was particularly glad that it was a girl, as this created less cause for jealousy. They did not mind all the fuss to which they contributed with the enthusiasm of two boys of eleven and nine.

The congestion in the apartment was dreadful. There was not a corner without toys, schoolbooks, music, or baby bottles. During George's short stopovers, it was impossible to create a restful atmosphere, and he screamed at everyone in the mornings when the noise woke him. Sometimes I thought he would move to a hotel.

But after the recitals came the Met tour, then he was off to Europe. So we decided that new lodgings could wait. The apartment was cheap, we could save money by staying there. I had decided to follow George to Europe as soon as the boys' vacation started, and we knew that the family's travels would be very costly.

From the very beginning I made up my mind, with George's approval, that I would take the children wherever he was singing for any length of time. I reasoned that if I did not do this, he would hardly ever see them and would miss these early years of togetherness. I had to plan and implement our summer trips. George could not get involved as he was busy traveling to keep his engagements. Besides, I preferred to take care of our travels alone. George was too nervous and impatient to tolerate the complications involving travel with small children. The bottles, the diapers, the special food. The restless toddlers running in the aisle of planes, one child getting sick during landings, another getting carsick when crossing half of Europe. These were my responsibility; he could not have coped.

It was not always easy to be together but, looking back, I am glad I managed it. George enjoyed spending his free time with Marina and later with our son Marc and became close to them. It was important for me, as well, to be surrounded by my family and yet to be able to go to George's rehearsals and performances.

After the summer of 1956, I went with George to Buenos Aires where he was to perform *Don Giovanni* and *The Marriage of Figaro* during an engagement at the Teatro Colón. We were there together with Lisa della Casa, her husband Dragan, and Birgit Nilsson. The performances were very glamorous. I returned to New York two weeks earlier than George with the intention of finding a new place to live. Nothing materialized; only after George returned did I find something. He was in the midst of a rehearsal at the Met when I called him. "I know I'm not supposed to disturb you, but it's absolutely essential that you come and see this apartment immediately, otherwise someone else will get it. I think it's ideal for us but I can't decide without you." He agreed. "I'll meet you at the address in half an hour."

He came, loved the apartment, signed the lease, and returned to the rehearsal. Some weeks later we moved into a penthouse at 262 Central Park West, a wonderful apartment with three large bedrooms, a library, and huge living and dining rooms all surrounded by a wide terrace with a magnificent view of Central Park.

As is usual in such cases, the moving day was traumatic. Nanny was taken ill with pneumonia, and I had to ask Andy and Philip to watch Marina while I was supervising the movers. The painters, in spite of promises, were not quite finished, and, as the boys were not too careful, baby Marina nearly landed in a huge pot of white paint instead of her playpen.

Eventually we all settled in our respective rooms, a big improvement over our previous cramped quarters. The large entrance hall, which had black-and-white vinyl tiles, led to the bedrooms on the left. Andy and Philip had a nice big room with ample space for two beds and two desks and their own bathroom. Completely separate, there was a bright and spacious room for Marina and Nanny, and down another hall was the master bedroom. This was our first very own room, large enough for our beds and George's desk, for he preferred to study and work in his room away from the bustle of the household. This is where he learned new music and reviewed older scores, rarely going to the piano except when working with an accompanist. Since he spent so much time in this room, it was decorated in subdued blues without any feminine frills.

On the other side of the entrance hall, an open arch led into the large living room, where the baby grand piano, French sofa, Louis Quinze chairs, and table fitted without crowding. The furniture was re-covered with French blue velvet, and our growing collection of paintings decorated the walls. I had a number of paintings by the French painter Maclet representing scenes from Paris, and George soon bought some Chagall lithographs, an Italian sculpture representing Don Quixote, and a Chinese bronze Kuan-Yin.

George loved art. Wherever we went, his time was divided among the hotel, the theater, and the museum if there was one. He always preferred the more dramatic subjects, spent long minutes observing period costumes and manners, and remarked in front of his favorites about how much he would love to have this painting in his home. Sometimes I looked around fearful that a guard would overhear and become suspicious of his intentions. I quickly said, "Darling, you can't have this, it belongs to the museum."

At times his desire was so strong that he bought large reproductions of his favorites (a Leonardo, a Dürer, a Murillo) and then admitted they were not good enough to hang in the living room. But wherever he went he bought art: German expressionists, Japanese prints, more sculptures. The walls of the apartment were soon filled. George did not want any pictures of himself, however. "I know what I look like and my friends can see me in the theater," he said. Later, however, he did accept a painting of himself as Boris Godunov commemorating his performance at the Bolshoi.

The years 1957 to 1964, which we spent in the apartment on Central Park West, spanned the most successful years of George's singing career internationally, and more particularly at the Metropolitan. The best measure of an artist's success in New York is whether he sings at the opening of the season. George sang at the opening in 1957 and 1958. Other coveted performances are new productions and the Saturday afternoon broadcasts, which are heard all over the United States and Canada (at that time there were no telecasts, which are now very desirable). George sang in twelve new productions and twenty-five broadcast matinees over the years. At one time it was also considered an advantage to sing on Monday nights, the so-called society nights, but their appeal was already fading during the 1950s. The artists felt that on society nights the people came mostly to look at each other, not to listen to the singers, and therefore there was little applause. A regular weeknight audience was much more enthusiastic and more knowledgeable and this was more satisfying for the cast. Of course, every major artist wanted to sing the openings, the broadcasts, the new productions. They also wanted an increase in their fees. In the 1950s and 1960s the Metropolitan Opera was the best theater in the world. It paid less than other houses, yet it could attract the best artists because it was prestigious to appear there.

By the mid-1950s George was paid twenty-five hundred dollars a performance; today he would receive much more, but at that time everything was less costly. The rent for our luxurious penthouse apartment, for example, was five hundred dollars a month.

At that time the solo contracts were signed two or three years in advance and in most cases the artists' managers did the haggling. George felt that his manager did not get the right kind of contract for him and believed he did better doing his own bargaining with Rudolf Bing, the general manager of the Met. He felt that if Mr. Bing promised certain conditions he always kept his word. On the other hand, George was an important artist, much needed in a specific repertoire. He was always on time, perfectly prepared, and not given to capricious behavior. No doubt all this weighed heavily in his favor at contract time. In some of his roles, such as the Flying Dutchman, he has not been matched to this day, twenty years after he stopped singing.

In the late 1950s and early 1960s, therefore, George went to see Rudolf Bing and discussed plans for the following seasons. He realized that the opera house needed to give some performances to those who covered his roles, in case he had to cancel, as well as offer important opportunities to other baritones, but he knew exactly what he wanted to sing and how long he wanted to be in New York (usually not too long). The Met was prestigious but George made more money on concert tours and guest appearances. The open and frank conversations usually ended to George's satisfaction. George criticized some of Bing's repertory decisions but not his business practices with the singers. Once an agreement was reached, George's manager took care of the details and exact dates.

Eventually George found that he was better off negotiating for himself at all houses, and did most of it for Bayreuth and the Vienna State Opera, as well. His European manager, Martin Taubman, took care of details there. He negotiated about repertoire and dates; however, everywhere, he left the bargaining about fees to his managers. He did not feel that it was good for him to argue about money.

On October 28, 1957, George opened the Metropolitan Opera season in the title role of *Eugene Onegin*. It was a new production, and his co-stars were Lucine Amara and Richard Tucker. The hero's part, a brooding and Byronesque character, suited George extremely well, and he had sung it many times with great success in Vienna.

I knew the libretto backward and forward; like every Russian, I was brought up with the poem by Pushkin on which the opera is based. My mother recited whole chunks of it to me while I was growing up.

I went to the rehearsals and, together with Paola Novikova, supervised every nuance of his interpretation and every detail of his costume and makeup. I found that his pants were slightly too short and that, although he had to look pale and bored, a deathly pallor was unbecoming on stage. Obviously he had to accept the instructions of the stage director, but sometimes I would tell George that I thought he was too far back on the stage for the best effect during an aria. He always listened and at the next rehearsal, I noticed that he compromised and stepped forward toward the audience without losing contact with the other singers on stage.

At the beginning of November there was a "close-up" about George in *Life* magazine. The article was titled, "I Prefer Villains and the Sinners," and showed George in various character makeups from *Faust* and *The Tales of Hoffmann*. There were pictures of him jogging in Central Park, lifting weights, taking a lesson with Paola, and at home, with Marina and with me giving him breakfast in bed. Much love and intimacy is captured in these photographs of us together by Gordon Parks.

George was extremely pleased with the article. He could not ask for better publicity, for at the time *Life* was one of the most popular magazines in the United States. These were good years for us. George could do no wrong in his career, and our family was flourishing. Indeed, these were good years for many Americans. During the 1950s everything seemed possible, the economy was thriving, the world was at peace. Our world of opera was enjoying a golden age with great voices capable of filling roles in any repertoire.

George's only complaint was that he was not doing enough recordings, but eventually he recorded all his roles, except Amonasro, a lack he always regretted. (Today there are available several pirated versions of this opera with him singing, and when I hear them, I am especially happy.)

In October 1958 George sang at the Met opening again, this time as Scarpia, with Renata Tebaldi, who was my favorite Tosca. He enjoyed playing the part, and not only because he died during the second act and could go home early. He loved Puccini's music and relished portraying the arrogant and ruthless Roman chief of police. He told me, "Scarpia is not only a vicious and brutal executioner, he is also a grand seigneur in love with the most beautiful woman in Rome and he has to have her." Sometimes during *Tosca*, as we were leaving, he would pull me back toward the wings when the third act had started. He wanted to hear the tenor sing his big aria that night or listen again to the soprano. He never ceased to be interested in other singers and loved all the music in the operas, not just what had been written for bass-baritones. We would stand backstage with the technicians and supporting members of the cast. They made room for us so that we could see. These were very special moments for me. George had his arm on my shoulder and when he was pleased, he murmured, "Isn't it beautiful?" as if it were the first night at the opera for him and for me.

During the following years, he repeated in New York the huge success he had in Bayreuth as the hero in Wagner's *Flying Dutchman*. At the premiere, George as the Dutchman and Leonie Rysanek as Senta generated such radiance and intensity that there were twenty-three curtain calls after the second act. The audience applauded right through the intermission. George wrote about this in a letter to his parents on January 14, 1960:

> The reception which Leonie Rysanek and I received at the Met last night following our big second act duet was the greatest I have ever experienced there. I had felt that there was a special atmosphere which we had created, and we were both in excellent voice, but we were quite unprepared for the way the house came down when we took our first bow together. As we stood before the curtain she turned to me, tears came into her eyes, and she threw her arms around me and embraced me before the whole audience. It was so touching and so spontaneous, I was deeply moved and the audience, too. There were over 20 curtains after the second act and about the same at the end. This was one of the most wonderful experiences of my career—one of those evenings that make up for so much of stupidity, common-place, and ups and downs of this profession. I shall never forget it. Of course Paola and Nora were in seventh heaven.

Obviously after such emotionally charged performances we could not simply go home and go to bed. It took a long time for George to "simmer down," as he put it. This was a good excuse for having parties at our house after the opera.

I became very adept at organizing such late suppers, which could be prepared during the day so that I could go to the performance without worry. I knew that everything was ready for our friends and that there would be plenty of food, particularly for the singers, who were always hungry after singing. There were stories circulating about singers arriving at postopera parties being served some cookies and soda by well-meaning but ignorant hostesses, obviously unaware that many artists do not eat before a performance. George was determined that no such thing would happen in *his* house, and I made sure that there would be one hot dish along with the cold food as well as plenty of drinks to choose from.

On party nights I went straight home from the opera instead of going backstage as usual. This way I was there to greet our friends. These included the singers Renata Tebaldi, Maria Callas, Leonie Rysanek, Birgit Nilsson, Richard Tucker, Giorgio Tozzi, and Nicolai Gedda. Also in later years the Russians, soprano Galina Vishnevskaya and the baritone Pavel Lisitsian, whom we first met in Moscow, came after their first performances in New York. We also invited conductors like Erich Leinsdorf, Dimitri Mitropoulos, Karl Böhm, and the composer Gian Carlo Menotti, in whose opera *The Last Savage* George starred. After the premiere of *The Tales of Hoffmann* George reported to his parents, on November 2, 1958:

> Following the opening we had an elaborate party which was intended as a celebration. Among our guests were Senator and Mrs. Javits, who are old friends of Nora's, Sidney Lumet the brilliant young movie and TV director and his wife, Gloria Vanderbilt, Mr. and Mrs. Billy Rose, Mr. and Mrs. Skitch Henderson, Steve Allen, Van Cliburn, the Soviet conductor Kiril Kondrashin, my colleagues Cesare Siepi and Roberta Peters, and the writer Joseph Wechsberg, and, of course, Bill Judd and Miss O'Neill of Columbia [Artists Management]. The party was really a great success with a relaxed atmosphere and excellent food. Everyone was delighted.

Many of our friends were journalists who came when they were in town. We became close friends with George Marek and his wife whom we met while my George was doing a recording for RCA of which Marek was the director. At the Mareks', in turn, we met Harry Belafonte and his wife and then spent many evenings together, during which Harry and George entertained the gathering with a succession of anecdotes told with multiplying details, getting dirtier and dirtier as they went on. This friendly competition could go on until three o'clock in the morning, leaving the audience exhausted from too much laughter.

Our apartment was well suited to these parties. The dining room was large enough to set up a buffet and several small round tables, each of which seated six. If necessary there could be more tables in the living room. This way everyone could eat in comfort; we hated the idea of balancing a plate on one's lap.

After a performance George was usually in high spirits. (In those days there were no bad performances for him. Some were greater than others; he was not a machine, but he was incredibly secure.) He loved to be surrounded by friends, show off his beautiful home, and make sure that everyone was provided with ample food and drink. He would remind me that one singer drank only beer after performances, another only white wine, another a special mineral water.

He also took care of entertaining our guests. No longer afraid to use his voice until the next performance, three or four days away, he talked at length. He delighted everyone with the latest jokes, doing his imitations of Italian, Jewish, Russian, or German accents. He expected his friends to stay until the early-morning hours, forgetting that some people had to get up the next morning for their businesses.

The day after a performance George slept late. He used earplugs and heard nothing. The boys left early to go to school and although I did not have to get up to make their breakfast, I listened to the noises of the household and soon got out of bed to see how everybody was doing.

In the summer of 1958, we went to Vancouver where George sang *Don Giovanni* for the festival in a staging by Günther Rennert, a director he admired a great deal. There was an excellent cast that included the Canadian debut of a young singer who overwhelmed us with the beauty of her voice and the ease with which she sang the incredibly difficult arias of Donna Anna. This was Joan Sutherland. George was so enthusiastic that he arranged an audition at the Met for her. Rudolf Bing was not present as he was on vacation in Europe, but his assistants who heard Joan did not engage her. However, she did not need any help from them. The following winter she had a huge success in *Lucia di Lammermoor* at Covent Garden. George cut out the reviews from the London *Times* and the *Manchester Guardian* and showed them to Mr. Bing. "This is the soprano I recommended last summer," he said. Joan made a triumphant debut at the Met the following year.

When Marina was two years old, we decided that we should have another child. There was too much of an age difference between her and the older boys, so that she was like an only child. I became pregnant during our stay in Vancouver.

Although I was feeling very well, I was unable to accompany George on a tour to Israel because it was too close to my confinement. He was enchanted by this trip during which he sang mostly excerpts from *Boris Godunov* with the Israel Philharmonic, conducted by Josef Krips.

George was back home by the middle of March and sang a series of performances at the Met: *Don Giovanni, Boris Godunov, Tosca,* and *Eugene Onegin.* Of course, I went to all of these, and trekked backstage at each intermission, but I was heavily pregnant and found the steep stairs to the dressing rooms in the old opera house increasingly difficult to climb.

Onegin is another long opera. The third act has two scenes and the hero is in both. That evening it was very late by the time we got home; there was no question of company, for I was very tired. We nearly had a repeat of Marina's arrival. I had to wake George again. This time he was not half as nervous but just as sleepy. However, I was in a greater hurry; there was no time for breakfast. The streets were deserted Sunday morning, April 5, 1959, as the taxi rushed us to Mount Sinai Hospital. A few hours later again I had the most wonderful joy of giving birth to a healthy baby, this time a boy.

We had some discussion about the name. George wanted David

but I preferred Marc, and we compromised with Marc David. A few days after the birth, George had to go away for a concert tour and wrote from Dartmouth College, New Hampshire: "I am grateful and happy and pray that my son will grow up in a peaceful world. That is all I have to yearn for. I have just about everything else." As for me, I had just about everything a woman could hope for. I had four beautiful children, I was madly in love with my husband. My life was rewarding and challenging.

The penthouse, which seemed so roomy at first, was slowly filling up. Daisy had gone back to her ancestors and we replaced her with a playful beagle. He had a sad and wise expression and was aptly named Socrates. Then my nephew Patrick enrolled at Riverdale Country School where Andy and Philip were going and came to live with us. He occupied one of the maid's rooms with a separate entrance at the back, an arrangement that suited him perfectly. He was almost grown up; Andy and Philip, too, were becoming teenagers, and the back entrance was convenient for letting girlfriends in and out. The three boys also took advantage of the apartment to give their own parties with loud music and dancing. When things got out of hand, they enlisted George's help as bouncer. Whenever undesirable youths tried to crash the party, the boys called George, who, incensed by such behavior, put on his most menacing expression. He threw the unwelcome guests out bodily with a thunderous "Don't you dare come back here!" The doorman overheard one of the outcasts saying on his way out: "Boy, they have a giant there who gets rid of people."

Between taking care of the older and the younger children and my desire to attend as many as possible of George's rehearsals, as well as all the performances, I had practically no leisure time, even though Nanny Buchler was wonderful with the children and our maid cleaned and cooked for our ever-hungry brood. During an interview, when a reporter asked me, "And what is your hobby, Mrs. London?" he was met by glum silence and an incensed look from me. George, who knew how I felt, laughed and saved me by lying smoothly. "She is a wonderful cook," he said, which I certainly never was or ever will be. As a result there was an article in *Vogue* magazine about my cooking skills, giving fancy Russian recipes stolen from my mother.

I never had a minute's free time or the vaguest desire to pursue "a hobby." Everything I was doing fascinated me and I felt no need whatsoever for outside amusement. No wonder, I was always in a good mood rushing around to the playground, the school play, or the opera. George asked me how I could cope all at once with the small fry, the teenagers, and a husband who worried about rehearsals, recordings, and performances. "I love everything about my life and about you," I answered. "It's like being on stage every day in my favorite play."

9

An Opera Singer's Routine

During the years 1956 to 1962 George's career as a singer was at its apex. He was offered more engagements than he could accept in the greatest opera houses of the world for the most interesting roles and productions. His appearances were greeted with enthusiastic applause from thousands of admiring people, and on a given night after the performance he was usually elated and well pleased with himself.

It was late at night or the next day that he started to question and doubt. Deep inside he knew his worth, yet he felt that to sustain his position he had to get still better. To this end he devised a series of routines that would ensure constant improvement.

He was very health conscious and every morning, without fail, he did his physical exercises. These included a series of breathing exercises with weights if he was home, a series of sit-ups, and an awesome number of push-ups, which he did with his feet up on a chest of drawers. After showering he examined his physique, then went on to look at his face with evident disapproval. He disliked his eyes, which were set too close for him; his nose, which he dubbed too small for his face; and most of all his "fleshy jowls." He was difficult to photograph and complained to me often that if he had been more photogenic he would have been able to make a career in the movies or in television. I answered that if he *had* perfect features in addition to all his gifts and general appearance he would be insufferable.

This did not satisfy him. He wanted to be beautiful, not out of vanity, but because it would promote his career.

His appetite was comparable to his size. He ate a copious breakfast while listening to records, preferably baroque music. He read *The New York Times* very thoroughly whenever available and complained that there was no news in regional papers when he was on tour.

When he was in New York, he went to Paola Novikova's apartment for a singing lesson almost every day and whenever possible I went with him. He would sing scales and arpeggios and other musical patterns, repeating them over and over to build the right physical position out of which the perfect sound could be produced. He sang arpeggios on the vowel *A* up through the *passaggio,* or passage tones, to the top of his range darkening the vowel as he proceeded higher. He perfected sustained notes on the *I (ee)* vowel until the legato flow of the breath met with Paola's approval. He made sure that he had perfect support of the breath, which was always necessary but particularly so for the long phrases of Wagner's music.

After the vocal exercises, which lasted about half an hour, Paola's husband, Werner Singer, came in for an hour. He often traveled with George as his accompanist and mostly played during the lessons. During this part of the lesson, they rehearsed new material or went over some Schubert or Brahms songs for the hundredth time until every intonation, every phrasing passed Paola's criticism. George also practiced new roles with her and wrote to his parents, after the premiere of *The Flying Dutchman:* "To Paola, I owe a great deal, because her insight into the vocal and interpretive aspects of the part were of incalculable help to me." Her knowledge in matters of voice and music was enormous, and I listened and watched carefully. I wanted to be able to help George during our trips when she was not there. Little by little his confidence in my judgment grew and eventually he trusted me completely.

After his lesson, if he did not have a performance the next day, we could loaf a bit, do some window-shopping, and have a late, late lunch because it was usually well past two o'clock by then.

He loved to go to the Russian Tea Room where he was pretty sure to meet an acquaintance, and after lunch it was just across the street to have a quick chat with his manager or check up with the patient Mary Crennon, who booked all the artists' travels, to make sure that he was not leaving anywhere "at the crack of dawn," as he said.

By four o'clock George wanted to be home to have time to study. He preferred to have a year's time to learn a new part and explained how he went about it in a speech to a young audience in 1968:

> I developed a system to prepare an operatic role which thereafter served me quite well. The first step was to master the text of a new role. If the language of the opera was one that I only partially understood (I didn't have too great a problem because I learned to speak French and German fluently and Italian serviceably; I am thinking in my own case of Russian), I wrote in the score above each foreign word the exact English equivalent so that while I was studying the part every time I went through the score with my pianist, the words were imprinting themselves in my mind and a time came when I knew what every word meant and thereby I could give the infinite colorings and the nuances to my interpretation.
>
> The thing that makes an artist interesting is the fact that he *can* give colorings and nuances, and if you don't know what the words mean or only have a general idea you cannot do this.
>
> Having memorized the words your next problem is to work on the pronunciation of those words. If there was a recording of the role sung by artists native to the part, I would study those recordings very carefully, listen for the genuine authentic inflection.

George was fanatic about diction. "In English, we have *tee* and *dee* sounds and we don't roll our *r*s. These are built-in handicaps in singing foreign languages." Further describing his methods for study, he added:

Having mastered the text, I was ready for the musical coaching of the role. If, in studying a worthwhile piece of music, you are scrupulously faithful to the printed direction and dynamic markings of the composer, you will as a result already have seventy-five percent of your interpretation. The interpretation basically and fundamentally comes from the music, and if you have paid attention to the sixteenth note, the staccato markings, the portamento, the contrast in dynamics that are written in the score, you will have gone a long, long way to having developed the style and the interpretation of the role.

George explained his good relationship with conductors as follows:

An outstanding conductor will take up your role where the coach has left off. He will have his own strong ideas about the character and at this point your advance preparation musically and dramatically will serve you well. You will be able to fight with conviction for certain things that you feel strongly about. The conductor may not always agree with you and in that case you must learn to compromise. I could usually find a *modus vivendi*.

George always tried to find a well-known protagonist of the part he was preparing and then persuade him to work with him. They were mostly retired singers who were flattered and pleased to transmit their knowledge and their artistry.

In my career, I was fortunate to find some truly outstanding people with whom I studied privately my important roles. Before I went to Europe in 1949, I sought out a Russian bass-baritone by the name of George Dubrovsky. He was a younger colleague of Chaliapin and he was a product of a school of acting which was typical of the Russian lyric theater and also of the Moscow Art Theater. From Dubrovsky I was able to learn an entire style of operatic acting, gestures and attitudes such as only one of his background could show me. It was Dubrovsky to whom I went to study *Boris Godunov* (a part with which I became somehow identified) and which I was privileged to sing in all parts of the world in later years. Dubrovsky had sung the part of Boris over five hundred times and he passed on to me all the treasures of his accumulated experience in the role. He taught me not only the details of my own part but particularly of the characters with whom I would work. He made of me a stage director should it have become necessary. He taught me the role of my son, the Tsarevich, and of Shuisky, people with whom I worked very closely.

He showed me how the boyars should bow, how the people should properly cross themselves in the Orthodox fashion, how the archbishop should bless me (how the archbishop blesses you is different than when your mother blesses you in Russia) and a myriad of such details. He assumed that the stage director would not know these details and experience proved that he was correct.

With Dubrovsky, I studied *Boris Godunov*, I studied Scarpia in *Tosca* and also Méphistophélès in *Faust*, and I worked with him every movement, every gesture, and I knew exactly what the people working with me were going to do. I was ready in those parts.

During the years in Vienna, I studied several of my important roles with a man named Alfred Jerger. He was a great singing actor at the Vienna Opera and in leading German theaters from the twenties to the forties. He had a demonic personality, reminiscent of the young Tibbett though he was not as fine a singer. Jerger was a Viennese, and he trained me for the role of Don Giovanni in the elegant tradition which had been typical of the administration of Richard Strauss, and this tradition was carried over into the postwar ensemble of the Vienna Opera. He saw Don Giovanni as a Renaissance man, a powerful, elegant and fearless person, and he helped me build a characterization which over the years I was to alter little.

For the role of Eugene Onegin, I also went to Jerger although it might have been more ideal to study with a Russian, but I never could find one who had actually sung it in performance. Onegin is a highly problematical figure and difficult to portray. I heard the opera when I was in Russia, both in Moscow and in Leningrad, and I was as dissatisfied with the two Russian Onegins I heard as I was with my own. I never really felt happy with my performance of Eugene Onegin although the critics thought that I was a good Onegin.

I was somehow always frustrated about my Onegin and in spite of the diligent work that I did with Jerger on this role I was not prepared for the events of the opening night performance at the Met of *Eugene Onegin* in 1957.

During the rehearsals, I had been warned. . . . There is a famous duel scene which takes place on the outskirts of Petersburg in the winter. Through an unfortunate, stupid set of circumstances, Onegin is about to fight a duel with his best friend, the young poet Lenski. It is a desolate scene, snow on the ground, and the stage director made a special point of telling me: "Now look, before you move into position for this duel, you must cock the pistol because if you don't cock the pistol it will not go off. Therefore you will have trouble killing Lenski."

So during all of the rehearsals I cocked the pistol and I walked back and I turned and I held the pistol and the music built up in crescendo and I lowered the pistol and pointed it at Lenski's heart and I pulled the trigger and it exploded and everything went fine. For the contingency that I should forget to cock the pistol, a stagehand had been placed in the wings also with a pistol and therefore should my pistol not fire, one could expect that his pistol would fire and give the same illusion.

Well, it was the excitement of opening night, I took the pistol, I walked into position, I raised the pistol, the music started building up to the crescendo, I started to walk towards Lenski, and I realized that I had not cocked the pistol, and so when I brought the pistol down and pulled the trigger nothing was going to happen and I was praying that my savior in the wings would be on the ball. I lowered the pistol, it was pointed directly at Lenski's heart. I pulled the trigger and of course nothing happened.

But nothing happened backstage either. Our stagehand friend was off having a smoke, I assume, or perhaps a drink; in any case he wasn't there. Now, I held this pistol in this position for a long, long time. It probably was only five seconds but it seemed like five hours, an eternity. The tenor couldn't take it, he couldn't stand the tension, there was no reason for him to collapse on the stage, nothing had happened, but he started to sink to the ground and the second he hit the floor the pistol went off, offstage. I rushed forward as I am supposed to. The only other person on the stage was Lenski's second, a character called Zaretski, and I said to Zaretski "Dead!" Lenski, of course, was lying there, Zaretski was kneeling next to him and Zaretski turned to me and as was also in the score he said: "Dead" and then under his breath, so that only I could hear it: "of a heart attack."

Mandryka in *Arabella* was another role that George studied with Alfred Jerger. Jerger had been the very first Mandryka under the baton and direction of the composer. In 1962, when he was preparing the part of Golaud in *Pelléas et Mélisande,* George consulted Lawrence Tibbett, who had preceded him in the role. He was very gracious and gave George his own costume for the part.

George was aware that people of different nationalities and different backgrounds moved in different ways, and he tried to implement this in his acting.

"The theater has its own rules and verities," he said. "One can borrow from and be influenced by life but should never try to substitute human for dramatic behavior. The performer who is moved to real tears by a scene he is playing succeeds only in troubling and embarrassing the audience. Between human and theatrical emotion there is a fine dividing line, and one may never cross it."

All together, George had a total musical and dramatic knowledge of his role by the time rehearsals started at the opera house. These took place in various rehearsal rooms a week or so before the performance, and on the stage if it was a new production or a first for the season. (If an artist was not singing the first performance there were hardly any rehearsals, just a short practice session with piano, possibly with some of the other principals.)

George insisted that by the time he went on stage the role had to be "like second nature to me." He preferred trying new parts in small theaters in Europe, but sometimes this was not possible and so he did his first Scarpia at the Met and his first Flying Dutchman in Bayreuth.

Because of the intense preparation preceding his performances, he was able to go on stage with a great deal of assurance. He did not endure the agonies that plagued some of his colleagues. It is said that soprano Lily Pons vomited before every performance. Another soprano prayed fervently in her dressing room before her entrance on stage, and a famous tenor held hands with his wife in the wings until the last second.

George did not indulge in such eccentricities; however, on the day of a performance he followed a special routine, always the same, which provided him with special security. Possibly it was his way of being superstitious: "if it worked last time it will work again."

He got up around ten-thirty and, after exercising, had his usual breakfast of coffee, one egg, toast, and salad. He believed implicitly that he would become ill if he did not eat salad twice a day. While eating, he listened to a favorite piece of music, Monteverdi or Vivaldi, or Schubert quartets, or a Mozart symphony; never vocal music on such days. Then he vocalized for about fifteen to twenty minutes. This took place either in the bedroom or more often in the bathroom with the water running. I once asked him why he sang in the bathroom, and he said, "In the beginning I always lived in hotel rooms and I was afraid to disturb the neighbors. So I ran the shower thinking the noise would cover my voice. Anyway, it *sounds* better in the bathroom."

When Marina was in nursery school, all the children were asked what their fathers did for a living and she answered, "My Daddy sings in the shower."

Although we had a piano at home, George preferred a pitch pipe and went through a series of scales, arpeggios, also making crescendos and decrescendos using different vowel sounds and taking his voice slowly to the highest notes of his range.

I could tell easily if he was satisfied with what he heard. If he stopped soon, all was well; if he kept on trying more exercises, he felt that he was not in good voice. I always listened and came in to tell him that I thought that he sounded wonderful. To which he replied each time, "Do you really think so?" Of course I insisted that he sounded good. Even if he didn't, I knew he would be fine by the evening, and thinking he sang well was a large part of the battle.

He used to tell me that a singer's misfortune was that he could not really hear himself because he carried his instrument within himself. I reassured him, for I knew that most of all he needed to feel good about himself. On the day of a performance George did not answer the telephone. I took the messages and generally left him to himself as much as possible. If it was nice weather, he went for a walk with the dog or enjoyed a short solitary stroll. By early afternoon he took a nap and after that he shaved, late in the day, as he had a very thick beard and wanted his skin to be perfectly smooth before applying makeup.

At five o'clock he had dinner, the same menu each time, consisting of rare steak, baked potato, the inevitable salad, and very light tea. I kept him company while he had dinner but did not eat with him. I did most of the talking and tried to tell him some amusing stories, preferably about the children.

Just before dinner he had once again gone over the score of the opera he was singing that night, probably for the thirtieth time. This was another ritual that gave him ultimate security and started the slow transformation of George London into the character he was to be onstage that night.

Already at dinner he was no longer completely with me. He left for the opera house immediately afterward alone. Exactly two hours before the beginning of the performance, he was in his dressing room, in front of the mirror, starting to do his makeup. Usually he did this himself; sometimes he enlisted the help of the makeup artist of the house if he thought he was talented.

Actually he loved to do his own makeup and engineer the changes of his eyes, his eyebrows, his cheekbones. He said his own features were too weak, thus ideal for stage makeup, which can be very heavy because the actor is far away from the audience. Most of the parts he played required a moustache and a beard, which were pasted on very securely with spirit gum so that there was no danger of their coming off in the course of the performance. As Boris Godunov, Mephisto, or the villains in *The Tales of Hoffmann,* he pasted fake bumps on his nose to make it larger and stronger. He insisted that the smallest detail was crucial in giving him the character he wanted. When he was finally satisfied with his work, he called for the person in charge of the wigs.

The look of a singer's wig is of the greatest importance, of course, but it is also important that he feels comfortable in it. George hated to have anything cover his ears, even partially, because it made it difficult for him to hear himself. Almost all the roles he sang required a wig; some he owned himself, like the beautiful white wig for the Count in *The Marriage of Figaro*, acquired in Paris, or his Boris wig; but mostly they belonged to the theater where he sang, in order to match others in the production.

The wig was combed and dressed freshly for each performance and pasted on with great care. For *Don Giovanni*, George kept his own black hair, penciled in to make his forehead somewhat lower, and wore a moustache and a small black beard. In later years, when his hair receded too much, he had to accept the fact that he needed a wig even for this role. "When you finally understand the part of Don Giovanni you are too old to play it," he said ruefully.

Once the wig was in place, there was a last check on the face, a line added on the forehead or a few hairs from the moustache cut off so they would not interfere with the movement of the lips. Then he would call the dresser to help him put on the costume, which sometimes was terribly heavy. Boris's coronation cloak, richly embroidered with stones, weighed nearly fifty pounds. He fiddled for a while with hooks, with belts, with the perfect angle of a sword, the ideal way of wearing a necklace. Suddenly he stood up very straight. *He* was ready; any trace of hesitation, anything tentative was gone—he *was* the character.

He started to vocalize again but not too much. It was said that some singers left their best notes in the dressing room because they vocalized too long—George sang only a few phrases from the text. By then I had usually arrived. I did not want to come at the last minute for fear he would worry about my absence. Also I wanted to be present when he vocalized to assure him once again that he sounded great.

If I thought he was not in such good voice, I wouldn't tell him anyway, but saying that all was well gave him that extra assurance that brought out the best even on a rare off evening.

However, he did not listen to any further talk. He smiled at me absently, never forgot to tell me that I looked beautiful, and then dismissed me with "I think you should go into the house." I wished him luck and left. He examined himself in the mirror once more; his gestures were the gestures of his character. The loudspeaker announced five minutes to curtain time and if he appeared right at the beginning, he walked slowly to the stage, clearing his throat one last time just before going on.

At intermission, I went backstage and reported that the performance was going wonderfully, that he was in great form, and that the public loved it. I did not go into details about the other singers' performance, for if they were not good, he was irritated anyway, and I was careful to avoid any conversation that might upset him. No matter what I thought, it was essential that he get the impression that all was going well.

He took off the costume, which usually had to be changed for the next act, and cooled off. He rested for a while or had a sandwich if it was a very taxing role, for he used an enormous amount of energy. If things had gone well, he was notably more relaxed and exchanged light gossip with me. He wanted to know which friends or well-known personalities were in the audience. Once, during the intermission of *The Tales of Hoffmann* Sir Laurence Olivier and Noël Coward came to congratulate him. He was thrilled. "My God, both of you!" he exclaimed.

I usually came back at every intermission unless I had special friends with me, in which case I warned him in advance so that he did not expect me. If someone he knew to be in the theater did not come back to greet him after the performance, George was deeply offended or he wondered if perhaps "he or she did not like the performance" or "did not think I was good tonight." Years later when George was director of the Kennedy Center, I noticed that some of the world's greatest classical artists reacted the same way.

After the performance, except when we had a party at our house, I rushed backstage. I wanted to be the first to congratulate him and be with him as soon as possible after the last bow in front of the audience. He radiated strength and joy, never fatigue, no matter how taxing the part. He was jubilant and smiled at me with delight. This was a high for him, the moment of achievement. As soon as he started to take off the costume and remove the makeup, the euphoria would dissipate.

He was still elated and smiling when he greeted the friends and admirers who came to his dressing room. By then he had already changed except if it was a complicated makeup that took a long time to remove. After many compliments and small talk for close to an hour, he was ready to leave.

If there was no party or no date with friends at a restaurant, we went home where a supper was ready for us. We ate lightly and drank some wine and I gave George time to enjoy the food, for he was always very hungry after a performance. Almost all his roles were dramatic and required strong, often tortured interpretation. These suited his personality but they were very costly—they took a great deal out of him.

When he relaxed at last, I suggested that we go to bed. While we were undressing he invariably started to ask me questions about the performance. He put me through the third degree: how was this particular tone in the big aria; how was this gesture in one scene; did I notice the change in his position at such and such a place? I had learned to observe the smallest detail, to hear the slightest nuance so that I could answer all his questions. He reviewed his whole performance again trying to pinpoint any possible flaw. He analyzed the character he had played in the most minute details and gained new insights into his behavior. This self-examination could go on for hours unless I managed to put a stop to it by begging him to go to sleep, assuring him over and over that he had been outstanding. He trained me to be so critical that I became a most discriminating and exacting audience, particularly for his roles. He wanted me to be aware of everything and often also discussed the performances of the other members of the cast, explaining in detail the reasons for their success or failure in their roles or singing technique. Added to my early singing experience, this indoctrination turned me into a shrewd connoisseur of opera, and he trusted my judgment.

To some extent I feel that he made me too critical. I could not just sit there and enjoy his performances. I had to be alert to any fault he might ask about later on. In those years I saw George and no one else perform Don Giovanni, Scarpia, the Flying Dutchman, Amfortas, Amonasro, Onegin, and Boris Godunov. Recently I have seen different artists, sometimes very good ones, in these roles and

I realize fully only now what an extraordinary performer George was. I see now that his interpretations had an added dimension born of sheer intensity, perfect timing, and inborn charisma.

George's quest for perfection was at its height during recording sessions. The best live performance leaves cherished memories but can never be re-created. Therefore the only permanent legacy of a singer are his recordings. George was aware of this and was eager to record the complete operas of all the parts for which he was known, as well as a number of solo disks. He had contracts successively with different firms: Columbia, London, and RCA. Then he ended up free-lancing. For each recording a separate contract was drawn, sometimes for a flat fee, sometimes for royalties. When George was asked to do the Wotan for the London recording of Wagner's *Das Rheingold*, he opted for a flat fee of two thousand dollars. He thought, "After all, how many people are going to buy a complete recording of a Wagner opera?" What he did not know was that this was one of the first complete opera recordings in stereo. The sound effects and the all-around quality of this set were so new and outstanding that it became one of the all-time best-sellers and was recently reissued as a digital recording after nearly thirty years. George used to laugh it off. "This was my worst business decision," he said.

There was also a difference between live and studio recordings. Occasionally a company decided to record a performance in the theater while it was taking place. Usually they spliced together parts from several performances to ensure perfect quality. In such a case, the singers received an additional fee as well as their fee for the performances, but there were no retakes and no control over the end product. Personally, I often prefer these recordings because they have an extra spontaneity and dramatic impact.

Most musicians prefer studio recordings, however, where they have the last say about each take. Thus for years, the conductor Bruno Walter did not permit the release of the Brahms *Requiem* with George and Irmgard Seefried because one phrase of the chorus did not sound right. Finally, after Walter's death, George persuaded his daughter to give permission for this outstanding record to go on sale.

George was not that fanatic about his recordings, but of course he cared very much and listened highly critically. After each take, which usually covered one scene or one aria, everyone involved went to another room where the technicians replayed what had just been recorded. Then the singer and the conductor decided if it was good enough for posterity or had to be done over again because it was either too slow or too fast, or the high note was not good or the orchestra and singers were not together.

I loved to go with George to the recording sessions. They took place mostly in London, Vienna, or Rome and afforded an occasion for a trip to these great cities. I enjoyed the special camaraderie between the artists that developed during long hours of rehearsals and takes. Sometimes there were big scandals: one famous Italian tenor beat the walls with his fists because there was to be a session on his birthday; and once the whole cast threatened to walk out because the recording company unjustly wanted to replace one mezzo with another during a *Walküre* recording.

In Vienna I could sit on a balcony overlooking the hall where orchestra, conductor, and singers were working. I watched the members of the orchestra doing crossword puzzles between takes. They were bored by all the repetitions; they had played these pieces hundreds of times with a long list of equally exacting conductors, slower or faster, louder or softer. It was quite a change for them when George did an all-Wagner recording with the famous Wagnerian conductor Hans Knappertsbusch. Kna, as he was called by his friends, was known to hate rehearsals. When he walked in, he said, speaking of *The Flying Dutchman,* "Gentlemen, you know it, I know it. Georgie! Let's start." And they proceeded to record the twelve-minute-long aria in one take. It was perfect. After they listened to it the technicians begged for another take for security, which was done. Then they went on to record the other Wagner arias planned for this record.

After the session, which lasted all afternoon, we went to have dinner at the Sacher and drank a lot of white wine, Kna's favorite, to celebrate the happy occasion. To this day I like this recording best of all, for I feel that George sounds fresh and enthusiastic, not dried out by endless repeats.

George also liked it, although like most artists, he listened to his recordings once when he received them, decided that he could have done better, and put them away on the shelf forever.

Shortly before his illness, at the request of some friends, he played the great Wagner monologues and a scene from *Boris Godunov,* listening intently. When the records were finished, he said, turning to me, "You know, it was not bad." I had tears in my eyes for I knew how much it meant to him "to leave my mark," as he said.

After he became ill, I found it very difficult to listen to his records at first, but as it was considered necessary for his therapy I forced myself. Little by little I found that it gave me pleasure. When I play his records now, I am moved on many levels. While I grieve anew that he can no longer sing in reality, I feel once again the excitement of years ago.

I am enchanted all over by the velvet, sonorous quality of the voice. I recapture his presence, his acting, his appearance. For a few moments he comes back to life. It is a profound joy mixed with the terrible sense of loss.

Then, when silence comes, I have a great feeling of victory; tomorrow and ever after I can play this record again; it will always be there. Beyond illness and death, his voice will remain a testimonial to his artistry for all to hear and, just for me, forever a testimonial of our love.

George, age three, in Montreal.

George and his singing teacher, Paola Novikova, in 1952. A picture of him as Amfortas is in the background.

ABOVE LEFT: George and I after a recital in 1956.

ABOVE RIGHT: Backstage during a performance of *Parsifal* in Bayreuth, 1956.

BELOW: With Marina, summer 1957.

Before the United Nations concert, 1959.

RIGHT: With George's parents, 1958.

BELOW: In rehearsal with Wieland Wagner for *The Flying Dutchman*, 1959.

FAR RIGHT: At home with Marina, 1959. *(Gordon Parks)*

BELOW RIGHT: George and I and the cast of *Boris Godunov* backstage at the Bolshoi, Moscow, 1960.

ABOVE: With conductor Hans Knappertsbusch and Wieland Wagner, 1961.

BELOW LEFT: On vacation in Jamaica, 1962.

BELOW RIGHT: Rehearsing *Parsifal* with Wieland Wagner and chorus master Wilhelm Pitz, 1964.

ABOVE: At home with the children, 1962. *(Photo by Eugene Cook)*

BELOW: Marina, George, and Marc, 1962. *(Photo by Eugene Cook)*

In concert attire, 1959. *(Karsh of Ottawa)*

10

Bayreuth

Every year in May I started preparations for our yearly migration to Switzerland and then to Bayreuth. George left at the beginning of May for Vienna, and I started packing after he had gone.

He had no experience in the care and transport of a family, but he always packed his own suitcase and did this to perfection, no doubt the result of years of practice. Shirts, pants, and suits were folded so well that they arrived without wrinkles. I had nearly as much practice but never achieved this kind of efficiency. But my own clothes were the last of my worries. I had to prepare three and later four children and a dog and make sure we would have the right clothes for boys and babies for the entire summer. Most important, we had to take along the formula for the baby. It was not available in Europe at that time, nor were the diapers, the baby food, the Kleenex, the perfect American toilet paper. Cases of these items were mailed at least six weeks ahead to the various places where we would stay and I prayed that nothing, and particularly the formula, would get lost. The dog came along mostly because I insisted he had to. Even with Nanny Buchler's help, this was quite an expedition. My friends and even George thought I was out of my mind not to stay in New York; but he agreed that as long as we all made it safely and met him as planned he was not going to interfere. Once we were there, he was happy, and spent every free moment with the children.

In spite of all my efforts and detailed lists and advance packing, something always seemed to go wrong. There were no jet planes yet. Commercial jet flights started only at the end of the 1950s. The transatlantic trips took over twelve hours and were often bumpy. Most of the time at least one of the children got sick on the plane; they inherited this deplorable fault from me. I found that a small baby is easy to travel with. It lies in its basket and if you're lucky sleeps peacefully between feedings. The airline stewardess caters to you and does her best to heat the bottles on time even when the plane is full.

But beware of toddlers! The instant they can walk, traveling becomes a nightmare. They do not like to sit for any length of time. They cannot be entertained for long, and my children, at least, never wanted to sleep. They ran up and down the aisle disturbing everybody and alienating the stewardess who obviously hated two-year-olds and despised the parent who is incapable of keeping her child glued to its seat for ten hours in a row.

With Andy and Philip, it was much easier. They read books, played cards, or could be entertained by word games, or the stories that I invented for them as there were no movies on the planes yet.

The dog was carried in a bag, its head sticking out. It stayed at my feet and did not move during the whole trip, shaking with fear. My feet were squashed and numb but all was well for I had remembered the vaccination and health certificate from the veterinarian. When this tired group arrived in Geneva, our usual goal, after a sleepless night, the customs officers commiserated with us and let us pass without inspection.

They never knew that Andy once carried some special stones from the United States to Switzerland, but Philip put things right by smuggling some shiny fresh chestnuts back to the States another year.

As soon as we had rested in the hotel in Geneva, I retrieved our car, which had been stored in Switzerland the preceding autumn, and took the family to Villars, the Swiss resort where we rented a house during the late 1950s and early 1960s. They stayed there with

Nanny Buchler for about a month while I went to Vienna to meet George. Then at the beginning of July I went back to pick up my gang and bring them to Bayreuth, so that we could all be together with George for six weeks.

The first year this expedition took place was the summer of 1956. Our car was still the convertible Mercedes we had gotten the previous year, but it was getting too small for our family. I knew I would have to convince George to give up this dashing automobile for a more pedestrian four-door sedan. In the meantime we squeezed into the convertible, Nanny with three-month-old Marina in the front next to me, the precious bag with bottles at her feet. Andy and Philip and Daisy were put in the back, which did not have a real seat but a kind of raised platform. I was driving, well aware that everyone was quite uncomfortable and would not hold out for long distances. We spent a night in a hotel on the way and I drove as fast as possible past Munich on the *Autobahn,* hoping to get to our destination before the next night.

Nineteen fifty-six marked my first trip to Bayreuth. I was excited about going to this famous festival town about which George had told me so much. I was to arrive a couple of days before George and get things organized. He had assured me that the director of the festival had rented a house for us, according to our specifications, and everything would be ready. After arriving in Bayreuth, I got my instructions from the festival's rental office and found myself driving into the countryside, farther and farther from the center of town, until we finally reached a house on top of a hill, with an unkempt garden.

The key that I had been given screeched in the lock. I entered reluctantly. The place smelled of mildew, had not been aired in months, and was furnished in the most primitive fashion. When I turned the faucet to get a drink of water, a rusty-color liquid came out, unchanged after running for a while. That was too much. How could we cook, how could we make Marina's formula, with the poisonous water? The baby was screaming, the dog barked, the boys sat down wearily, stretching their cramped legs, and Nanny stood in a corner with pinched lips and a disgusted expression.

I started to cry. "So this dump is the famous Bayreuth!" I grabbed the phone, which by some miracle worked. I reached George in Vienna and revealed to him the horrors I had encountered. "I'm ready to leave," I said, sobbing. He consoled me as best he could and persuaded me to go to the hotel in Bayreuth until he arrived and then we would look for another house together.

The festival season had not yet begun. This was the beginning of a three-week rehearsal period, and we had no trouble getting rooms at the Bayerischer Hof where we were comfortable and waited impatiently for George's arrival. I felt forlorn and wondered if I had not been stupid to come with my brood after all. But George was so happy to see us that I soon forgot my misgivings. Eventually we found an acceptable house, but there were few distractions for the older children and in subsequent years I did not take them along.

George knew his way around. This was his fourth summer in Bayreuth but once he, too, had gone there for the first time under exciting circumstances, which he described himself in a letter to his parents dated September 11, 1950:

> I was met yesterday in Munich and was driven the 100-odd miles to Bayreuth and was greeted at the door by Wieland Wagner, the grandson of the composer, and the man who will be in charge of next year's Bayreuth Festival. He is a vital and charming man who looks to be about 35 and of a sympathetic nature. I was entertained in "Haus Wahnfried" which Richard Wagner built so many years ago, and which still bears the imprint of his personality and of the colorful figures who passed through those rooms.
>
> After a chat and tea, I was driven to my hotel where I took a bath, rested up a bit, and was then driven to the famous "Festspielhaus," the theatre which has seen the presence of so many great singers of the past and which has housed all of the Bayreuth festivals since the 1870's. The house is not unusually large and ideal to sing in. The acoustics are marvellous. During the performances the orchestra plays in a deep pit in front of the stage and cannot be seen by the audience.
>
> In spite of my long journey I felt rested having slept well on the train from London, and in good voice.

In a *Saturday Review* article from 1967 about Wieland Wagner, George completed the story:

I found myself on the stage of the Festspielhaus excited and awed, singing a long audition of arias and monologues of Wotan, Hans Sachs and Amfortas. Afterward, Wieland invited me for supper at the "Eule," a restaurant located in an alley of the old part of Bayreuth and frequented by the artists of the festival since its inception. We ate venison and talked of many things other than my audition. It was late, and I was exhausted, having sung the Count in *Figaro* in Edinburgh barely twenty-four hours earlier.

I retired to my austere room at the Bayerischer Hof, too tired to care whether I had made a good impression. At seven the next morning I was awakened by Wieland in the lobby asking if I would breakfast with him. Over rolls and coffee he said, "Mr. London, I must tell you I haven't slept all night. I have searched all over Europe in vain, and I want you to sing the Wotan at the festival next year."

I was deeply moved, utterly disarmed. Yet I knew that I had neither adequate time to prepare such a gigantic assignment nor the vocal maturity to assume such demanding roles. I told him so and hoped he would not consider me ungrateful. "You are a phenomenon," he said. "You are the only singer I have ever known to refuse a part." We settled on my singing Amfortas in *Parsifal,* which was to be the premiere of the 1951 festival. Wieland later drove me to the station and I felt we had, in a short time, established a warm relationship. Indeed this ripened into a friendship which I cherished over the years we worked together.

George did not mention that 1951 was the first time the festival was open since being closed by the Allies after the war because Winifred Wagner (an Englishwoman who had married Richard Wagner's only son, Siegfried), who was the director of the festival during the war, was a supporter and great admirer of Hitler. Indeed, Bayreuth had been considered a Nazi stronghold. Winifred was banished immediately after the war and six years later her sons Wolfgang and Wieland were finally authorized to reopen the opera house, when she gave up her right to direct the festival.

After Winifred was allowed back to Bayreuth, she occupied an

apartment in a wing of Haus Wahnfried, the palatial villa Richard
Wagner built for his family. She took a fancy to George and invited
us for tea. Several times we were able to get out of it, but finally we
could no longer decline. We entered the house through a huge hall
filled with pictures of Wagner and his family and were led upstairs
to a separate, quite cozy apartment. Winifred greeted us, clearly
pleased by our visit. As we sat balancing delicate china cups on our
laps and chatted amiably with this pleasant old lady, I could not help
thinking that less than twenty years earlier, she had been sitting this
way with Adolf Hitler. She was tall, with white hair pulled back in
a chignon, and had white skin with handsome features. We spoke
German, for she had been so completely assimilated into German
culture that she rarely used her native tongue. We talked mostly
about opera and past interpreters of the great Wagner roles. She was
obviously knowledgeable and opinionated; but then she had been
the wife of Richard Wagner's son and had known Cosima Wagner,
Richard's wife, and thus was a direct link to the nineteenth century.
I felt that I was speaking with a part of history. Although the subject
was never alluded to, it became clear to us in the course of the
conversation that her political opinions had not changed over the
years and that she still revered the recent past. George felt that if we
had met her then, and he had not been a singer she admired, she
would not have hesitated to send us to the gas chamber. When we
left we breathed in the cool summer air and knew we would never
visit her again.

In 1951 George climbed the hill to the festival house every day
for the rehearsals. Although he had a car by then, he lived nearby
and thought the walk would be good for his health. He enjoyed the
well-kept gardens that led to the theater, built according to Richard
Wagner's instructions and perfectly preserved.

As usual, George prepared himself fully for the role of Amfortas.
The part is not very long, but is central to the plot and includes two
lengthy outbursts that are very difficult and in which the voice is
very exposed. Hans Knappertsbusch had seen George in *The Tales
of Hoffmann* in Vienna and had been the one to recommend him for
the part to Wieland Wagner. George was particularly eager to fulfill
his expectations; he sensed Kna's support from the pit and was

thrilled by the beautiful sounds coming from the orchestra, particularly during the introduction to Amfortas's complaint.

During the rehearsal period, Wieland received several menacing calls because George was Jewish. He paid no attention. The day before the first performance he was warned that the Holy Grail, which George would hold up in his hands during the first act, would not light up as directed in the score. Wieland again dismissed the warnings and told everyone that the show would go on. George was aware of the threats; they added an extra tension to the first night, and when the moment to hold up the Grail came, he raised his arms with some trepidation. Wieland and the electricians were standing in the wings. There was an instant of suspense, then little by little the Grail lit up and the performance continued without incident.

The performance was a tremendous success. Wieland's staging was a landmark in the development of his craft, and his *Parsifal* production was given in Bayreuth with minor modifications for over twenty years. George had a huge personal success and was identified with this role in Bayreuth over the next decade. *Parsifal* was recorded twice with George as Amfortas, in 1959 and 1962, showing the "almost intolerable intensity" (as one critic put it) of his interpretation.

After a *Parsifal* performance in 1961, he wrote to his parents: "I feel that I am able to reach people in a human way that evades most of my colleagues. It is a great satisfaction and the people let me know that they have gotten the message."

It seems almost prophetic that he could feel so close to this operatic character, who suffered a "wound that would not heal." Very often during his illness, as I sat next to his emaciated Amfortas-like figure reclining in his chair, I thought of the similarity and of Amfortas's impassioned plea for death and redemption.

Parsifal was given every year in Bayreuth, while other Wagner operas rotated on different summers. George returned to Bayreuth to sing Amfortas every summer from 1951 to 1965 except in 1954, 1955, 1958, and 1960. In 1956, 1959, and 1961 he also sang *The Flying Dutchman*. Each appearance in the summer festival included a long rehearsal period and a commitment to a number of performances in each role.

George had told me repeatedly about the high level of the performances and about the special atmosphere in and around the Festspielhaus. My turn to experience the spiritual impact of Wagner's shrine took place at a rehearsal of *Parsifal* soon after my depressing arrival in Bayreuth. Not surprisingly, I was much in awe. I had met Wieland Wagner the preceding summer at the Vierjahreszeiten, a famous restaurant in Munich. We had dinner with Wieland and Hans Knappertsbusch; the next table was occupied by the Duke and Duchess of Windsor and a large party. The conversation at our table was entirely in German, which at that point I had hardly spoken in twelve years. Although I understood everything, I had trouble finding my words and said little the whole evening. I explained my silence to George later. "They must have thought that I am a moron," I said. "Nonsense," he answered, laughing. "They enjoyed the food and thought you were a beautiful and perfect wife who knows better than to interrupt an interesting conversation."

I was tremendously impressed by Wieland. He was of average height, with prematurely graying hair, and bore a strong resemblance to pictures of his grandfather. He exuded strength and assurance, which came from his encyclopedic knowledge of all kinds of subjects, from Greek mythology to Germanic legends. He commented with scorn about his youthful experiences in Hitler's time. His political ideas were liberal and he had an innate distrust of heroes, the police, and the military. His major interests were the festival and his own stagings. In an afterword to Victor Gollancz's book *The Ring at Bayreuth,* written in 1966, Wieland wrote,

> We are no longer prepared to accept the aesthetic theories either of Richard Wagner or of his immediate successors as sacrosanct in relation to his works.
>
> My generation has been, and still is, concerned not to luxuriate in aesthetic conceptions as if these were defined immutably for all time but to seek out the inner laws inherent in a work of genius and to interpret it uncompromisingly, as we find it mirrored in our souls.

In answer to this search Wieland produced a succession of provocative, not always successful but always fascinating, stagings for Wagner's operas.

George wrote in *The Saturday Review:* "When I first met Wieland Wagner [in 1950] he was thirty-three years old. He died on October 19, 1966, at the age of forty-nine. His entire career covered a brief span of fifteen years. Yet in this period he completely revolutionized the staging of Wagner operas and profoundly influenced the style in which many contemporary operas are produced."

No wonder George found Wieland "the most fascinating individual I ever met."

Wieland had the reputation of being difficult and abrupt if he did not like you. For instance, when George introduced to him a young soprano with a beautiful voice but who was not overly bright, he commented, "What is this voice doing in this woman?" and dismissed her summarily.

It was difficult to get close to him. However, he was always very courteous to me, no doubt a reflection of the respect and feelings of friendship he felt for George.

As I entered the auditorium for the *Parsifal* rehearsal, I felt intimidated. I was about to sit down somewhere toward the back when Wieland spotted me. "Frau London, come and sit here," he said, pointing to the seat next to him. This was unusually friendly on his part for I knew he did not like people in the halls during rehearsals and George had to ask for permission to bring me.

There were at most ten people in the audience when the lights went out. I had the impression that the performance was given just for me, as once the king of Bavaria had demanded a private performance of Richard Wagner, the composer.

Soon I was surrounded by the music, which I had never heard played quite like this. George wrote for *The Saturday Review:* "The entrance of the Knights of the Grail is unforgettable: From the deepest recesses of the vast stage, seemingly from infinity, an army of swaying men moves closer as the music grows in almost unbearable intensity until they have assumed their places around a huge circular table in the center." Then the Knights of the Grail intoned the Grail motif. The voices, chosen from Germany's best choruses, seemed to come from heaven. Then Amfortas was carried onstage on a litter. Instinctively I clutched my hands in a tight grip. Soon George's voice rose strong and faultless, in his long "complaint." I was close to tears and shattered by emotion.

When the lights went on at intermission, I could not say a word. Wieland, perhaps aware of my feelings, turned to me and said: "Grandfather could not have visualized anyone greater than George." He always spoke of Richard Wagner as if he were in the next room and would come over at any moment to give his opinion.

This rehearsal remains in my memory as one of the greatest musical and theatrical experiences of my life. I returned to *Parsifal* each time George sang it and every performance had a degree of excitement and fervor I found nowhere else. For an artist in the 1950s, being part of the festival was like entering a religious shrine. The singer felt part of an elite that performed artistic feats worthy of the heroic figures he impersonated.

The Wagner family reinforced this impression.

It was impermissible for an artist involved in any of the operas to behave obnoxiously in public. For example, after it was reported that a soprano had been drunk at the Eule, Wieland declared, "The Bayreuth Isolde cannot be an alcoholic," and she was not reengaged.

I felt privileged to be a part of this special world. Although I wondered why Richard Wagner had picked so drab and undistinguished a town for his Festspielhaus, I cheerfully accepted the uncomfortable housing and rainy climate.

George loved to work there. The artistic level was high and he enjoyed the weeks of rehearsal that built up to challenging performances. During these weeks there were many meals taken together with other artists. Everyone relaxed, ate large quantities of the heavy German food, and swapped outrageous jokes. As soon as the festival began, the town was invaded by tourists, the restaurants became crowded, and we no longer went out.

Because the artists expected to stay for a long time, most of them came with their families. We often visited each other and also entertained friends coming from nearby Munich. The first summer, in 1956, George invited all his colleagues to come over and admire his four-month-old daughter. The tenor Ramón Vinay came with his camera and captured Marina's big brown eyes and long eyelashes. George was bursting with pride.

The weeks of preparation went by too quickly and soon the festival began. Every performance started at four o'clock, and the crowd milled around the opera house in evening dress and tuxedos in the early-afternoon sunshine. After each act there was an hour-long intermission, which allowed everyone to strengthen his endurance by fortifying himself at the adjoining Festspielhaus restaurant.

Because of this custom, George was faced with a dilemma during *Parsifal* performances. He appeared in the first and the third act but not at all in the second. This act lasted one hour, the two intermissions took another two hours. So there was an interval of three hours between his appearances on the stage. He tried to sit around in his dressing room and have dinner brought to him, but the food was cold and distasteful. He reviewed the score one more time, then paced around the hallway visiting with friends and other singers, generally not knowing what to do with himself and, as he said, "losing the concentration." Finally he found a solution. As soon as the first act was finished, he removed costume and makeup. I went to get the car and drove him home where he had a good hot meal, then a quiet nap for an hour. Then I drove him back to the theater where he still had an hour to put on a fresh makeup, vocalize briefly, and put on the costume. Now he was rested and full of energy for the last act.

I returned the car to the parking lot and rushed back to the opera house just as the crowd was coming in. For this reason, I almost never saw the second act of *Parsifal* in later years.

The first year in particular, George encouraged me to see as many of the operas as possible, for he wanted me to experience the entire magic of Bayreuth, not only his performances. It was a period that boasted many good singers, and I had a glorious time. Unfortunately, George could not go with me too often as he was especially busy that summer.

He was to sing the role of the Flying Dutchman for the first time in a staging by Wolfgang Wagner. Wolfgang, co-director of the festival with Wieland, was very knowledgeable as well, but eclipsed at that time by his brother's genius. He is now the sole director of Bayreuth's opera season. George spent long hours working with Paola Novikova, who came to stay with us to prepare with George this role, which he termed "terribly demanding, vocally covering the widest scope of dramatic and lyrical singing."

I got along well with Paola and we provided a harmonious

atmosphere for George. The first performance was a tremendous success, and George wrote to his parents: "I felt that I had done, vocally and dramatically, a first-rate job. This role really suits me, and I feel in time that I can become especially identified with it."

The Flying Dutchman became one of his most successful parts. In 1960 he repeated his success in an inspired new staging by Wieland Wagner. In the *Saturday Review* article of 1967 George described as unforgettable

> the entrance of the Hollander's ship; a vast blood-red sail descends from the heights of the stage to meet a gigantic prow which rises from the floor, giving the impression that the ship, in its hugeness is bursting into the auditorium; the Hollander, himself, during his entire monologue, crucified on the prow of the doomed vessel, arms outstretched, motionless throughout the scene, only his face bathed in a ghostly light revealing his torment and his tragedy.

Although George preferred the role of Boris Godunov, the Flying Dutchman became my favorite part for him. Perhaps he was more handsome as Don Giovanni or more dramatic as Boris; but I felt that he identified most completely with the Dutchman who was condemned to roam the seas like a wandering Jew. The role suited him vocally, covering exactly the range of his voice and showing it off at its best. In the Bayreuth production, he wore a black leather costume, high boots, and a long cape made of netting, which made him look still taller. He was made up to look older than he was, with a gray wig, a gray beard, and lines in his face, and I thought how handsome he would be in later life.

After the premiere, which opened the festival, there was a reception at the city hall given by the Wagners for the principal stars and specially invited guests, including the German head of state, ministers, and some well-known international figures. The city hall was the former castle of the margraves, and the supper took place in a long dining room by candlelight with a waiter in livery standing behind each of the high-backed tapestry-covered chairs. It was a fairyland evening enhanced by all the compliments that George received. I felt elated, happy for him and for myself to have the good fortune to share these hours with him.

In 1961 George sang again in Wieland's staging of *The Flying Dutchman* in Venice at the Teatro La Fenice. This is a lovely small baroque auditorium, heavily decorated with gilded carvings, that has extraordinary acoustics.

The engagement was in May and for three weeks we lived in the Grand Hotel overlooking the Grand Canal in an apartment furnished with precious antique furniture. I called our stay the honeymoon we had not been able to take after our wedding. The rehearsal schedule was light, the weather was mild, and we took long walks in the narrow alleys of Venice.

One night after a performance, we were walking back to the hotel, and, as usual, the gondoliers were trying to attract customers by shouting "Gondola, gondola, Signore." Suddenly one of them, recognizing George, called out to him, "But you, sir, you don't need any boat, you already have your own ship even if it is a ghostly one."

Every summer when we arrived in Bayreuth, Wieland Wagner sent over a score of *Die Meistersinger,* with a note hoping George would consider the part of Hans Sachs. Each year George replied that he did not see himself as the benign, poetic German shoemaker. But George was learning the Wotan roles for *The Ring of the Nibelungen,* to prepare for a new staging of the *Ring,* which was to be shown in Bayreuth in 1965. It was decided that there would be tryout periods for the productions in Cologne during separate years, first for *Siegfried,* then for *Rheingold,* for *Walküre,* and for the complete *Ring.* Wotan does not appear in the last opera of the tetralogy.

Thus Cologne became an extension of Bayreuth with the same conductor, Wolfgang Sawallisch, and many of the same performers who were supposed to take part in Wieland Wagner's 1965 *Ring.*

The first opera given was *Siegfried,* in January 1962. There were nearly three weeks of rehearsals and I came with Marina, Marc, and our new nurse, Marie Claire De Reyff, to keep George company. Our beloved Nanny Buchler had retired after Marc's birth; she was old and frail and could no longer handle my large family. Marie Claire was a competent and affectionate Swiss nurse, in her twenties, who stayed with us for eight years. George missed the children acutely during his travels and when he did not see them he mentioned his longing in every letter. During our stay in Cologne the weather was miserable, cold and icy rain nearly every day. After a visit to the cathedral and shopping in the beautiful toy stores, there was not much to do.

I decided to take Marina and Marc, only six and three years old then, to part of a rehearsal. I timed it so they could see the dragon in *Siegfried*. They had a great time and shrieked with fear and delight. I related their reaction to Wieland with some hesitation, for he could be quite forbidding, but he was extremely pleased. "Yes, that is what I want; after all, it is also a fairy tale," he said.

This was the period of the closest collaboration between Wieland and George. They never tired of the rehearsals and went on discussing the operas at lunch and dinner in a small Italian restaurant they had discovered. Wieland went into detailed psychological analysis of each character in the *Ring* and wanted to stress the subconscious impulses of good and evil in his new production. George found him absolutely brilliant, continually inventive, and later wished he had had a tape recorder to preserve everything he said.

He wrote in his article for the *Saturday Review:* "My personal debt to Wieland Wagner cannot be overstressed. He opened up for me a world of insight into dramatic characterization. His ideas about Amfortas, the Hollander, and the three Wotans, all of which I sang under his direction, were endlessly fascinating."

After the opening performance in Cologne of *Walküre* on May 26, 1963, which happens to be four days after the composer's birthday, George commented in a letter to his parents: "Last night was vocally and artistically one of the most perfect performances of my career."

Wieland wrote to him the next day: "I must congratulate you for your extraordinary achievement on Sunday. You have fulfilled completely my expectations for your Wotan, yes, even surpassed them. I am very happy and I thank you. That was a really worthy birthday celebration for Richard Wagner. Stay the way you are and remain faithful to me."

The Ring of the Nibelungen was given in its entirety in Cologne in the autumn of 1963. George sang the three Wotans for the first time in the same week. There were some cuts in the tirades of the *Siegfried* Wotan to which no one seemed to object. It was a major achievement for George and the new stagings were well received, promising even greater success for the festival production of 1965.

George and Wieland, who came from such different backgrounds, were linked by a common devotion to their art. But their precious friendship lasted only another three years. Wieland Wagner died of lung cancer in 1966 and George never sang again in Bayreuth.

11

Russia and
Boris Godunov

On September 17, 1960, *The New York Times*'s front page carried the following headline: "George London Sings Boris Role in Moscow and Wins an Ovation." The article went on:

MOSCOW, Sept. 16—The American baritone George London received a standing ovation at the Bolshoi Theater tonight for his performance in Russia's greatest national opera, *Boris Godunov*.

It was the first time that an American had been starred in an opera on the stage of Moscow's large opera. Mr. London sang the dramatic role of the medieval Czar Boris in Russian.

At the end of the third act of the Mussorgsky opera when Boris dies, the audience of more than 2,000 persons rose and applauded the forty-year-old singer for eight curtain calls. Even the remainder of the all Soviet cast that filled the stage joined in the accolade to Mr. London's stirring performance.

"This is the climax of a life's dream," said Mr. London in his dressing room after the opera. "It is like Mohammed going to Mecca. I have played Boris many times and it is one of my favorite roles. It is a great honor at last to be able to play it here in Moscow—in its original setting."

As we were both in Russia, we were not immediately aware that the story was front-page news. But George was truly jubilant that night and the glow remained for a long time. I, too, was exultant, as I applauded, lost in the crowds of Russians. I kept thinking, "He did it, he did it, now no matter what happens, his wish has been fulfilled." Once he had told me, "I will sing Wagner in Germany, French opera in Paris, and Boris Godunov in Moscow." I thought the two first projects were very likely but was doubtful about the third. The Russians were proprietary about their opera, and it was extremely difficult to get an engagement there for a foreigner, let alone a singer wanting to perform their own favorite by a Russian composer.

George's friend and manager at Columbia Artists Management, Herbert Fox, knew how much George wanted to perform in Russia. Herb is a man who doesn't easily take no for an answer. While he was in Moscow negotiating for Columbia Artists to get the Red Army Chorus to do a tour of the United States, he told the negotiator from Gosconcert, the agency in charge of all the productions and concerts in the Soviet Union, "Mr. Supagin, you know that every manager has a favorite artist for whom he wishes a special engagement. I have a favorite bass-baritone, an American named George London, and I would like him to do some guest appearances in the Soviet Union. His greatest ambition is to sing Boris Godunov at the Bolshoi." "Dear Mr. Fox," replied the other, "I also have a favorite artist, an American, a bass-baritone called George London." And to Herb's amazement, Supagin proceeded to tell him that while stationed in Vienna during the Soviet occupation, he had heard George perform the role of Boris Godunov on Christmas night, 1949.

Supagin agreed that George should come to the Soviet Union and sing the role of Boris in Moscow. This being exactly what Herb wanted, they drew up a contract for a number of opera and concert appearances in Moscow, Leningrad, Riga, and Kiev, a tour that would take about four weeks.

In a return gesture, Columbia Artists engaged a well-known

Russian baritone, Pavel Lisitsian, for performances at the Metropolitan Opera and a tour of recitals.

At the beginning of September 1960, we packed for a month-long trip to the Soviet Union and said long and tender good-byes to the children. The younger ones were left in charge of Marie Claire. Andy and Philip, now fifteen and thirteen years old, went to Riverdale Country School daily on the school bus and could be trusted to behave under Marie Claire's benign supervision and occasional visits from my mother.

I was warned to take winter clothes and bought a gray suit with a long fur-lined jacket, which would keep me warm without being too conspicuous and which turned out to be perfect most of the time. In preparation for the long waits for transportation and many evenings in hotel rooms, Paola persuaded us to learn a card game, which proved very useful when we got too impatient. We played constantly in Moscow, in other towns, in airports, and never played again in our lives. I don't even remember the name of the game. We took powdered coffee, tea, soups, and the indispensable immersion heater, which George took everywhere so that he could have a hot drink late at night in hotel rooms after performances. He was always thirsty and did not want to drink anything cold after singing, as this was considered bad for the throat.

After the long trip, we were greeted by our special guide from Gosconcert, which is of course government-owned and has total control over everything and everyone connected with the arts in the Soviet Union. Olga, our guide (or private spy, as we called her), turned out to be quite nice, spoke astonishingly good English, and followed us everywhere during our stay. We were able to get rid of her only now and then, by visiting our embassy or our American friends, or in our hotel rooms.

We were booked at the Hotel National, which was the best in Moscow at the time and is still considered the most comfortable. We were given a large suite with a huge bathroom containing an old-fashioned bathtub standing on four legs. We had been warned that every room was bugged and started out the first evening whispering our first impressions to each other.

We were struck by the drabness of the airport, the city streets, and the hotel; everything was gray. Even the hotel suite adorned with welcoming flowers was depressing.

We continued whispering as we got into bed. Suddenly, in the dark, George shouted, "To hell with it, they can listen if they want. I'm not going to whisper for a whole month." That was the end of that and we spoke freely for the rest of the trip.

We were so open, and so loud, that one day, while visiting Israel Shenker, one of our journalist friends in Moscow, and exchanging political opinions, our friend raised his voice and addressed the suspected microphones: "This last opinion was expressed by George London, visiting here, and not by myself."

Everybody believed that the only places safe for conversation were cars or the streets. Relatives of friends whom we were asked to see would not come to the hotel but met us on the street in front of the post office. The streets were extremely crowded, with throngs of people rushing in all directions. There were hardly any cars on the broad avenues at that time. Everyone stood on line for food and for almost all other goods, yet the theaters and the concerts were packed. The price of tickets was cheap and the entertainments provided a much-needed relaxation for these people whose life was so difficult and so constrained.

I was excited to be in Russia, about which I had heard constantly from my mother. Also, I spoke the language sufficiently well to converse about any subject I wanted; but it was immediately evident that I was a foreigner, for I had a strong accent. I wondered whether I would feel some real bonds with these people or if whatever Russia had been like in the past had disappeared completely.

I found that the people we met were friendly, outgoing, eager to share a good meal and whatever they had. But it must be said that we met only other musicians or artists, well-educated people who had relatively privileged positions in society. The people in the streets and the crowded shops were rude and boorish. They shouted insults at each other, pushed and shoved, but were always relatively polite to me, for they knew immediately that I was a foreigner from the look of my clothes.

Even my most ordinary outfit was much better than what they had, and I found myself giving away whatever I could spare. Even our incorruptible Olga accepted my hairbrush and stockings before we left.

In 1960 Russia was still suffering from terrible shortages of every kind. It got better on subsequent visits, but I understand this situation still exists today. In Leningrad the people still talked about the war and how terribly they had suffered from hunger during the siege of the city. The gray clothes and the short gray days made me forget that the war had been over for fifteen years.

I liked the people very much and was sad to realize that the terrible regime under which they lived would make any prolonged friendship impossible.

The day following our arrival in Moscow, George went to the Bolshoi Theater for the first rehearsal. I went along, and so did the inevitable Olga. The opera house was a short walk from the hotel. We went in through the small artist's entrance and were immediately introduced to some singers waiting there. Then we went to a rehearsal room where the conductor, Melik Pashaev, was waiting with the stage director. Both greeted us cordially.

The rehearsal began and as usual the director made several suggestions. Some George accepted, but he expressed reservations about others. Olga interpreted dryly: "He does not want to do that." I saw immediate hostility spreading over the gathering and, though I had first kept away from the artists, I decided to interfere. I explained in Russian to the director that George thought that his ideas were excellent, that only in one or two places was he used to making different gestures, and that if he, the director, did not mind, George would like to do as he was used to.

Everybody smiled again and, from then on, I did all the translating, avoided hurting any feelings, and conveyed George's diplomatic utterances to the Russians. I thought if the translators were as maladroit in affairs of state as they were with us, it is no wonder people never get along with each other. Anyway, we parted great friends, with everyone looking forward to the next rehearsal.

George remembered this rehearsal in a speech to students given in 1968:

I went to my first musical rehearsal with the conductor. He did not speak English—we conversed in German—and he paid me the very great compliment that I sang in the Russian style. And then there was a staging rehearsal on the rehearsal stage the same day with the stage director, a little man by the name of Baratov. Mr. Baratov had been in America, had done a tour with the fabulous Moscow Art Theater in the U.S. in the 1920s. We sat there with my wife sitting between us acting as interpreter, and he told all about his tour in America: "Oh!" he said. "I played New York, Chicago! Terrible! Gangsters! Boom, boom!—Gollywood [the Russians have no *H*, so every *H* becomes a *G*] John Barrymore! John Barrymore, wonderful actor! played every night for six months in *Gamlet*."

He was an amusing little man and he had some ideas about *Boris Godunov* that were very helpful to me, not much, just a couple of really important tips and suggestions that helped to strengthen the character. He pointed out to me that in a few places I was being too self-pitying, that I should be more aggressively bitter, and this helped strengthen those scenes.

Baratov had just restaged *Boris* in Leningrad and described with pride some new pieces of business he had introduced. For example, when Boris enters for his scene with the Fool in front of St. Basil's, the hungry populace implores him for bread. Baratov had the Czar's retinue toss coins to the people, which they were to pick up and angrily hurl back. No doubt this was intended to endow the people with socialist dignity in a presocialist era. I told him, tactfully, that I did not feel it was true to life. Although he disagreed, he left this out of the Bolshoi production.

The dress rehearsal was onstage the next day. George had been told not to bring his Boris costume: they had their own, which conformed to their staging. He tried the costumes, which had been made for a Russian bass and they fitted him almost perfectly. I stayed with him until I was sure that he did not need me anymore. Then I walked across the stage to go to the auditorium. The stage was immense, the deepest I had ever seen.

George was rehearsing the scene in which Boris first appears, on his coronation day. According to the stage direction, Boris walks slowly from the very back of the stage to the front accompanied by the music and the sound of church bells. Again, from George's speech:

> This was the dress rehearsal of all dress rehearsals because I came out in the coronation scene and that was my first contact to the greatest star of the Bolshoi Theater and the star of this Opera, and that is the chorus. It is the greatest chorus I have ever heard, it is overwhelming. I finished the coronation scene and then I came out for my big scenes in the second act, and as I looked out into the theater, it was packed. As I later learned, it was filled with practically every singer, actor, dancer, theater person in Moscow. Most of these people didn't have tickets for the performance; that was mainly for the fat cats, it is generally hard to get in. I went through these scenes in Russian at the Bolshoi, in Moscow, in a kind of a trance, and when I finished the scene on my knees, the house came down. It was an ovation, at the dress rehearsal. I got up feeling embarrassed and a little foolish and I found myself taking bows as if it had been a performance. It was very thrilling and very exciting and I was superstitious about it, lest it be too wonderful, lest the performance be not as good.

I rushed backstage, for I knew everyone would speak to him in Russian, persuaded that he understood. They congratulated him and embraced him in the effusive Russian way. Even the conductor came to praise his performance. George asked me to speak to the young woman who played Fedya, the Czar's son. There are two scenes in the opera where the Czar is very close to his son and the singer was wearing such a heavy perfume that George could hardly breathe and had a terrible urge to sneeze. I went over to her dressing room and explained George's allergy and she immediately promised not to wear any perfume on the night of the performance.

George was moved by the approval of his peers: they were his colleagues and they knew best. If they thought he was good, he would surely win the approval of the Russians.

Still, we both faced the next evening with some trepidation.

This was it—the big night George had anticipated for so many years. I was unusually nervous, although I did my utmost to seem totally relaxed in order not to add to his own fears.

We walked to the opera house together, two and a half hours before the performance. I went backstage with him, as he needed me as an interpreter. He had discussed the makeup the day before and decided to let the makeup man help him, for he seemed extraordinarily capable. The result was remarkable indeed. George added a line here, a shadow there, and had a picture taken on stage during intermission—his best Boris picture ever. I sensed that he was satisfied with what he saw in the mirror and he seemed in good voice. He did not need me anymore and I went to my seat.

I felt terribly alone in the huge auditorium. The curtain rose and soon there he was, walking slowly upstage in his splendid golden costume, holding the scepter against a background picturing the beautiful Archangelski and Uspenski cathedrals with their colored domes, and the Kremlin walls. He was doing something so difficult in such a foreign environment and I could not help one bit!

In his 1968 speech, George described his feelings about the performance:

If my reception at the dress rehearsal augured well for the performance, it did not succeed in stilling the nervousness that assailed me. I felt that this was the supreme test of my artistry to date.

I made that first long, long walk to center stage where I sing my first aria. The stage of the Bolshoi is enormously deep. When you start out for the entrance of the coronation scene, you start at the very back of the theater. It is like sitting at a baseball game and looking out at center field, it is just about that far. There is a little peasant woman up in the flies and she is running back and forth and is ringing two cathedral bells which are part of the permanent equipment of the Bolshoi. They don't have some poor desperate assistant conductor hitting some chimes as they do in most theaters. These are cathedral bells, which is a fantastic effect except when you are standing back there ready to go on, it just about takes your head off.

As I slowly came into view of the audience, I was greeted

by waves of applause and suddenly all nervousness vanished. From that moment until the end of the performance I was in a state of complete euphoria. At the final curtain I received a standing ovation. Huge baskets of chrysanthemums were brought up on the stage. My colleagues applauded and some embraced me. Even Mrs. Khrushchev stood up. Her husband wasn't there, he was at the U.N. endearing himself to everybody by pounding on the table with his shoe. My dear friends, the baritone Lisitsian and the conductor Kondrashin and their wives, came backstage to compliment me, as did Ambassador and Mrs. Thompson and the entire American press corps. The soprano Galina Vishnevskaya (the wife of Mstislav Rostropovich), whom I had never met, rushed over, threw her arms around me, gave me a resounding kiss, and just as abruptly left. And then it was over. I was quite in a daze. Having finally divested myself of costume and makeup, I walked slowly with my wife back to the Hotel National where we celebrated quietly on caviar and sweet champagne and went to bed.

I was awakened about five o'clock in the morning by a cable saying that the story had hit the wires in the States, that there was a big headline story on the front page of *The New York Times* with a profile about myself inside, and I guess this was just about the happiest moment of my life.

When the crowd was gone, George removed his makeup and we left the deserted theater. We walked back to the National arm in arm, an anonymous couple among late pedestrians in a Moscow street, thousands of miles away from California where George first dreamed of performing Boris. I thought how much this meant to him and how glad I was that it went so well. I loved him so much and squeezed his hand very tight. We did not speak a word and felt closer than ever.

The following week, he was again greeted with ecstatic applause at a sold-out recital in the concert hall of the conservatory. The audience was clearly knowledgeable. We later found out that Russian audiences did not applaud without discrimination, but if they approved, they were enthusiastic and affectionate. George's accompanist, Leo Taubman, had arrived from the States to play for him during the forthcoming concerts of the tour. During each recital, George sang a group of Mussorgsky songs or an aria by Borodin in Russian.

After the first concert, I was accosted by a Russian journalist who told me he did not believe that George could not speak Russian, that he was just pretending. I became quite annoyed but restrained myself. At George's very last appearance in Russia, the same writer came up to me again and apologized. He had followed George everywhere and established for a fact that he did not speak Russian. I had to laugh at such perseverance, but decided that the Russians were so used to being deceived they could not believe anything.

After Moscow, we went to Riga, where George again sang Boris and gave a recital. Riga was the capital of Latvia, an independent country until World War II, when it was annexed by the Soviet Union. Since then the population had been forced to speak only Russian and to submit to Soviet rule. Only fifteen years had passed and the people were far from being assimilated by the Russians. The concert hall was packed and when George sang the aria from *Prince Igor* in which the prince, taken prisoner, laments about his fate and sings "Give me freedom," the whole audience rose and applauded until he repeated the aria.

It was a moving moment. We were well aware that the applause was not only for him but for the incarnation of freedom that he represented. After the concert, when he left the hall, hundreds of people were waiting backstage to greet him, some just to touch him. "Come back, please come back," they begged. He talked with groups here and there for a long time in the cold night and when we finally left many people were crying. We, too, had tears in our eyes, wondering why people had to be so cruel to each other.

From Riga we flew to Leningrad where we arrived toward evening. The taxi driver who drove us to our hotel pointed out some landmarks. At the Nevsky Prospekt, which was sparsely lit, he turned around, grinned and said "Broadvai" with great satisfaction.

George was to sing several performances at the Maryinsky Theater, which had been preserved exactly the way it was under the czars. I thought it was one of the most beautiful halls I had ever seen. The walls were gold and the seats and curtains were aquamarine. It was not as large as the Bolshoi and had wonderful acoustics.

George and I saw a wonderful performance of Tchaikovsky's *Pique Dame* there, and the next night I was in the same box sitting with Leo, while this time George was on stage singing Méphisto in *Faust*. There had been just a short rehearsal covering only scenes in which he was involved. All went well and the opera was coming to its close. We were expecting the last scene where Marguerite ascends to heaven. Suddenly, however, to my astonishment, Marguerite was led away in chains by an irate mob. Because Marxist dogma does not recognize religion, Marguerite could not be redeemed and Gounod's heavenly music accompanied her death march. I looked at Leo, who raised his arms in dismay. This was *Faust* Soviet-style.

We decided not to tell George right away, for we knew he would be furious at the desecration of this masterpiece. He was not onstage at that point so he did not see it; I told him only some weeks later. He was very angry indeed but could do nothing about it.

George loved to go to museums and we spent as much time as possible at the Hermitage. I was awed by the wealth and majesty of the czars' palace, not to mention the collection of paintings. I thought Leningrad very beautiful and the people more European and more gentle than in the rest of Russia. In 1960 in the West, we had long ago put memories of the war to rest; yet in Russia it seemed still very close and was talked about very frequently. These people were frightened at the idea of another conflagration, and the government constantly refueled this feeling with their propaganda about American "imperialism."

Some of the artists we met were permitted to ask us to their homes. We became friends with Pavel and Mara Lisitsian. Pavel was the baritone who came to the United States in exchange for George's trip to Russia. They always managed to have fruits and salad, which were unavailable anywhere else, on their table. They toasted us with sweet wine and strong vodka, which I could not swallow. I kept changing glasses with George when no one was looking so as not to offend them, and they admired my taste for their drinks. Meanwhile George had double rations and was becoming more and more enthusiastic about the food and the company.

We liked the Lisitsian family. We met their married daughter and their twins, a boy and a girl, all with beautiful velvety dark eyes and warm smiles. For many years we exchanged notes at Christmas, but in the long run it is impossible to cultivate a friendship with postcards. When we returned to Moscow the last time, in 1966, Pavel was ill with serious back trouble. We went to see him in a hospital on the outskirts of the city. The hospital was clean and roomy, situated in a lovely park, and Pavel was immensely pleased with our visit. He told us he had been overworked; he was forced to travel and perform constantly in remote provinces. Pavel was an honored Soviet singer and entitled to first-class care. His services belonged to the state and as a useful subject of the state it was advantageous to restore him to good health. We reflected that although Pavel was guaranteed engagements he could not choose them and we preferred the Western system. "It is true that artists often have a hard time getting work in our country, but we always have freedom of choice," George proclaimed, "and that is essential to artistic growth."

We said good-bye sadly to Pavel and his family, fearing that we were not likely to see each other again. There was little chance of our returning to Russia and the Lisitsians had no prospect of coming back to the United States.

But that first year we had good times together and saw each other often. Through Pavel we met an Armenian sculptor who made a striking bust of George. Our friend Igor Markevitch, the conductor, who was in Moscow at the same time, introduced us to a young painter called Zverev with the advice, "He is very talented, but he paints only if you give him a bottle of vodka." So we invited Zverev to our hotel room for a drink, he liked George and admired him and agreed to paint us.

A few days later we went to his place, which consisted of one room, with a mattress in one corner and a chair in another. He proceeded to make a fascinating likeness of George, full of tormented insights, and also a charming but glib portrait of me. We carried these aquarelles with us to our house in Switzerland, and they hung there until one day in May 1977, when George's portrait fell from the wall and the glass broke into many pieces. I was terribly upset and beset with frightening premonitions even though I am usually not superstitious.

Today the portraits are in my room, treasured evidence of the long-ago voyage that took us around Russia.

Our last stop before returning to Moscow was in Kiev, capital of the Ukraine, where George was to give a recital. My mother had told me that Kiev was famous for its baked goods and that I must absolutely taste the rye bread, which she remembered from her childhood. I went to a bakery. Like everyone, I had to stand in line. The Ukrainians were pushing and shouting insults, but when they realized that I was a foreigner, they yelled, "Let the stranger go forward" and I was served immediately. I thanked everyone profusely and left with a fragrant round loaf. It was delicious.

While I was shopping, George had an interview with a young journalist who spoke perfect English, having been raised in Canada where his father was the Soviet ambassador. As they were walking along the wide but bleak avenues of Kiev, the young man tried to convince George that his city was as beautiful as "Paris in the spring." George accepted this statement but told me about it later and we both laughed about the extent of self-deception people are capable of. Forever after when a place was gray and depressing we would say it was "like Paris in the spring."

By now it was the beginning of October, almost winter in Russia. It was unusually cold in Kiev, we were told, and there was no hint of heating anywhere. For George's recital I decided to wear a blue satin dress from Paris with a matching coat lined with mink. I thought it was a bit showy but I had nothing else sufficiently dressy and warm at the same time. I was quite shocked when I entered the large concert hall and discovered that I was seated way up front, in the middle of the center aisle in an armchair that had been placed there especially for me. The local organizers felt they were doing us a great honor this way.

I felt terribly conspicuous. Everyone in the audience would know at once who I was and when George arrived on the stage and bowed to the audience, he could almost touch me. I could tell he was surprised to see me there, but controlled himself and just winked imperceptibly at me. Then he proceeded to perform with his usual passion and dedication. I thought that I detected an extra warmth in the voice, an extra depth in his expression, and soon I was convinced that this one time he was singing just for me. It was the only time I ever felt this, and I will never forget the sensation. How fortunate I was, I thought. I was deeply moved and forgot all about my awkward seat. Indeed, only after a while did I realize that it was so cold I could see George's breath while he was singing.

I started to worry that he would catch a cold, a dreaded event for a singer, especially since he was due to sing another recital in Moscow. He was concerned, as well, and demanded hot tea during the intermission and at the end of the recital. The demand had not been foreseen and created a tremendous crisis, but in the end someone managed to bring some tea from a nearby restaurant.

On the following day we were supposed to fly back to Moscow. When we arrived at the airport, it was covered with fog: no plane could possibly arrive or leave. Then we discovered that the airport was not heated, that there was an electrical breakdown, and that for some unknown reason no food was available. Dejected, cold, and hungry, we waited all day, George getting angrier by the minute. I managed to keep his temper under control by playing cards with him. We played in coats and scarves with gloves on, barely able to see in the gray daylight, and blessed Paola for having taught us our game.

Finally an Aeroflot plane managed to land and carried us to Moscow. Olga apologized for the mishap and accused the Kiev officials for this inefficiency.

We loved the Russian people but we resented the oppression of this iron regime upon them, although most of them seemed used to it. Our Armenian friend told us with contempt, "The Russians are like sheep, they follow the leader blindly." All the people we came in contact with were warm, outgoing, and fun-loving. I felt great empathy for them because of their strong family ties and their love and understanding of music. However, I did not identify with them. I found that they had very little in common with me and my Russian refugee relatives. Besides daily use of the Russian language and a strong Russian accent in every language they spoke, my mother and my uncle were definitely sophisticated Western capitalists.

The Soviet people were suspicious because of their lack of freedom and lack of information. They were constantly frustrated and exhausted from their efforts to procure daily necessities or obtain permits to travel, to change apartments or jobs. After a month in this stifling atmosphere, deprived of news (all the Western news came from an occasional paper from the U.S. Embassy), we could not wait to go home, in spite of all the honors and the success. George decided that we had to leave immediately after his last concert.

He asked me to call the Gosconcert people and tell them that he wished to go that Thursday, instead of Saturday as originally scheduled. They informed us that this was impossible because there was no Aeroflot plane leaving that particular day. I replied that I knew that an SAS plane was going to London on Thursday. The answer was: "Impossible." We could not leave, no reason given. I knew they wanted us to use Aeroflot because the fare would be collected by the Soviet government. Furious, I said, "If we cannot leave on Thursday, my husband will not sing on Wednesday."

I knew that the concert in the huge Tchaikovsky Hall was completely sold out and that it would be a great scandal if the recital did not take place. I was told, "Please wait a moment." There was much discussion at the other end of the line. In the meantime, I explained the conversation to George, who waited anxiously unable to understand what was going on.

After a short pause, the answer came back, "You can leave Thursday with the Scandinavian Airlines." I breathed a sigh of relief; my threat had worked. I don't know what we would have done had they refused, but with our Western outlook we could not tolerate being told that we could not go somewhere when it pleased us.

The last concert was very moving. The audience applauded on and on and shouted to George, "Come back, come back." George wondered if he would ever be able to return to sing in Russia. He loved the audience even if he detested the government. He would always remain ambivalent about Russia. He had tears in his eyes as he bowed and applauded them, as is the custom in Russia. We left the next day, on a gray morning with snow flurries, full of love and sadness. Yet already in the Scandinavian plane we felt as if a weight had been lifted, and when we arrived in London we appreciated to its fullest the meaning of democracy and freedom.

We returned to Moscow in May 1963. This time Herb Fox had negotiated for George the recording of *Boris Godunov* with Mezhdunarodnaya Kniga, the Soviet state organization that does all the Russian recordings as well as the publishing of books. George was to record all the scenes in which Boris appears, and these scenes would be incorporated into a recording of the whole opera. The complete recording with George as Boris was then sold in the United States by Columbia Records. Boris appears only in four scenes in the entire opera and has fewer than thirty minutes of singing. It took three sessions to record his role.

We spent nearly two weeks in Russia and were happy to see all our friends again, including Kiril Kondrashin and his wife, Nina. He was a well-known conductor who eventually defected to the West. George indulged again in his passion for caviar, which he ordered every morning for breakfast while Mara Lisitsian managed to bring him some salad leaves from their *dacha*. She knew of George's addiction and we were deeply touched by her solicitude. George wrote in the notes for the recording:

> May in Moscow was delightful and balmy. The trees in the parks were in full bloom. Young girls in gaudy summer prints, walking arm in arm with their swains, were to be seen everywhere. The city looked brighter and more prosperous than the last time we had been there. At the large recording studio of the Mezhdunarodnaya Kniga (International Book), which produces all records in the Soviet Union, I renewed my acquaintance with Melik Pashaev, who this time eschewed German and insisted on conversing in French. I was warmly greeted by my colleagues, all of whom had sung with me at the Bolshoi. But my most profound impression of these recording sessions was of the Bolshoi chorus. The women's voices possess a quality of what may be described paradoxically as cultivated vulgarity. It is a folk sound so well suited to the scenes of the populace in such operas as *Boris, Khovanshchina* and *Prince Igor*. And yet

there is a perfect discipline of musicality and intonation. The tenor voices are high and lyrical, but cutting, and the basses are of unequalled sonority and profundity. Mussorgsky felt that the true protagonist of his opera was the chorus, the Russian people.

Our sessions went smoothly and without incident. We listened to the final playback on May 10, 1963.

The days went by quickly and we did not have time to get homesick. When we left, the Kondrashins surprised us with the gift of a large lacquer box representing Boris Godunov against a colorful background of St. Basil's Cathedral and the Kremlin. We had admired this box while visiting the Gum department store with them and we were deeply touched by their thoughtfulness.

Back in the States, George suggested that a picture of the box be used for the cover of the *Boris Godunov* album, and Columbia Records adopted his idea.

George expressed his feelings in the conclusion of the *Boris* album notes when he wrote: "I felt that were I never to sing another note, I would at least have this unique documentation of my most beloved role."

LEFT: George, Julius Rudel, and the Honorable William McCormick Blair at the dedication of the John F. Kennedy Center, 1969.

BELOW: Coaching a student during a master class, 1972. *(Copyright © Henry Grossman)*

ABOVE LEFT: With Roger L. Stevens.

ABOVE RIGHT: George receiving the Litteris et Artibus decoration from the Austrian ambassador Arno Halusa, November 1976.

BELOW: The children, Marc, Andy, Philip, and Marina, in Armonk, 1980.

At the Washington Opera Ball, 1976.

Title role in Mozart's *Don Giovanni. (Sedge LeBlang; courtesy the Metropolitan Opera Archives)*

RIGHT: Amonasro in Verdi's *Aïda*.
BELOW: Dr. Coppelius in
Offenbach's *Tales of Hoffmann*.
BELOW RIGHT: Title role in
Tchaikovsky's *Eugene Onegin*. *(All
by Sedge LeBlang; courtesy the
Metropolitan Opera Archives)*

ABOVE LEFT: Title role in Wagner's *Flying Dutchman*. ABOVE RIGHT: Baron Scarpia in Puccini's *Tosca*. BELOW LEFT: Count Almaviva in Mozart's *Marriage of Figaro*. *(All courtesy the Metropolitan Opera Archives)* BELOW RIGHT: Title role in Menotti's *Last Savage*, 1964. *(Louis Melançon; courtesy the Metropolitan Opera Archives)*

Title role in Mussorgsky's *Boris Godunov.*

Amfortas in Wagner's *Parsifal. (Courtesy the Metropolitan Opera Archives)*

12

Loss of His Voice

During the summer of 1959 we rented a house near Geneva. Our family was complete: Andy and Philip, aged fourteen and twelve, were two handsome, healthy boys doing well in school; Marina was a bright, enchanting three-year-old; and Marc was a beautiful three-month-old baby. George and I celebrated our fourth wedding anniversary that summer more in love and closer than ever. I admired and applauded his accomplishments, and I was always ready to share his dreams, his hopes, and his disappointments. In turn, I was fulfilled by his passion, his tenderness, and his obvious admiration.

There was really very little to complain about. George had more offers than he could possibly accept; his only regrets were that often he had to forgo a prestigious offer at La Scala, for instance, because he had already committed that time slot to Vienna. He never went back on his word and insisted on having enough time to recuperate between engagements. The intensity of his performances was costly to his nerves and he needed several days to unwind. No doubt, his involvement in his roles was part of his success, and he could not have behaved differently had he wanted.

By the time his summer vacation came around he was in need

of complete rest. I was aware of this and convinced that a summer house, shared by the family, was the solution. Long periods in Bayreuth together were difficult, because of the lack of distractions for the children and the climate was not great for anyone. In 1959 George did *The Flying Dutchman* with Wieland Wagner but he did not sing *Parsifal* that year and was free after August 5. We both loved Switzerland and decided that there we would find the ideal place for all of us. There was entertainment for the children, the air was wonderful, and above all Switzerland would provide the calm and relaxation that George needed.

The Villa Bella Vista in Bellevue overlooking Lake Geneva had a fabulous view, as its name suggested, but was in fact a white elephant. No one would buy it, in spite of its location on the water, because it was a huge mansion, with innumerable rooms and the second floor was inhabited by bats. For this reason it could be rented at a reasonable price. I decided that if we closed off the upper part of the house, including the bats, there were enough rooms left for us all. Making the house habitable was well worth the effort for it came with a marvelous garden and private beach.

I had arrived after a plane trip with Marina and Marc. Nanny having retired, I traveled alone with the children and was met at the airport by Marie Claire. She took the baby from my arms, but Marina did not want to go to this new person at first and held on to me while we moved into the big house. The next day our family's maid came from Paris and helped me to get everything organized. Eventually I also engaged a cook who provided excellent meals for the family, which also included Andy and Philip, and their friend Gerard. After a week's time Marina got used to the nurse and I could meet George in Bayreuth, leaving everybody happily ensconced in the house under my mother's supervision.

My mother had become George's greatest fan and was prepared to do things for him she would never do for anyone else in the family. Geroge had grown very fond of her. He liked her *air de grande dame*, he said, mixed with a good sense of humor, which "made up for her faults like being superficial and prejudiced." She adored the children, most of all Marina, for she openly preferred girls. Although she lived partly in New York and partly in Lausanne, close to her brother Senia, she spent part of the summer with us.

When we returned together, George was delighted with the place. He loved to be with the children all day, enjoyed loafing on the beach with the older boys and Marina, and admired his infant son. He had grown to love Andy and Philip as if they were his own and was involved with their playtime as well as their school curriculum. The summer started perfectly. We hardly ever went out but many friends visited: the conductor Eugene Ormandy and his wife, Gretl; Henry and Ginny Pleasants; and some childhood friends of mine from Paris. George was relaxed and enjoying himself. He laughed a lot and joked a lot and was acutely aware of his good fortune, for he wrote to his parents, "One must always count one's blessings and be grateful for every good day in one's life."

During the end of August he returned to Rome for a few days to complete some minor scenes for a *Tosca* recording started earlier. When he returned he looked tired. Even after a week of rest and sleeping twelve hours each night he did not feel better and could not digest his meals. He did not look right to me and his eyes seemed blurred. I inquired about a doctor and he agreed to go. The diagnosis was clear: George had viral hepatitis and was immediately hospitalized in Geneva. The staff in the hospital was extremely kind and efficient and the doctor assured me that after three weeks in the hospital and an equal amount of rest at home, George would recover completely.

I couldn't believe that George was so ill. He always seemed so strong and took such good care of himself. I was shattered but could not allow it to show. I made sure that George had the best specialist and then I concentrated on making George feel as secure as possible.

I knew he would be horrified at having to cancel some engagements and that he would worry about it. His peace of mind was very important to his recovery, so I reassured him as energetically as I could. I argued that this was his vacation period and that by the autumn he would be well again. I promised I would contact his managers. I told him everyone would understand that it was not his fault if he got sick and I begged him to relax.

He lay in his hospital bed, quite jaundiced and weak. He agreed to everything I said and promised not to worry. I was desolate to see him so subdued.

Once at home, I called his managers in New York and Europe to inform them of his illness so that they would cancel George's engagements for the coming six weeks. We agreed that he would hold on to a planned *Don Giovanni* in San Francisco for October 20, which would give ample time for a full recovery.

We were inundated with get-well wishes from all over the world. While trying to respond, I wondered how George could have contracted this disease. He was too despondent for serious conversations and in my daily visits I confined myself to superficial chatter, news about the children, who were not allowed to visit, and reassurance about future engagements.

When George felt somewhat better, we talked over his experiences during the past three months and found that during the arduous tour in Israel he had been given vitamin B injections, which he believed gave him added energy. He had noticed that the needle was not new and did not seem too clean (disposable needles were not in common use at that time), but he was assured that they were sterile. No doubt the needles were the cause of his illness, for the time between the injections and the hepatitis was the exact incubation period for the disease.

The summer was coming to a close and as soon as George was strong enough to be moved, we decided that he would be more comfortable in our apartment in New York. School was about to start for the boys and now I transported the whole family back to the United States, including the new nurse but leaving behind our beloved Sasha, the maid, who returned to Paris.

George recuperated quickly. There was a lovely Indian summer in New York and he spent lazy afternoons on the terrace overlooking the changing colors of Central Park. The children were delighted to have Daddy home for such a long time. He played for hours with Marina and watched the development of baby Marc, now six months old. He wrote to his parents with great perspicacity: "Marina has a simply devastating personality, enormous charm and humour and great warmth too. Marc has a very special sweetness."

He spent more time with the boys and helped with their homework, especially English. He had an unusually large vocabulary and perfect command of the English language; he prided himself on being able to finish the crossword puzzle in *The New York Times* every

Sunday. He tried to inculcate his love for words in all of us, although he declared with a tender smile that I managed to confuse everybody's English with my idiosyncratic pronunciation. However, in the end I think he succeeded in teaching us a reverence for the wealth and power of the language of Shakespeare.

Soon he became impatient at being condemned to inactivity. He argued with me about his ability to exercise and to go out and I complained that he needed a gendarme, not a wife to take care of him. To keep him entertained, I invited his friends to visit and distract him with political dissertations or opera gossip.

When he felt stronger, George started to vocalize and found with relief that all was well with his voice. In fact, soon he was again his former self except that he had to forgo all the sweets and desserts that he loved. I tried to invent palatable pastries based on angel-food cake and jelly rolls, all made without cream and fats. It was a challenge and I never really succeeded; but although George sighed with frustration, he was quite good about it. He was never again able to eat two banana splits in a row but he did recover completely from the hepatitis.

We left our cozy domesticity to go to San Francisco for performances of *Don Giovanni,* which went very well. In fact, the 1959/60 season turned out to be one of George's most successful ones. It was the season of the triumph of the first *Flying Dutchman* at the Met and the creation of the role of Golaud in Debussy's *Pelléas and Mélisande.*

All through the autumn George worked hard to prepare the Golaud role. Because I spoke French with my mother and most of the time with the children, George had become fluent in the language. This made the study of a new Gallic work easier, but, as usual for him, he had to delve deep into this new character. Golaud is another one of those complex, tormented personalities with whom George could identify because he understood them and had the ability to project their inner conflicts on the stage. Golaud became one of his most moving roles and a great personal success for George, although the opera is never very popular.

The Flying Dutchman premiere took place in January 1960. It was followed by one of George's longest seasons at the Met, during which he sang in a variety of his roles: Amonasro in *Aïda,* Méphistophélès in *Faust,* Don Giovanni, and a number of *Flying Dutchmans*. His singing was so secure that I could attend his performances without apprehension.

In April he left on the Met tour, doing the Count in seven performances of *The Marriage of Figaro* all over the United States. He did not travel with the tour but flew home between performances. After the second *Figaro* he came back and I could tell right away that he was disturbed. He told me that the previous night his voice cracked on the F-sharp, the high note, toward the end of his third-act aria, "Vedrò mentr'io sospiro." This had never never happened before and he was terribly upset. He had prepared for the high note as usual, supported the voice perfectly, and could not understand how the crack had happened. "Such an accident," he said, "should never happen to a singer of my standing. I am mortified."

I talked with him for hours, mentioning his tiredness from traveling, uncomfortable housing, heavy meals, all the possible reasons. Finally, at wits' end, I said that after all, it could happen to anyone and that one single note could not erase the accomplishments of his entire career. I knew I had to remove the fear that the accident had implanted in his heart. I had seen in many singers' eyes the look of terror when they approached a high note they dreaded. I was afraid for George; I wanted to protect him from such trials.

I knew he would have to go back and sing more *Figaros* in the next few weeks. So I told him over and over that this F-sharp was unimportant, that the whole aria was the thing, that he was a magnificent Count, that the people came for his interpretation of the role, not to hear one note. I managed to calm him down. He practiced the dreaded phrase over and over in the bathroom until he was partially reassured. He went off again and finished the tour without further mishaps, but for the first time fear had entered his singing. The performances, which came in close succession, were a trial for him and took a heavy toll on his nerves. When the last one, on May 25, was behind him we were both greatly relieved.

I was glad that we were going to Europe. Our first stop was Geneva. We stayed at our favorite Hotel de la Paix, with a view of the lake and Mont Blanc, to celebrate George's birthday. He wrote to his parents on May 29, 1960, "Tomorrow I shall be forty years old. I'd just as soon not go into details about this or even to philosophize. I hereby leave my youth behind and take the first timid step into middle age. On the other hand I feel a flowering of my vocal and intellectual powers which previously had eluded me."

Switzerland did not have its usual soothing effect on him. Although he seemed to be in good health, he was traumatized at the thought that he was leaving behind his thirties, during which he had been so fortunate. He still worried about the *Figaro* incident. Did he have a foreboding of what was to come? He was terribly gloomy and I consoled him as best I could, pulling out all the jaded arguments about the forties being the best years of a man's life. Eventually he emerged from his depression, yet I was concerned about his strained nerves and approved his decision to cancel a concert in Vienna and six performances in Bayreuth. This way, he argued, he would be in perfect condition for the forthcoming recording of *The Flying Dutchman* in August and for the all-important Russian tour in September.

He talked to me again and again about needing complete relaxation and total rest for his nerves. I thought that, in spite of appearances, he had not completely recovered from his bout with hepatitis. He became very quiet and gloomy, kept to himself, and read. Gone was the boisterous, gregarious man so full of life that I had called my fifth child.

I decided that a prolonged stay in Switzerland would provide the right atmosphere, and George agreed.

This time we rented a chalet in Villars up in the mountains about an hour from Lausanne. I thought the mountain air would be beneficent and invigorating for all. Our good friends, the conductor Igor Markevitch and his wife, Topazia, lived nearby, and they would be of help, because I knew that George could take just so much nature and would need intellectual and artistic stimulation before long. George spent two weeks alone just resting while I went back to the States to fetch the family.

Everyone including Socrates, our wise beagle, moved safely from New York to Villars after the usual packing, last-minute expired passports, and missing baby formula. Nurse Maire Claire, always calm and cheerful, was a great help during our travels.

The summer turned out to be a great success. George and the two younger children were soon beautifully tanned. Marc was walking, holding on to George who seemed gigantic next to him. Philip had his first flirtation, with the daughter of the family in the chalet next door, and Socrates begged around the kitchens of nearby hotels for additions to his meals. Marina and I were dressed up in dirndls: George had bought these for us, deciding that I was the perfect Aryan type. He did not get bored thanks to evenings with Igor and Topazia, during which we argued about the merits of various pieces of music (they did not like Rachmaninoff as we did) or about politics. They were more indulgent toward the Soviet regime than we were; they had been there and gave us advice about our forthcoming trip.

Soon George was rested, optimistic, and his usual noisy and joyous self. He forgot about the shame he always felt when he canceled a performance and began to look forward to the *Dutchman* recording. I stopped worrying about him. I, too, enjoyed the carefree mountain life and the family's daily routines, uninterrupted by rehearsals. The glamour of George's career, in my eyes, did not always make up for all the sacrifices, the tension, and the frequent separations. The love and care that George lavished on the children made me specially happy, for this was what I had always dreamed about. Here was a man who could love and fulfill his wife and also give plenty of love to his children.

At the end of the summer we left our mountain refuge. By then George was eager to go; he was ready for work. His vocalizing was going well. As we had no piano, he went to practice with an accompanist at the Markevitches every day and was pleased and confident with the results: He would be in top form in London and in Russia.

We went to London where *The Flying Dutchman* was to be recorded. There we met Leonie Rysanek, who sang the role of Senta, and Antal Dorati, the conductor. In spite of uninterrupted rainy weather, the recording went extremely well. After the sessions, which were long and strenuous, there was much togetherness and joking among the artists. George was full of verve and swapped jokes with Toni Dorati and Giorgio Tozzi, who was also part of the cast. When the recording was finished, we went back to New York to prepare for the Russian trip. After that, George had a somewhat shorter season at the Metropolitan, which included *Boris Godunov*s, *Arabella*s, *Don Giovanni*s, and *Tosca*s. No *Figaro*s were foreseen, and I believed that the last year's incident had been forgotten.

George left for a long and profitable concert tour that kept him away for weeks in a row. He hated to be gone so long and swore that next year, he was going to insist that his concertizing be cut into two separate periods.

In May I went with him to Stuttgart where he did a television performance of *Tosca* with Renata Tebaldi, which was seen all over Europe. He wrote about it to his parents: "To be known by the average person one needs either TV or films. It depends on what you want out of life. Believe me, I'm aware of these things and I'm proud and ambitious too. I am sure I will leave my mark in operatic history and that is what counts."

In spite of the Russian triumph a certain wistfulness crept into his outlook. He was no longer the young singer ready to climb mountains. He had been wounded, and it was not quite the same again.

During the summer of 1961, we went back to Villars, renting a more comfortable chalet for four months. There George spent happy periods before and after his performances in Bayreuth. Once, as we left to go to Germany, we drove off in our new four-door white Mercedes and we both kept waving at the children standing in front of the door. We waved so frantically that George forgot about the driveway and drove down the four steps of a footpath. There was a clatter and tremendous laughter as everybody ran over to assess the damage. Miraculously the Mercedes went on without a murmur and served us perfectly for ten years. The mishap postponed our departure for a few minutes and afforded an excuse for more kisses and good-byes.

It was one of George's busiest and most satisfying summers in Bayreuth. He sang Amfortas twice and the Dutchman three times, and we came back in a great mood. A few weeks later he went alone to Munich for some performances of *Don Giovanni* and brought back a surprise especially for me. In his arms he carried a small basket, which he put on my lap with a look of great joy and expectation. He could not wait to see my face when I discovered that the basket contained a two-month-old wirehaired dachshund, silver and black, brown eyes like shiny buttons, a tiny wet nose, and a pink tongue that licked my hands with immediate devotion. I was overjoyed.

George knew how much I loved this breed, and had driven from Munich without stopping to be sure to get home with the little dog on the eve of our anniversary.

At the end of the summer, just before we came home to New York with the new family member, we started to look for a piece of land near Lake Geneva where we could eventually build our own house. The couple who had rented us the chalet in Villars lived near Lausanne and knew of land for sale not far from their own house. So one day we stood proudly on our own property, six acres overlooking a vineyard, some rolling fields, and below, Lake Geneva with the Alps on the far side. Far away you could see Mont Blanc when the weather was clear, and just to our left was a fourteenth-century castle that gave the name of Vufflens-le-Château to our village. We stood arm in arm on the property making plans for the house and our future life in it. Someday we hoped to spend most of the year in Switzerland, just keeping a small pied-à-terre in New York for the Metropolitan Opera season.

During the following winter George caught a cold and, as usual for a singer, he went immediately to see his throat specialist. Dr. Leo Reckford took care of most of the Metropolitan Opera's artists. In addition to being medically expert, he also knew how to handle his patients' delicate psyches. After George's visit Dr. Reckford called to warn me that one of George's vocal cords was not responding. He was not sure, because the throat was inflamed, but if it was the left cord that was injured, it could have serious implications. The nerve to that cord loops around the aorta, the main artery leaving the heart, and George might be seriously ill. Dr. Reckford had not said anything to George, expecting to see him again in a few days when the swelling went down, but he told me to keep George home and prevent him from getting agitated. I barely heard the physician's advice. My mind was racing. What did this mean? What kind of heart problem? Could it be fatal? How could this strong giant be so ill? How would I keep this secret to myself these next few days? But already George was home giving a report about his sore throat, and I smiled and went about the household chores as if nothing had happened. This was my first apprenticeship of laughing through tears; I became a master at it in the future.

A few days later George went back to Dr. Reckford and I went along. The swelling was gone; the cold was cured. Dr. Reckford asked me to look over his shoulder into George's throat while he was examining him with his instruments. George's throat was so wide and open that I could clearly see his vocal cords, two short rather thick membranes that met in a central position when he said the letter *a*. I could also see what the doctor now diagnosed: that the left cord was moving back and forth diligently while the right one seemed sluggish and vibrated only slightly when touching the left. The doctor explained to George that because the right cord was the affected one, it had nothing to do with the aorta. Still, it seemed that the nerve which activated the right cord was paralyzed. Possibly the nerve and cord were affected only temporarily, as a result of the throat infection, and would recover in time. In the meantime he advised as much vocal rest as possible.

I was somewhat relieved to be free of the terror of the past few days—at least it wasn't his heart—but we left the doctor's office in silence, each wondering what this meant for the future. I took George's hand and caressed his small elegant wrist, unusually delicate for such a tall man. I wondered if there was anything seriously wrong in the magnificent vocal apparatus I had just inspected.

Evidently George had the same thoughts. He did not know the exact prognosis of his ailment. Of course he was deeply disturbed by the doctor's discovery, but it was not in his nature to accept any misfortune without a fight. His voice was his capital and he was determined to take any measures needed to preserve it.

He remained as loving and considerate as ever with his family but his nerves paid a heavy price. He had to resort to sedatives more and more frequently. At night I often heard him get up, to read for hours, and my heart sank for I could not help. The constant search for a cure kept him busy at best and sustained him with hope of improvement.

At first the diagnosis had no influence on his singing. His cold was cured and he went back to his busy season at the Metropolitan, his recitals and the performances in Cologne. But from that time on, between operas and concerts, wherever we were, he would consult every throat specialist he heard about. I would take the familiar position behind the physician and look over the shoulder into George's throat. In the beginning it often seemed that the right cord was moving, and the doctor and I could reassure George. Then he went back to the stage and performed as if nothing had happened. In 1964 Dr. Zimmermann, a German doctor, convinced him that an operation to straighten the septum in his nose would help. I was opposed to this, feeling that it was useless torture. For once I intervened and begged George not to do it, but he went ahead and was disappointed once again. As the years went by, it became obvious that the right cord was definitely not moving; would never move again. Another operation opening the base of the neck to find out if some muscle was pressing on the nerve proved useless; the laryngeal nerve was not functioning. No valid explanation could be found. Perhaps the paralysis stemmed from the hepatitis.

Because the cord was not moving, it eventually became atrophied. The left cord compensated and moved over farther and farther to meet the affected one. As long as the cords met sound was produced and George could continue to sing. Because of his excellent technique and breath support, he was able to perform for a few years without too much trouble. On January 19, 1963, Winthrop Sargeant wrote in *The New Yorker*:

> George London, in his role as the Dutchman, ought to be commemorated by a statue in the lobby. I have never encountered a finer interpretation of the Dutchman, and I suspect it will be many seasons before any other artist anywhere undertakes this brooding, romantic role with comparable authority, either in voice or in physical presence.

This extravagant praise was particularly welcome at that time. Yet I could tell that some high notes were becoming increasingly difficult, and then little by little I noticed that he did not have the customary thrust in the voice. I tried to reassure him and tell him that he sounded fine, but I knew he was not fooled.

At the end of 1963 we sold the apartment on Central Park West—the building had gone co-op the previous year—and moved to 1155 Park Avenue. We also started building our house in Switzerland, hoping to go there within two years. Andy started at Yale that year and Patrick had gone to Cornell a year earlier. So we were left with only three children. Philip was picked up every morning by the Riverdale bus and Marie Claire took Marina to the French Lycée two blocks away on her way to the park with Marc and Zorro, the dachshund.

The apartment was very roomy with four bedrooms, living room, dining room, and den. There was a rumor that Caruso had once lived there. More important for us, it was quiet; the master bedroom, which George also used as a study, was at the end of a long hall and George did not hear any of the household noise. With the increasing strain he was experiencing, he needed more rest than ever and became extremely irritated when he was disturbed.

In January 1964 George sang the title role in *The Last Savage,* a new opera by Gian-Carlo Menotti, which was given at the Metropolitan Opera. George was carried onstage in a cage where he stood dressed in a leopard skin, showing his splendid physique. During the remainder of the story he became exposed to the benefits of civilization. The libretto was rather silly but there was some charming music. After his entrance George had a lovely aria, set fairly high in his range, which gave him trouble, and he was nervous about it. However, at the general rehearsal all went well and we had a party full of good cheer in our new apartment with Gian-Carlo Menotti, Samuel Barber, and Thomas Schippers, the conductor. We had just moved and everyone sat on boxes and cases, eating delicious food displayed on a huge buffet. At the premiere, three days later on January 23, the cage was brought in to great applause and set down center stage. When George started singing, the cage, which had evidently not been well fastened to the floor, began to sway alarmingly and it appeared to be falling over, righting itself at the last moment. There was a sigh from the audience. Sitting at the front of the orchestra, I thought I would die. Remembering George's fear of the aria, I knew the incident would throw him off even more. He managed to finish the aria decently but afterward he came to dread his entrance more and more.

By the end of 1964, every appearance was an ordeal for him. The carefree performer of the past was gone; his instrument was no longer dependable and all his know-how could not help. He took tranquilizers before each performance, and I watched with a sinking heart the heroic battle of my beloved husband against his awful fate. He never complained and forced himself with superhuman dedication to try different tricks: take a deeper breath, or place the tone preceding a high tone somewhat higher, or cheat with the pronunciation of a vowel to make it sound like *A,* which is easier. I could only encourage him when he asked my opinion. At times I suggested that he transpose an aria one tone down, but he would not hear of it and I did not insist.

I could not tell him what to do. I had never interfered with his career. I always felt he was the expert and knew what was best for him. I did not want to be the singer's meddling wife. Now I felt that psychologically I had no right to interfere.

I could not be the one to tell him to quit the profession to which he had given all his life and energy. Even if sometimes I wanted to scream "stop torturing yourself," I said nothing: he had to decide his own fate. I was determined to be cheerful and constructive at all times and to hide my distress.

The situation was all the more difficult because besides the doctor and Paola Novikova, his teacher, no one knew that there was anything wrong with George, since that in itself would have been damaging to his career. No one would engage a singer who had trouble with his vocal cords!

At home, he was quieter than usual and would stay for hours in his room with a book. He was always affectionate with the children, who did not suspect anything. He worked on many of Philip's English compositions; they were a challenge to both. Then he waited anxiously for Philip's marks to find out if they had done well. He was naturally competitive in everything he did and had strong opinions in literature and politics. He was furious if the teacher did not like his/Philip's work. I encouraged these outbursts; they were good outlets for all that pent-up frustration and I teased him about his school marks.

In September 1964 George went on a four-week tour of recitals in Japan. He tailored his program to his current capacities, performing arias without too many high notes and relying on relatively easy song cycles. We went to Tokyo, Kyoto, and Osaka; the faithful Leo Taubman was his accompanist. The concerts were a success. George was fairly relaxed and we loved Japan. But this was to be the last extended tour abroad.

During the season 1964/65 at the Met, George had a fairly

heavy schedule, which included his first *Walküre*s in New York, *Tosca*s, *Last Savage*s and a number of *Flying Dutchman*s. The *Walküre* performances were in February and the beginning of March. Miraculously they went rather well. Although the voice lacked luster and carrying power, he had some good nights, but each performance took a heavy toll on George's nerves and required twice as much energy as usual.

The atrophy of the affected cord progressed faster during these months, and by the spring of 1965, George's singing voice was a fraction of what it had been. I remember his last *Flying Dutchman*, at the Met, in mid-April. I sat with friends in a box, soaked in perspiration, almost unable to listen. I sensed George's panic and his agony and just prayed he would get through to the end.

When the opera was over, our friends did not say anything and went backstage where everyone played the usual comedy of lavish compliments. Later on we went through the ritual analysis of the performance and I managed to lie fairly convincingly. I knew he had to sing three additional *Flying Dutchman*s on tour and I had to bolster his confidence. However, he knew how costly each appearance was for him and what a dreadful torment each high note had become.

He was, in fact, acutely aware of his condition and realized that he would not be able to sing opera too much longer. When he was offered a role in a Broadway musical, he jumped at the opportunity. It was scheduled for November 1965. George was to play the male lead in the story of Anastasia, the daughter of Czar Nicholas who allegedly escaped the massacre of the imperial family during the revolution. The show sounded promising and was to be directed by George Abbott. I was glad of George's decision and hoped he would be able to do this kind of singing without problems. Also, he would be well paid and that would be a big help, for the cancellations had mounted steadily and consequently George was earning only a fraction of his former income. At the same time our expenses were increasing: the children were going to school and we had started to build our house in Switzerland.

In the summer of 1965, we rented a house in Bayreuth for two months in preparation for *The Ring of the Nibelungen* in Wieland Wagner's new staging. George was scheduled to sing the role of Wotan. This had been planned for years with great expectations both from Wieland and George. The trial performances in Cologne had gone well in previous years. I moved our family to Bayreuth, knowing that now it was too late. How could George possibly get through those grueling parts? The weather did not help. It rained nonstop from the moment of our arrival. George immediately got a cold that would not go away. Karl Böhm, the conductor replacing Wolfgang Sawallisch, the Cologne conductor who had been more accommodating, insisted on opening up some cuts in Wotan's declamations, cuts that had been promised to George in his contract. This situation gave George the opportunity to withdraw gracefully from the whole engagement.

The atmosphere in the house was heavy with sorrow. This was the first major disaster resulting from George's infirmity and we had to face it. I packed up our belongings and prepared the family to leave as quickly as possible. George had the sad duty of taking leave of Wieland. Both men were heartbroken to see their dreams shattered. Wieland could find another Wotan but it would not be the same. George was dejected; this was one of the worst moments of the long, tormented path from stardom to the end of his career.

Still, we left the gloomy, wet town for the Swiss mountain resort of Gstaad carrying with us the secret of George's real malady. I felt sure that by now many people in the music business had guessed that there was something wrong with George, but no one knew what it was. Over the years we were forever inventing new excuses—sometimes a hernia, sometimes colds, or various indispositions—but never mentioned the sacred words *vocal cords,* a death sentence for an opera singer.

We both hated the lying, the cover-up. It was particularly difficult for George, who was such an extrovert and liked to talk openly about all his concerns. He became gradually more uncommunicative and less sure of himself. I was devastated to see the change in him and I didn't know what to do.

During the fall of 1965 George's voice became less and less dependable. From time to time I noticed that even his speaking voice was a little hoarse. At last George realized that he could not even go through with the musical-comedy project. The doctors suggested an operation to free possible pressure on the paralyzed nerve. It was announced to the press as a hernia operation and George withdrew from the musical. He had pinned his hopes on the operation, but it turned out to be useless. Once again the doctors had found no cure. I visited him in Lenox Hill Hospital and he smiled at me bravely; he was still hoping that there would be some improvement, but the cord did not move. I hated to have him submit to surgery but I felt that if there was a millionth of a chance for the operation to succeed, I had no right to interfere. I could only admire his perseverance and stay at his side.

On his forty-sixth birthday he wrote to his parents, "The current season has not been very agreeable. But I've had a lot of success and joy and fulfillment in my life and I should not complain too bitterly." And he added, "There is so much to be thankful for—it's true I've had my share of bad luck this past year, but I've developed a good broad back and have most certainly grown and become wiser and perhaps better for the experience."

After his supposed "recovery from the hernia operation" he sang one last Amfortas at the Met. The voice was no longer there but the performance was deeply moving. Inevitably George identified with the wounded knight. I thought what a great actor he was and what a loss his retirement from the opera stage would be. We did not know that this would be his last opera performance.

In the spring he was asked to be the American judge for the singers' contest at the Tchaikovsky competition in Moscow, June 10 to 26, 1966. The two weeks in Russia provided a wonderful change for both of us. We could forget about George's voice and just think about the voices of the competitors. George again had caviar every day for breakfast and spent most of his free time advising and helping the American contingent, which included the eventual gold and two bronze medalists, Jane Marsh, Veronica Tyler, and Simon Estes. George was received with great honor by the Russians, who listened respectfully to his opinions. Watching his interest in the young singers, I had my first hint of an activity that might satisfy him after his career was over.

And suddenly the voice problem became even more serious than before. Now his speaking voice was getting weaker from day to day. A visit to a specialist in Moscow resulted in the usual diagnosis and sad shaking of the doctor's head. He, too, could offer no cure.

Although he knew that Soviet medicine was generally backward, George wanted to try every possibility; at that point he would have consulted a witch doctor.

After Moscow, we planned to go to California to visit George's parents. On the way, George had been scheduled to give a recital in San Francisco, which he had to cancel, using a sore throat as his excuse. Although he did not suspect the seriousness of the disease, Kurt Adler, the director of the San Francisco Opera, recommended that George see an outstanding throat doctor in Los Angeles. Dr. Henry Rubin not only realized what the trouble was but could offer a remedy. He proposed to inject the paralyzed right cord, now much shrunken, with silicone. The implantation of plastic material into the atrophied cord fills it out and pushes it back to the center; then the two cords meet as if both were healthy.

We took a long walk along the ocean in Santa Monica to discuss the proposed treatment. I had no faith in it; all else had failed. Healthy youths and tanned children were playing in the waves. We walked in the shallow water. George was talking to me and I could not hear what he said. The great voice that had sung on stages all over the world was reduced to a whisper. I did not want him to know that I did not understand him and just mumbled some answers. I wiped off some tears as if the water had splashed in my face. It was for me the lowest point of our ordeal.

The next morning George had the injection, and two days later he could talk almost normally. It was miraculous. Dr. Rubin advised him to start vocalizing slowly to see how he would progress. Neither George nor I was overoptimistic, but the immediate result of the injection was so spectacular that one could have high hopes. George was still a little hoarse, but both the speaking and the singing voice retained the same quality and exact tone as before the paralysis.

Encouraged, we returned to Switzerland and our village of Vufflens-le-Château. We had moved into our new house the preceding spring with the two younger children. Both Andy and Philip were at Yale now. All our belongings were sent over from New York, where we now kept just a two-room apartment on Madison Avenue. The house was everything we could have hoped for, and George adored it. He picked the colors of the walls, the wallpaper, the curtains, and the furniture, and I was delighted to see that the joy of having his own place made up a little for the torture that he was enduring. He was in a good mood, as loving and playful as ever with the children.

When the moving truck arrived with our furniture from the United States, I thought, "Now I am moving here forever." But even then I had a sad premonition that I was wrong.

George's vocal progress was astonishing and he could realistically think of singing again. He did not talk about opera but recitals seemed perfectly possible. His voice sounded good, as caressing and rich as ever, but I wondered if it had the strength and the sustaining power. I was worried about his return to singing. How would he take the pressure? What if it was a disaster? He had more stamina and courage than I. Once again I could not refuse my support. How could I be the one to decide whether he could sing?

In March 1967 he gave a recital, which was respectable and got good reviews, at the Metropolitan Museum of Art in New York. Paola Novikova had the great joy of hearing her Georgie sounding his old self again. She died a few months later. George was guardedly optimistic. He had been able to complete this recital without too much hardship. I did not know what to think. Could he sustain the effort and how long would the improvement last? There was a problem with silicone injections: they were sometimes reabsorbed. I dreaded going through another cycle of anguish and disappointments.

On May 17, 1967, he was scheduled to give a recital in Vienna and I decided that I would drive there from our home in Switzerland and take Marina, Marc, and Marie Claire. I wanted the children to see Vienna and above all I wanted them to see their father on the stage and witness the cheering crowds, the applause, the flowers. I was hoping that at eight and eleven they were old enough to remember the concert when they were grown.

The house was full. George ended his program with the "Farewell and Death of Boris," and although the voice did not have its former power, his artistry was such that the audience was as enthusiastic as always. Marina and Marc watched the applause with starry eyes and George described the concert in a letter to his parents:

My concert here was a great success. I had a wonderful reception from the audience when I first appeared and the applause grew in intensity after each group so that at the end it was quite frenetic. Certainly the Viennese public has remained faithful to me.

Marina and Marc came. It was the first time they had ever heard me in a recital. They sat so quietly, quite transfixed. It was such a pleasure to look out at those four intense, chocolate-brown eyes. Afterwards, Marc helped carry my flowers to the dressing room. He asked Nora how come nobody asked for his autograph. Nora explained that Daddy had sung and that he was the one who should sign autographs. Marc said to this, "But I'm daddy's son"—it's quite an argument. Marina looked so grown up—really a young lady. We took them with us to the restaurant where we had supper afterwards with close friends. When she kissed me good-night, Marina whispered in my ear, "It was just great."

Sitting in the restaurant across from three pairs of shiny eyes, watching George's delight, I was glad that I had brought the children. I, too, would remember this day.

Some weeks later, back in Vufflens, I sat on the bed looking at the familiar landscape of fields, lake, and mountains in front of our window. George came in and sat down next to me. He put his arm around my shoulder and for a while we sat in silence. At last he said quietly but with a strong inflection, "You understand, what I can do now is not good enough. I have come to a decision. I will not sing anymore."

Tears came to my eyes. In a few words he put an end to six years of torture and concluded his career as a singer to which he had dedicated his life. I identified with him so completely that I felt physical pain at his decision, yet, at the same time, a great weight was taken away. I said that I understood and approved totally anything he decided. I embraced him passionately and held him in my arms for a long time.

In a letter to me after two last concerts in Germany that had been booked earlier, he summed it up:

Giving public appearances on this basis is simply not worth it in terms of morale and personal satisfaction. I know I gave the people great pleasure. I was also relaxed and able to concentrate on my interpretations. However, for me the experience was not exultantly satisfying—as it should be—and can only be if I have vocal strength to spare. I may never again achieve that—and then again I may—but I will go ahead now—without pressures or deadlines. I'm sure you agree with this. And believe me I'm not depressed in any way, truly not. I just feel that when I sing in public it must be representative of my best standards. Otherwise I harm my inner self even if the public buys it.

This paragraph was George's own epitaph to his singing career; it marked the end of his struggle. I could not bear to go with him to those last concerts for I could not endure any longer to see him diminished and watch his hopeless struggle. I might have wished him to stop sooner but I understood that for him, it had to be a slow process.

He had told me that without his voice he felt emasculated. Thus he could not stop singing all at once. He had to give up first the opera, then the recitals, until at last he was able to face the world without his voice but with his soul intact.

A few years later, in November 1971 George gave an interview to Bob Sherman for his WQXR "Listening Room" and talked openly for the first time about the end of his singing career. He said:

You reviewed a concert [at the Metropolitan Museum] in which I sang a varied rather substantial program where I was working with a paralyzed vocal cord which had been artificially reconstituted with silicone. It's a miracle and therefore we ask ourselves, Where does the quality of the human voice come from? What is the secret of that special sound? because I have always flattered myself that people who are keyed to voices could recognize George London if they heard him on a record. They say, "That's the sound that *he* made."

From a hoarse resonanceless state I went to a situation where a reviewer of *The New York Times* can say "Well he has made a fine comeback and this is the voice we always knew." That is a miracle.

I continued to work in this way for the better part of two years but by the very nature of the situation, which is not a normal thing—this is like working with a prosthesis of some kind, with a crutch—structurally the voice is not what it was, and therefore under stress and under certain conditions I could not be expected to maintain the top standard with which I believed I had been identified. And so rather than do less than what was expected of me, I decided to give it up and so I went into other areas that interested me. It is an unfortunate thing but I had about sixteen years at the very top, I made a lot of good recordings and I think I left my mark on certain parts in a rather special way and so I have a great deal to be grateful for. It's regrettable because singing was great fun and a great satisfaction.

13

A New Career—
Washington

We loved our Swiss house which we called Les Muses. It was our first house and George was immensely proud of it; we had designed the floor plan with the architect. Our large corner room, in blue and white, was on the main floor far away from the children's and guest rooms, which were on the first floor. This way George could sleep late, undisturbed by the youngsters. His sleeping habits were a constant problem for our household and they were best solved in Vufflens.

During the school year, Marina and Marc had to leave the house before seven, since school started at eight o'clock in Switzerland. Marie Claire drove Marina to her school in Lausanne, twenty minutes away, and Marc was dropped off at the village school in Vufflens. In the summer months Andy and Philip came to visit. I was happiest when we were all together. We played different games in which George also took part. Most of all we enjoyed touch football and Ping Pong, at which we were all very good. There were fierce battles; each of us was very competitive and no one would give up, including the adults. The games sometimes ended with tears from one of the losers.

On hot summer days the children and I went swimming at the pool near the lake and often stayed for lunch. George was content to remain at the house. He could spend hours on the terrace reading and watching the vineyards below our property, or the white mountaintops beyond the lake, or the little Disneyland train climbing across the fields from the coast to our village.

I think that George's pleasure in the ownership of the property helped him face the loss of his voice. The solid brick house, the peaceful landscape, everything proclaimed a beloved tangible possession that no one could take away from him.

During the inexorable progress of the paralysis George became more and more aware that he could no longer support his family by singing. Having been deprived as a youth, he always worried about financial security and had taken life insurance and even health insurance that covered his voice. So he did receive some compensation when he could not perform, but it could not compare with what he was earning when he was well.

In 1965 he began looking at positions for which he would be qualified. He was best prepared for the directorship of an opera company. He had a thorough knowledge of the whole repertoire; unlike some of his colleagues, he had not been content simply to perform his own part. Frequently he listened to the other artists and gave them advice about their careers. As a result he was unusually well informed about the capacities and availability of most singers.

Aside from this, George was also interested in all forms of music; his taste was eclectic and if he preferred classical music, he also loved jazz, the Beatles, and Broadway musicals. At that time, there were fewer opera companies in the United States than at present and the important ones, such as San Francisco, Chicago, and the Metropolitan Opera were all in charge of capable directors. Another possibility was as director of a music school: there had been precedents of singers appointed to such positions. George enjoyed teaching, particularly coaching young singers. He found out how good he was at this during classes in Cincinnati in February 1968.

In May of that year George was approached by Julius Rudel, director of the New York City Opera, who intended to recommend him for a position at the John F. Kennedy Center for the Performing

Arts in Washington, D.C. Julius had been engaged as artistic director of the Kennedy Center, but his obligations with the New York City Opera, a position that he intended to keep, would make it impossible for him to give full time to Washington. For that reason, another artistic expert was needed to reside in the capital.

The Kennedy Center was scheduled to open in 1971, but the staff had to be in place long before, as planning for any artistic event had to be done years in advance. George would be in charge of artistic matters, Rudel told him, and although the offer was not definite yet, it prompted him to write to his parents on May 30: "Today is my birthday [his forty-eighth] and in spite of all the setbacks which life has presented me with these past couple of years, I still consider myself a most fortunate man. My children are happy, healthy and well adjusted, I have an excellent marriage and I am perhaps on the threshold of challenging new activities."

George met William McCormick Blair, Jr., the director of the Kennedy Center, in Europe and apparently the meeting went well. As a result Roger L. Stevens, chairman of the board of the Kennedy Center, its founder and animator, signed a contract appointing George artistic administrator in June 1968. He was to start in September of the same year.

The title was a compromise as there were already an artistic director and a general director. George was hired on the basis of his artistic expertise; he could not boast any previous administrative experience. However, his conversations with Bill Blair and Roger Stevens had evidently convinced them that he had enough intelligence and common sense to implement the artistic plans for the future of the Kennedy Center.

I was immensely relieved by the news. This would be an interesting and stimulating position for George with a measure of prestige. At least it would make up a bit for the terrible blow that had hit him, and it would guarantee us a steady income. George had invested in real estate in California but this was not an auspicious time to sell. We could not bear to sell our house in Vufflens, where every stone, every tree meant so much to us. True, we would have to move to Washington, but we planned to return to our Swiss house every summer for a few months. Marina and Marc were growing; the older boys thought that the younger children's education should be continued in the States. Otherwise, they said, we would make foreigners out of them and they would never "belong."

I knew this problem from personal experience, so I doubly welcomed the opportunity to take them back to the States.

On August 28, 1968, I wrote to George's parents:

> The difficult adjustment will be for George who is going into such a different kind of work under difficult and challenging circumstances. I am sure that in time with success he will find it exciting and satisfying but I know that for the time being he still feels much heartache at leaving his artistic career. But he will see little by little that he is just as needed in this type of work where his knowledge and his enthusiasm will be so important.

Once more we were moving with a complete household. We had rented a house on Chain Bridge Road, in a beautiful residential part of Washington. The house was not furnished and we had to decide what furniture to take and what to leave so that the house in Vufflens would remain comfortable. We decided to transport only a few pieces of furniture but George could not part from his favorite paintings: a large dramatic Appel, a poetic Chagall, colorful Jenkins, and several sculptures. I added a small oil representing the Sacré-Cœur and *Montmartre in Wintertime* by Maclet, a minor impressionist, which I had bought after the war in Paris and which accompanied me to all my homes.

I was eager to make the new house as pleasant as possible for George. For myself, I was not too concerned about going to an unknown city. I had been to so many places; surely I would adapt again, as long as I was with George. I was worried about him. He had been self-employed, at the top of his profession, recognized by all those he came in contact with. Now he would be an employee in a large organization and in a city where most people knew nothing about him. It was almost like starting from the beginning, and I realized how difficult it would be for him to be in a subordinate position, no matter how cheerfully he seemed to accept it.

From the time of our move to Washington, I tried to think of ways to make up for his loss and of ways to shield him from further distress. Before the voice problem, I helped him when he needed me, but felt that he was secure and could do without me. Now I became extremely protective of him, feeling that I was responsible for making his life bearable. There was something fragile in him that frightened me and that I was perhaps the only one to see.

It was impossible to pinpoint exactly the cause of my concern. He could no longer digest huge quantities of food and he slept more fitfully than ever. Suddenly he looked his age, his waist was a little thicker, while his wrists and ankles seemed even more delicate. But when I persuaded him to have a checkup, he was found to be in perfect health. He was full of enthusiasm and could work long hours without tiring. I convinced myself that all was well, that I was just an overanxious wife, yet from time to time I experienced the same fear.

We had found a fine school for Marina and Marc, the Maret School, which emphasized the teaching of French. I hoped that this way the transition would not be too traumatic for them. Our dear Marie Claire remained in Switzerland; the children were too old for a nurse now. The farewells were very difficult for everyone as Marie Claire was like a member of the family. I decided that I could not bear to leave my dogs behind. That meant taking Zorro, the intrepid dachshund, which posed no problem; and Tessa, our huge Bernese mountain dog, almost the size of a Saint Bernard—which meant a big problem indeed. We ordered the largest possible cage at the airport in Geneva for the flight overseas. But Tessa had no intention of entering it. Since I could neither lift her nor push her, my only hope was that she would follow me, so I went into the cage and crouched in a corner until she came in too. The airline employee watched in disbelief as this middle-aged woman entered a cage with her dog.

The problem solved, I rejoined my family ready to embark in the same plane in the normal fashion. For once the four of us were traveling together. Marina was a grown-up twelve-year-old and Marc a serious nine. We felt very close and adventurous. The trip was uneventful, but we arrived at Kennedy Airport just after Labor Day, and it seemed that the whole world had arrived on that same day.

We had ten pieces of luggage that required customs inspection, and I had to retrieve the dogs from a special section. It looked as if it would take hours. When I opened Tessa's cage, the huge black dog jumped with joy on me and anyone nearby while Zorro barked incessantly. We created havoc. The customs officials couldn't get rid of us fast enough. They glanced at our passports, declined looking at our luggage, and showed us out in five minutes. We laughed about the scene for days. Washington, here we come!

Our nine years in the capital turned out to be happy ones for me. George traveled less; we were together a great deal; I saw more of the older boys. Our life-style was comfortable and interesting; we made great new friends and kept in touch with old ones. Looking back, this period seems like a bright bulwark between two abysses.

Yet, it was clearly a better period for me than for George. I was relieved to know that his whole life no longer depended on his voice. The constant tension was gone and I was content with an undisturbed family life. But he was fighting new battles daily. His job was a test of unknown capabilities; and his voice, even for speaking, gave him problems from time to time. He was surrounded by turmoil. Once he asked me if I thought he would ever achieve the repose of maturity, and I answered that it would be very difficult for him.

However, I was not given much to brooding as I went about settling in the rented house. To Tessa and Zorro's delight, there was a large garden that led directly into a public park, and there were a series of reception rooms perfectly suited for our active social life. The day of our arrival Bill Blair and his wife, Deeda, paid a friendly call with flowers. I was touched by this gesture and thought it augured well.

I was glad to have met them. The following Saturday Roger Stevens gave a cocktail party to introduce George to Washington society. Except for the Blairs, I did not know anyone of the hundred fifty guests, not even the host and his wife, Christine. We circulated bravely among the crowd, which included Senators Fullbright and Percy, Chief Justice Abe Fortas, several ambassadors, and other influential Washington personalities. There was much talk about the forthcoming presidential election. The host and most of the guests were Democrats, and everyone hoped that Senator Humphrey would be elected, although they all feared that it was unlikely.

George, as always, was completely at ease. He was interested in politics and he had testified before Congress in favor of the establishment of the National Endowment for the Arts. He was well informed and had an excellent memory so he could converse intelligently with this political crowd. For me it was much more difficult. I was definitely not a social person. I felt at home in the lyrical theaters of the world but not in Washington's drawing rooms, at least at first. However, I established an immediate rapport with our hostess, Christine Stevens, who is committed to saving endangered animal species. I volunteered at once to work for the Washington Humane Society.

A few weeks after our arrival, George was invited to tea at the White House by Lady Bird Johnson. She was interested in the arts and wanted to know all about George's plans. He found her very charming and intelligent. Sometime later we were both invited to a reception at the White House by President and Mrs. Johnson. For the first time I experienced the glamour of these official dinners. There are extensive security checks when you drive through the gates of the White House and once more as you enter the house itself, but afterward you can walk around quite freely. At the entrance level there are several rooms with exhibits of the china used by various presidents and a gallery of portraits. As you go up the marble stairs to the reception rooms, the marine band is playing. We stood in line and an aide introduced us to the president, who shook hands with George and then with me and said a few pleasant words.

Later we were invited to the White House quite often, particularly by President Carter, who was fond of opera. We also went to special performances there, such as the Alvin Ailey Dance Theater or concerts by Vladimir Horowitz or by young singers. No matter how often I went it was always with some excitement. I could not help thinking that this country, which had accepted me as a refugee, had been so generous to me.

The social highlights were only a small part of our Washington life. I spent a great deal of time with Marina and Marc, who had to get used to a new school. They were old enough to take care of themselves, but such adjustments are difficult. It was particularly hard for Marc whose English was not too good after three years in

French-Swiss schools. I helped him with his homework every day during the first year, and then his English became better than mine. I drove the children to and from school like all American suburban mothers.

George, of course, was away from home all day like any businessman, so I spent much less time with him than in the past. He launched into multiple projects all dealing with music, to which he brought imagination, hard work, and tremendous know-how. Aside from his activities at the Kennedy Center, he directed a number of operas culminating in Seattle with Wagner's complete *Ring of the Nibelungen,* in both English and German. He coached young singers, he created and supervised a grants program, he gave numerous master classes here and in Europe, and finally he became director of the Washington Opera Company.

I never questioned anything he did. I favored any activity that involved opera and singers since I knew that was what he enjoyed most. In retrospect, it seems to me that he crowded as many activities as possible into these years, as if he were racing against time.

I was afraid that his forceful and exuberant personality would create problems for him in Washington. George was given to strong statements and outbursts, which might lead people to think of him as mercurial and difficult, whereas actually he was just the opposite, infinitely serious and totally dedicated. In the end he proved to all that he was not a temperamental opera singer but a reliable and successful administrator.

Those who knew him realized that the rhetoric was just an outlet for his theatrical personality. Although he was getting older, he remained slim and elegant. To his dismay, his hairline was receding but he still had plenty of hair.

He was quite vain about his figure and exercised religiously every day. He loved good clothes and occasionally indulged in flashy blazers and bright ties. I encouraged him to buy new things; I was eager for him to have pleasure in life.

When George expressed interest in vintage cars, I encouraged him to buy one, first a white Bentley convertible dating from the 1950s, then a four-door Bentley sedan, both of which required constant repairs but gave him enormous satisfaction. I called them his mistresses and watched with amusement while he spent hours polishing them with special wax and chammies on Sunday afternoons. It was great therapy for him.

Meanwhile the work at the Kennedy Center was interesting but often frustrating. George had to discuss most decisions with Julius Rudel, who did not spend too much time in Washington. George was very grateful to Julius for recommending him for the job and told me at first that "Julius and I see eye-to-eye in all musical matters."

The Kennedy Center, as conceived by the architect Edward Durell Stone, is composed of three theaters enclosed in one building. There is a concert hall with twenty-seven hundred seats, an opera house of twenty-three hundred seats, and the Eisenhower Theater for dramatic performances. George was in charge of the first two halls. He had several ideas for the opening season but the actual opening spectacle had already been planned by Roger Stevens before George's arrival. This was to be a Mass commissioned specially from Leonard Bernstein to be performed in September 1971 at the opera house. A good number of events had already been booked in the concert hall by the Washington Performing Arts Society before his arrival, as well. This organization had existed in Washington for many years; formerly their concerts had taken place in cavernous Constitution Hall or the theater of George Washington University, which were the only halls suitable for music in the nation's capital.

Three evenings weekly were taken by the National Symphony Orchestra, which also moved into the Kennedy Center's Concert Hall, eventually under the dynamic leadership of our close friend Antal Dorati. On free evenings, George was eager to arrange for some special events in the concert hall but the Kennedy Center's budget was small. Roger Stevens's efforts had managed to convince Congress to vote for the funds necessary to build the Kennedy Center; now there was not much money to run it.

In 1969 George was able to persuade friends and colleagues from the classical and popular music world to perform during the opening season of the Kennedy Center. The artists most generously donated their performances. In return they received a replica of the Kennedy Center in white marble and silver and the assurance that their names would be engraved in the building as "Founding Artists." Thus George put together an extraordinary series of thirty-five concerts divided into a jazz series, a pop series, and a classical series. The concerts included many great names in music, from Dionne Warwick to Pearl Bailey to Dizzy Gillespie, from Isaac Stern and Van Cliburn to Joan Sutherland, Beverly Sills, and Placido Domingo.

As time went on, there were disagreements between George and Julius Rudel, and Roger Stevens was put in the position of mediator between the two music administrators. Eventually there was friction about every important decision. George was used to adapting to the desires of conductors or stage directors and could adapt to the wishes of the different directors of the center, but he resented being interfered with when he felt that the interests of the Kennedy Center were at stake.

For example, he conceived a plan for bringing great European opera companies to the Kennedy Center Opera House. This would generate great prestige for the new theater, he felt. This idea was opposed by Julius, who intended to bring the New York City Opera to the Center and feared the competition. George felt that the foreign companies would not interfere with the American opera company. He thought that if the Washington public became acquainted with international-caliber grand opera, it would only whet its appetite for more opera at home.

The greatest difficulty in realizing such ambitious plans was financial. Even sold-out houses have never been able to support the lyric theater and there was an added problem because the Kennedy Center Opera House, which is a perfect size acoustically, is very small as far as financial returns go.

La Scala, the Vienna State Opera, or the Berlin Opera would be able to come to Washington only if the Italian government, the Austrian government, or the West German government heavily subsidized their appearance. George talked to his friends at the Vienna and Berlin operas and started negotiations with the director of La Scala with the help of the Italian ambassador, Egidio Ortona. The negotiations progressed slowly; and George traveled to Milan to meet Antonio Ghiringhelli, the director of La Scala. It was hoped that La Scala would open the second season of the Kennedy Center.

George's efforts came to fruition a few years later, when he was no longer head of the Kennedy Center. All the big European companies eventually came—the Berlin Opera arrived with *Lohengrin* under the baton of Lorin Maazel in November 1975.

For that opening, there was a gala performance in presence of the German ambassador Berndt von Staden, a friend of ours. George and I were seated in the center of the orchestra and as usual we were early, for George hated to be late to any performance; he felt it was an insult to the artists. While we were getting settled, George noticed that two young men immediately in front of us were wearing swastikas in their lapels. George was incensed and asked the men who they were. They answered rudely and said it was none of his business. George said it was very much his business. The men snickered malevolently. Now George was furious. He got up from his seat, towering over the short youths. He took both of them by their coat collars, lifted them out of their seats, and literally carried them to the door where the police took over.

Later it was established that the two individuals were indeed part of a plot to disrupt the performance. Ambassador von Staden sent George a formal note of gratitude.

As for me, I could hardly believe George's rage and his enormous strength. The incident must have been an outlet for years of pent-up anger besides his hate of Nazism.

Most of the time, however, there were no incidents like this one and I enjoyed going to concerts and operas *with* my handsome husband instead of meeting him backstage and sitting alone in the audience. I was proud to enter receptions and embassies at his side, and noticed with pleasure that with time Washingtonians liked and admired him.

We were still very much in love. Whenever he went on a trip, I met him at the airport with as much anticipation as fifteen years earlier. At night when he came home from work he told me at length about his problems and his plans. He wanted me to know every detail, and was extremely articulate. Often he asked my opinion and listened to my advice.

Still, I had a less intimate knowledge of his work. Whereas formerly I knew when and how he took every breath during performances, now I did not see his "performances" at the office. I could only judge what he was doing by what he told me. It was often difficult to give constructive advice.

On Christmas 1968, the whole family celebrated together. Philip, Andy, and Patrick had come and everyone helped decorate a huge tree in the living room. To spite us the furnace broke down on Christmas Eve, which was a bitter cold night, and we huddled together around the tree until a good-hearted repairman mercifully arrived that very evening. We applauded and thanked him profusely.

I watched proudly our three young men who were ready to start life on their own. But I knew they would always remain close to us and I felt full of love and contentment. I looked at Marina and Marc, so much like their father. They needed us for some years yet but I was sure that they, too, would grow into special people. I thought it terribly important that they all be close to each other; it would be a great strength in their lives and I welcomed any opportunity that brought us together.

At the end of December, George wrote to his parents, "Our children are wonderful and make up so much of what I am feeling grateful for as this old year passes."

But with the new year, there were renewed concerns about his voice. It seemed that the silicone was slowly being absorbed in the tissue. Consultation with Dr. Rubin confirmed this, and he recommended another injection into the vocal cord. However, as this could not be done too frequently, he advised George to wait a few months.

George went to California in February to have another injection. The result was good but he had more difficulty recovering than the first time, becoming hoarse on and off. I wrote him suggesting that perhaps Dr. Rubin had overinjected the cord a little but that it would settle soon and added, "I got your long, sad letter last night. . . . I am so dreadfully distressed that you continue forever to have troubles and tortures. You, who are the nicest, dearest, most humane person I know. I miss you acutely at all times and must watch myself not to talk about you all the time."

During the following years, the quality of George's speaking voice varied. Sometimes it was clear and strong, sometimes less weighty, sometimes slightly hoarse. He had two additional injections, the last one with Teflon, a newer substance that was not expected to be absorbed.

This constant concern was agony for George. I stood by helplessly as he tormented himself. He had to use his voice all day, on the phone, teaching, coaching, staging, for an occasional speaking engagement, in interviews. During interviews on radio, or television, he always asked me anxiously afterward how he sounded. With his trained ear, he was conscious of every variance in his speaking voice. I thought that most people did not notice and told him so again and again. It was difficult for him to believe me.

Fortunately, his voice was no longer crucial for his livelihood and in time we learned to live with his problem. But over the years it remained a recurrent torment that George was never allowed to forget.

14

The Lure of the Met
and the
National Opera Institute

George found his work at the Kennedy Center interesting and challenging. It provided him with valuable new experience. However, he could not help feeling that he was spending too much time on administrative duties and not enough in dealing with artists. He complained to me that he missed direct contact with opera. I could understand that he felt deprived without the singing and the music, for I felt it as well. Although at first we were glad to be removed from the sources of our pain, we began to be aware of a great void in our lives.

The long reign of Sir Rudolf Bing as general manager of the Metropolitan was coming to an end in 1972. There were several rumors about his successor and George's name was mentioned repeatedly, even though he had made no effort to approach anyone for the job. Obviously the prospect of the Met excited him, and eventually he started making inquiries and talking to people he knew on the Met board. George was bursting with new ideas, while aware of the Met's financial problems. But the people in power had no confidence in George's managerial capabilities. It became clear to him that he had little chance to be nominated and he did not expect anything to happen. It was 1970, and he had as yet no references as an administrator. Bing did not feel that he could recommend George, and it was questionable that his support would have helped. The board's attention turned to Goeran Gentele, the successful director of the Stockholm Opera, and in December 1970 Gentele was appointed general manager starting in the 1972–73 season.

Because opera seasons are planned many years in advance, the new general manager had to begin working in New York in the fall of 1971 to ensure a smooth transition. He needed to assemble a new staff and to set as soon as possible the repertory and the casts for the 1973/74 and 1974/75 seasons. (The 1972/73 season had already been booked by Rudolf Bing.) Therefore, Gentele started looking for assistants in the beginning of 1971, and George was recommended to him. He contacted George and they had a number of conversations. I never met Gentele but evidentally he was a charming and cultured man. Following their meetings, George reported to me that they were in agreement on all artistic subjects and became extremely hopeful that he would be hired.

On April 16, 1971, Gentele wrote him a letter with the following paragraph:

> As to the specification of your job at the Met, I want you as "assistant manager." One of your tasks will be to take over part of the planning job, which is now handled by Bob Herman. The chief stress should be laid upon the casting problems— to find the right persons with the right voices for the right parts which, up to now, not always has been the case—besides the fact that you should take part in the planning and proposing operas for the repertory in consultation with the music director, an eventual other assistant manager and myself. In other words: you will be holding one of the key positions in the team of persons, who will handle the artistic side of the theatre.

The proposal was very attractive to George. We discussed the possibilities during the spring of that year. George reasoned that he would be giving up a more glamorous title at the Kennedy Center to become assistant manager at the Met, but that he would be doing what he loved best, involved once more with opera and opera singers.

I thought that he would be happy at the Met and encouraged him to accept.

In the beginning of May George was in Germany and decided to go to Sweden and see Gentele once more. When he returned, he was convinced that the matter was settled. He encouraged me to look into schools and housing in New York and decided to resign from his position at the Kennedy Center. I was somewhat worried, for besides the April letter George had not received any written commitment; but he assured me that all would be well. My intuition proved correct. I have found often that I have accurate premonitions of coming events, but since I am basically a realist, I resist my forebodings.

Unknown to George, Gentele had approached Schuyler Chapin as early as February for the position of assistant general manager. Schuyler Chapin had suggested Gentele's name for the general manager job to Lowell Wadmond, a member of the board. On March 18, 1971, Chapin accepted the position.

Therefore, when Gentele wrote the April letter to George he had already appointed Schuyler Chapin, but he never mentioned anything about it to George.

On the other hand, Chapin does not mention George's name at all in his memoirs. Possibly he did not know of Gentele's offers to George, or felt that *post factum* it was not worth mentioning.

Suddenly there was the announcement that Gentele had appointed Schuyler Chapin assistant manager and the conductor Rafael Kubelik music director. There was no mention of a position for George. When he asked, he was informed that he would work with Chapin and have some position to be decided in the future.

The memory of George's disappointment on hearing this hurts me to this day. Once again he had been ready to change his life, hoping to be involved in opera, which he missed terribly. He could not understand why he had been misled or why a commitment turned out to be just idle talk. We sat on the blue velvet sofa in the spacious living room of the house on Edmunds Street where we had moved from Chain Bridge Road and lived for the past year and a half. Outside we could hear the children playing with their friends around the swimming pool and on the steps leading to the garden, Tessa was sunning herself with her new pup, a ball of black and white fur.

Although the setting was idyllic, we were engaged in desperate conversations concerning our future.

It was hard to believe that George had been hit by yet another blow. I felt like taking him in my arms and stroking him like a child to make him forget. He was more angry than sad but discussed the situation calmly. We talked at length and he consulted a number of friends. Some told him he should sue for breach of promise but I felt that he should not, as this would only cause him further grief and would prolong the pain. We discussed the possibility of his accepting a lesser position at the Met. I was inclined to encourage him to do it, but everyone else told him that he should not consider it. I did not pressure him for fear he would be unhappy if he accepted.

Schuyler, who had been an old friend and had been with George's management at Columbia Artists, must have known about Gentele's conversations with George by then. He begged George to work with him. But George had made up his mind and refused. Schuyler tried to change his decision but George could not be persuaded.

Looking back, I think that Gentele never intended to give George a position of control. He was probably frightened by George's strong personality. Schuyler Chapin wrote in his book *Musical Chairs*: "Gentele had one bothersome habit: he hated making final decisions." But I think that if he had openly explained his intentions to George from the beginning, George might have considered a lower position.

As it was, George felt betrayed and suspected Schuyler Chapin or Rafael Kubelik of having conspired against him when in fact it seems to have been entirely Gentele's doing. We will never know exactly what happened. In July 1972 Goeran Gentele was killed in an automobile accident and Schuyler became general manager of the Metropolitan. As it turned out, Kubelik was not able to spend enough time in New York and did not get along with the rest of the staff. He resigned from his post in February 1974.

Ten years later, when I first returned to the Metropolitan Opera House in New York, I was amazed to find how much beloved George still was by everyone, even after such a lapse of time. I could not help reflecting that he might have been happy there, working with people who admired and appreciated him. It would probably have been stressful for him to be in a subordinate position, but perhaps he was stress-prone under any circumstances and at least he would have lived in the opera world.

The board of the Metropolitan and particularly its president, George Moore, had accepted Schuyler Chapin as general manager by default and kept looking for another candidate on and off. By the spring of 1974 there was a new wave of rumors and soon an article in *The New York Times* predicted the demise of Chapin and named some front-runners for the position, one of whom was George.

Our phone started ringing. George answered truthfully that he had not been approached. However, he asked our friend Gabor Carelli, long-time tenor at the Metropolitan and active with the Met Auditions, to find out what was going on. Gabor met with several members of the board and discovered that indeed they were thinking of replacing Schuyler and that George had been mentioned, but that George Moore did not favor George's candidacy.

Eventually Gabor met Mr. Moore and convinced him to consider George and meet with him. George had several meetings with Moore and evidently made a very good impression, for the two men agreed on many points. It seems that Moore had decided to recommend George for the position of general manager when he went to the next meeting of the board of directors in the summer of 1974. By then, however, Moore was no longer president of the board. He had been replaced by William Rockefeller, and his influence no longer prevailed. Rockefeller seemed to like and respect George. But there was a new mood among the board. One of their own, Anthony Bliss, became general manager and the young conductor James Levine became music director.

George remained sanguine during these months of suspense. The heartbreak had occurred in 1971 when he really believed that he was going to the opera house and was looking forward so eagerly to casting and choosing repertoire. Three years later he no longer believed it would happen. He did have a moment or two of hope, but it always remained remote. I encouraged him to be skeptical, for I doubted that anything would materialize and I did not want him to be hurt the way he had been earlier.

I feel that for George being in charge of the Metropolitan would have been the only position that would have made up for the loss of his voice. I think he would have been an excellent administrator and a fine artistic influence on the house, as he proved he could be for smaller organizations. "It is not in the cards—I am not a member of the establishment," George said with some sorrow but with newly acquired serenity.

When Gentele's appointment fell through in 1971, we were greatly distressed. What would happen to us? George had resigned from the Kennedy Center, there was no job at the Met, and he suddenly found himself out of work for the following autumn.

In June I went alone to Switzerland with Marina and Marc. George came only briefly, but we were together for our anniversary on August 30, 1971. I gave him a small lithograph of Sarah Bernhardt by Mucha that he admired and wrote apologetically: "Only something very beautiful could celebrate the beautiful relationship between us—How could I ever find anything which could even begin to express my love, my devotion and my admiration which has grown continuously over the years." We could really celebrate, for George had arrived with good news: he had another job.

In 1969 Roger Stevens, with George's help, had incorporated a new organization, named the National Opera Institute, which was dedicated to the support and encouragement of all matters pertaining to opera. Now he had appointed George as director of the institute, with an office in the Kennedy Center. George was pleased and greatly relieved. He was beginning to do more and more stagings, and those together with the institute job would provide him with enough income; on the other hand, his duties at the institute would allow time for stagings. He threw himself into his new occupation with his usual enthusiasm. The institute started giving grants for apprentices in all fields of opera, management, staging, composing of new works; but the program that was closest to George's heart was the one designed to help young singers.

George said, "No one ever helped me when I started my career," but he remembered his long and painful road to success and he wanted to help devise a way to make the road a little easier for future generations of singers.

George created a grant program whereby young American singers with some professional experience could receive financial assistance during the difficult and expensive early years of their careers.

The program started modestly. In the first year, 1971, there was only one grant recipient, Richard Stillwell. Richard turned out to be a model for many of his followers. He was hardworking as well as talented, developed rapidly, and now has an important international career. The awards program grew rapidly and established the routine that would subsequently follow.

There were yearly auditions in several cities: Chicago, Washington, New York, and Los Angeles or San Francisco. Each singer had to be a professional with some opera experience to qualify for a grant. Every year there were ten grants of five thousand dollars each. George went to each city and heard all the candidates, an average of two hundred fifty singers each year. He was assisted by local judges who were asked to mark each candidate's description sheet with their recommendations. Back in Washington, George would go through all the lists and pick the ten best artists. These artists could receive an equal grant for a second year if the results of their coaching or their engagements showed serious efforts and progress.

After a few years George found that there were some artists who were not quite ready for a career and did not qualify for the prize but were talented. He hated to deprive them completely and so he started one-thousand-dollar encouragement prizes. The recipients also could come back another year and compete again.

During the following six years I often went with George to the auditions in New York and Washington, and sat next to him. As with everything he did, he was intensely involved in the proceedings. He greeted each singer very pleasantly, but I sensed that they were awed by his presence and obviously nervous. Each performer sang one aria of his or her choice and then would be asked to sing another chosen from a list that he or she had submitted to George and the other judges. Sometimes George did not agree with the choice of a particular singer and would suggest some other piece. I could tell immediately when he liked an artist; he became more absorbed in the performance. He was delighted with the discovery of talent, and he always talked with the candidate, asked questions about his or her experience, teacher, and repertoire.

The grant program was the beginning of a new phase in George's career, for now young singers entered our lives. George was not content to give the grants and check on the use made of the money. He insisted on getting reports of the activities of each grantee, and often got in touch with them personally. This started a personal relationship with a number of young artists. They came to our house or to the office and George gave them advice on their teachers and their repertoire, and help with possible engagements. Occasionally he would get an accompanist and coach a singer in a special aria or show him some special technique that would improve his vocal production. After he worked with a young singer and future teacher, Erik Thorendahl, who was preparing the role of Siegmund in *Die Walküre,* he followed up with a letter on February 27, 1971:

> The pianissimo involves exactly the same production of tone as for forte; the position is identical. Try practicing crescendo and decrescendo. If the soft tone is right, the crescendo should work smoothly as well as the decrescendo. If not, it will be difficult to crescendo the tone smoothly. In decrescendoing one must think very high and increase the support.

His influence was powerful. For example, he convinced Rockwell Blake, a timid young tenor with a wonderful high voice with exceptional flexibility, that he could do all the Rossini and Bellini repertoire in opera. Rocky now has a successful international career. He says: "George told me that what I was doing was all right for oratorio but that I had to give more sound if I wanted to be an opera singer."

One night the phone rang. A young artist, on tour in Switzerland, had become ill and called for advice about a doctor. We found what she needed through friends and within a short time George called her back with the information. A few days later he called her again to find out how she was doing.

The young people became almost part of our family. George was very fond of many of them. To some degree he was reliving his own beginnings through them, and he was most eager for them to succeed. He wanted them to be aware of his support. Whenever they were engaged, he tried to attend the performances and gave encouragement and sometimes constructive criticism.

An avalanche of calls began coming in from young hopefuls who begged to be heard. If George had the time he obliged. These auditions often filled his weekends, and I complained to him but he answered, "You know, they are so anxious for my advice." He could also be very abrupt and uncompromising at times. After listening to a young man who had come with his parents all the way to Washington from Cleveland, he told them nicely but unequivocally that the youth had neither the voice nor the talent to make a career. Later I told him that he had been cruel to squash the youth's hope. "Not at all," he said, "I prevented him from paying teachers and coaches for years, saving every penny to be able to live and giving up in the end anyway because he will never make it."

George was realistic and down to earth when necessary. He thought of music making as serious work that required total commitment. He detested dilettantes. I could never get him to accept the concept of nice young girls playing the piano or singing for pleasure, although he acknowledged that people did this in past centuries. However, when someone was serious about a career and showed real talent, George had tremendous patience.

At the end of his speech to young singers during a master class in Cincinnati, George spelled out his credo:

> I would urge every young singer to immerse himself in all the arts—everything which stimulates the aesthetic nature. An understanding of life is important to the developing artist whatever his field. Human development and artistic development are concomitant. The cultivated and versatile human being can be sensed in the work of every distinguished artist. So I urge you to be content not merely with producing mellifluous sounds but with building a fully rounded human and artistic personality. It will be the attention to such details which will make the difference between the talented singer you are now and the compelling artist you can become.

When George became director of the Washington Opera in 1975, there were some murmurs about conflict of interest and in 1977 he felt forced to resign from the National Opera Institute. One hundred twenty grants to young singers were given between 1971 and 1977. The Awards Program has continued to provide help to the young performers whom he loved and protected as long as he could, and today it is called the George London Grants for Singers.

John Ludwig, the current director of the Institute, wrote in the program notes to George London's memorial gala:

London founded the Singer Career Program in 1971 and until his retirement in 1977, he supervised it personally, giving its grantees the benefit of his artistry, managerial expertise and great warmth of spirit. His career had been built on talent, knowledge, and perseverance, and he made it his mission to pass on to the singer grantees what he had learned and—more importantly perhaps—some of his own spirit.

Metropolitan Opera soprano Catherine Malfitano, one of George's grantees, said in a television interview in 1982: "Each one of us received from him this gift and we all think that we were special. And each one of us was special to him. But the amazing thing was that he was able to give this to so many people."

Ruth Welting, another young soprano, added in the same interview: "George gave me criticism but it was with love, it was with encouragement. He said 'You can work on this but you are like a raw diamond that needs to be polished.' He was one of the few people who gave me the incentive to keep going at all."

In spite of his involvement the National Opera Institute was not a full-time job and George made other commitments during those years. In the summer of 1972, he gave a master class at the University of Southern California and while there investigated the possibility of founding an opera company in Los Angeles. With this in mind, he signed a contract with the Music Center Opera and was involved in a concerted effort with his friends Larry Deutsch and Lloyd Rigler to raise enough money in southern California for such an enterprise. But their efforts were not successful. At that time Los Angeles did not appear to be ready for a major opera company.

Since George was to spend six weeks in California, I decided that I would come, too, and take the children along. We could rent a house there and drive from Washington to save the fare for all of us. This way we would have a car in Los Angeles and Marina and Marc, who had been brought up in Europe, would get a good look at the United States.

Once I made the decision, no amount of arguing could change my mind. When told that it was too long a drive for a woman alone with two children, I replied that Marc was already fourteen and that Marina was seventeen, and able to drive.

I encouraged her to get her license, which she did just weeks before the trip. She invited her girlfriend Reed Sutherland to join our party, which I thought a wonderful idea. So the four of us embarked on the long cross-country journey in our green Mercury station wagon.

I twisted my right ankle while stepping out of the house in Washington and I was in agony during most of the trip. I was glad that Marina could drive and relieve me whenever there was little traffic, such as on the roads of Tennessee and Oklahoma. For the second time I measured the immensity of this country: together we stood in awe on the edge of the Grand Canyon and enjoyed a leisurely stop in Santa Fe where Philip joined us briefly.

The rented house was in Pacific Palisades, five minutes from the beach. George was very busy and could not spend as much time with us as I would have wished, but walking on the beach with him I remembered our time there four years earlier when we had de-spaired of his singing. Now we were in good health, the children were all doing well, and as George wrote to his parents: "One must constantly count one's blessings, particularly when one has health and wonderful children. That is more important than the search for glory—especially when one has had it in good measure. I'm a lucky man."

Marina and Reed had a good time together. They had met at the Madeira School for Girls in Virginia where Marina had gone since the ninth grade. Marc continued to go to Maret, where he was doing well and slowly making solid friendships, although he was shy and retiring as opposed to his outgoing sister. I encouraged the children to invite their friends and the house was always full of young people. When George was home he greeted the kids and chatted with them. Marina and Marc explained to me that he had no idea how intimidating he was to their friends because of his height and his authoritative manner. Marc often found it difficult to talk with his father. He was aware of George's strong opinions and did not dare speak up unless he could agree with him. They shared a great interest in baseball and football, which they watched together with total involvement, and laughed at me because I did not understand what was going on.

George expressed to me his frustration about being unable to converse with Marc. He had always been very close to Andy and Philip and wished to have the same relationship with his son. I told him that it would come with time when Marc grew older and became more sure of himself.

There were no such problems between George and Marina. They got along famously, both being extroverted and loquacious. They went shopping together and brought back outrageously expensive items, which they showed me with excited but guilty laughter knowing full well that I would disapprove. Inevitably I complained but could never be angry for long.

In June 1973 Marina graduated from high school and was accepted at Yale, where she was determined to go to follow in the footsteps of her older brothers. We had rented out our house in Switzerland the previous year, but we spent that summer there with the children.

We were both elated to be back and George expressed over and over his love for the house and the landscape. As soon as we arrived, he installed himself on the terrace with his binoculars and looked at the lake and the chain of mountains behind it. Every now and then he called me over and thrust the binoculars in my hands, "Look at Mont Blanc, isn't it incredible? Can you see the little cabin near the top?" Then he ran for his camera and took pictures of sunsets on the white slopes.

At the end of July, George went to Salzburg to give a master class and had the courage to go back to Bayreuth for the first time since Wieland's death. Although he was very fond of Wolfgang Wagner and was received with great respect, he found a lack of great voices at the festival. He left, disappointed and sad, after a few days.

While he was away, Gene died in Paris, after a year-long battle with cancer. George urged me to go to the funeral to give support to Andy and Philip. When I arrived in Paris, I was glad that I had gone. The boys were very shaken because Gene's last days had been particularly distressing and I was able to comfort them somewhat.

I went to the burial of this man with whom I had lived for ten years with mixed emotions. Nearly two decades had gone by. I had lost all recollections of intimacy but I had also forgotten most of my animosity. I felt truly sorry for Gene who had pursued life's pleasures so frantically and died so young, leaving nothing worthwhile in the end except the two wonderful sons we had together. After all, I was grateful to him for that.

I went back to Vufflens where George had returned, as well. He understood the ambivalence of my feelings and found just the right words to console Andy and Philip, who came for a few days. More than ever, I was aware of my happiness with George.

The month of August was beautiful that year. We had many friends in the region and there were dinner parties with much joking and good food. George's cousins, Ed and Lorna Mann, who came to live nearby, even convinced him to go on a picnic with all of us, to the delight of the children. His horror of ants and other insects was overcome only with the promise of a portable table and a sophisticated picnic basket, so that he sat on a lawn in the middle of nowhere just like at home, declaring, "I am definitely not a nature boy."

But he could sit for hours on the terrace and be content. The vineyards below our property were heavy with golden grapes and behind our house the wheat in the fields swayed in the wind. In the evenings we took long walks on the deserted country lanes to the nearest village and back.

I saw how much George enjoyed this life and I had visions of us, many years later, being able to retire there to spend our old age together in this ideal setting.

When we returned to Washington in the autumn, we decided to move again. The house on Edmunds Street was too big and too expensive now that our circumstances were less affluent. We moved to Bethesda where Marc could go to the excellent public high school. We found a pleasant house on Glengallen Road, which had the advantage of a huge playroom in the basement with enough room for a bar, a pool table, and living quarters for Tessa and her son Samson who grew to a size commensurate with his name. The disadvantage was that the house sat on top of a hill and on cold winter nights we had to crawl up to the door on all fours to avoid slipping.

During the last two years we had been helped by a warm-hearted Haitian woman who followed us to Bethesda. Ricilia worshiped George, she was a great worker and constantly made special dishes for him. She could also whip up an elaborate buffet dinner for forty people. She stayed with us until 1978.

This was our third move in five years, and in spite of Ricilia's help, and although I was becoming a specialist in relocating our family, it was an ordeal.

Finally we relaxed in our new living room with the furniture freshly re-covered in French velvet. George was pleased because he heard that some of his records were being reissued. He was prompted to write to his parents: "If I have achieved that, it is more important than whether I was able to sing some years longer than I did." He was in his fifty-fourth year, and I knew that, although he would always regret that he could no longer sing, the acute pain had gone; he was at peace with himself.

15

The Stagings:
The Washington Opera

As we have seen, very soon after George gave up singing, he became actively involved in staging. His first assignment was in 1971, when he directed *The Magic Flute* for the Juilliard School in New York. It was well received and opened opportunities for more engagements.

In 1973 he staged *The Marriage of Figaro* for the Dallas Opera Company with a distinguished cast headed by Evelyn Lear and Sir Geraint Evans. I went to Dallas with George for the rehearsals and attended the premiere. As is often the case with regional companies, one of its benefactors gave a party afterward for the cast and members of the board. We were taken by car on a twenty-minute ride to a palatial home in the outskirts of the city and arrived with mighty appetites. George had waited for the singers to remove their makeup before leaving the theater, so the party was in full swing when we arrived.

There were some dainty finger sandwiches and the single ham supposedly meant for the cast was almost gone. Barely greeting the hostess, the singers ran to the buffet, but in vain; within minutes not a grain of food was left. The drinks too were distributed grudgingly and in small glasses. After a very short visit, a group of us left the mansion, to return to our hotel where we managed to get a late meal. We ate and drank and joked into the morning hours. Much bitter humor was directed at wealthy patrons too stingy to feed starving artists. George proclaimed that there was a residue of eighteenth-century haughtiness that allowed the artists in the drawing room only when they were performing.

During the same year George directed Wagner's *Die Walküre* in Washington, a performance that brought together the forces of the Washington Opera and the National Symphony with great success. In the beginning of 1974 he staged another *Walküre* with a different cast for the San Diego Opera. Again I traveled with him and went with him to all the rehearsals. It seemed a little like old times, although he was sitting in the hall, not standing on the stage.

We felt closer and more attuned to each other than ever. A few weeks before, for my fiftieth birthday, he had written: "You have approached this impressive birthday with more beauty, more grace, more charm and more elegance than anyone I have ever known or heard of. My love, admiration and respect for you has grown constantly from the day we first met. Your adoring husband."

When he looked at me, I did not feel a day older than at Chaliapin's Russian Easter party. We had gone through hard trials and heartbreaks but we emerged from each test more thoroughly devoted to each other and more deeply in love.

I enjoyed our stay in San Diego. The weather was beautiful and we spent a lot of time walking around, just the two of us. I persuaded George to visit the famous San Diego Zoo with me and at night I went window-shopping with him.

We were in a good mood, for George's successful stagings had prompted Glynn Ross, the director of the Seattle Opera, to engage him to direct a complete *Ring of the Nibelungen*.

Glynn was a friend of George from early days in Los Angeles. In 1964 he had single-handedly created a successful opera company in Seattle, and by the 1970s had a yearly winter season, as did most regional companies. Now, at a time when there were no complete *Ring* productions in the United States, not even at the Met, Glynn conceived a daring project: he was going to create an American Wagner Festival. Each summer the Seattle Opera would present *Der Ring des Nibelungen* on consecutive nights, as in Bayreuth, and to make it more attractive to American audiences there would be a *Ring* in German one week alternating with a *Ring* in English the following week.

George agreed to stage both versions with two different casts, to open July 15, 1975. He was touched by Glynn's confidence in his talent. It was a tremendous challenge. He was excited at the prospect and sure of himself: he knew that he could draw from his years of work in Bayreuth. "But the time for abstract stagings is past," he said. "Nothing can be added to Wieland's concepts and we must go back to realism."

This idea has been upheld by subsequent stagings of the *Ring* in the last ten years, including the recent stagings in Bayreuth, which returned to naturalistic interpretations. It is not inconceivable that, had George lived longer, he could have returned to Wagner's Festspielhaus as a director.

I wonder if he fully realized that he would be staging eight operas, all performed for the first time, within a period of two weeks— a feat that, I believe, had never been done before or repeated since.

He did know that he would need at least six to eight weeks of rehearsals to accomplish his task, particularly as a good number of the artists had never performed their roles before. So he decided that he would need to spend June and July in Seattle.

As usual, he wanted his family with him and some kind of living quarters that would permit him to eat home-cooked meals instead of depending solely on restaurants. By then all our children were almost grown up and arrangements were no longer so complicated. Marc elected to stay in Washington and go to the seashore with friends. Marina wanted to come with us and take a summer counseling job in Seattle. By now Andy had his own information business in New York and Philip had started to make documentaries for television. They could no longer spend summer vacations with us.

The Seattle Opera Company found a pleasant apartment for the three of us and I started keeping house. Fortunately my duties were not very time-consuming and I had plenty of leisure time to go to the rehearsals with George. He had an able assistant director, Lincoln Clark, but I was pleased to find that I could be helpful in many ways. George told me what he wanted and I took notes on a yellow pad throughout the sessions. He trusted my advice and listened when I voiced an opinion. Since he had so much to do and was so absorbed in his work, the singers sometimes found it more convenient to come to me with their problems.

At first the rehearsals took place in rooms, in lofts, anyplace where a piano could be installed. A few chairs and props marked the limits of the stage. Theaters and orchestras are expensive so most rehearsals for opera take place in small rooms with piano accompaniment. Onstage rehearsals with orchestra are reserved for the last two weeks or less of a production, depending on the wealth of the opera company.

George worked long hours with incredible energy. He coached every performer separately, then in groups like the Rhinemaidens, then put together successive scenes. I watched for hours as he demonstrated what he wanted and explained the importance of the text to the young singers.

He lavished special care on the role of Wotan, which had been his own and which was now sung by a young American bass, Noel Tyl. Noel has a beautiful voice and a tall, commanding appearance. George taught him every phrasing, every gesture. He told him never to make an aborted movement with his arms. "Do nothing or make a wide, sweeping gesture."

I was not surprised that he knew all about *Rheingold, Walküre,* and *Siegfried:* after all, he had appeared in these operas many times. But I wondered how he could handle *Götterdämmerung,* the fourth opera of the *Ring* cycle. As I watched his progress, I asked him how he had become so familiar with it. "I saw it many times, in Bayreuth," he told me. "I studied the score and I remember all my discussions with Wieland."

He wanted to infuse his own knowledge and intensity into his cast. He proved to have patience and did not mind repeating the same scene over and over. Eventually when the artists did not duplicate his instructions, he became frustrated and angry and shouted, "No, no, that's not the way." He would jump up and run on the stage and demonstrate what he wanted.

I calmed him down and when he complained to me later that he would never achieve the right effects, I told him that the performance was already very good, that it would improve, and that he was too exacting. Pacified, he admitted, "I know. I'm a perfectionist and will never be satisfied."

He had demonstrated his fanatic sense of detail the previous year while working with Sherrill Milnes. The Met had asked him to coach Sherrill, who was to make his debut in the role of Don Giovanni that season. So Sherrill came to Washington and George taught the part he had sung so many times in his own career. He was thrilled to be able to bequeath his knowledge to the young baritone who had such a beautiful voice. He was terribly eager for Sherrill to have a great success and later went to the rehearsals at the Met. After the first dress rehearsal, he stormed backstage and argued with the lighting director, complaining that the Don did not have enough light while singing his aria. "But, Mr. London," replied the attending engineer, "this is exactly the same lighting that *you* had in this scene." "That just shows you that I didn't have a maniac like me watching in the hall when I was rehearsing," George said, and he did not give up until there was more light on Sherrill.

In Seattle he pursued the same kind of thoroughness. He checked every detail of the costumes: the tunic was too long for the tenor; the sandals had to be a darker shade. Brünnhilde's hair was too light, she looked like a bleached blonde, not a natural Nordic. Used to the lavish facilities of the costume and wig ateliers in Bayreuth, he was frustrated with the production level provided by Seattle's modest budget and tried his utmost to make things look their best, coaxing Glynn to get a handsomer wig or another new costume, as if the whole show depended on it.

Finally it was time for the premieres. George could not do anything more except be nervous for everyone. It was worse for him to be a spectator than to be on stage. We sat together in the third row and watched on successive nights the four operas of *Der Ring des Nibelungen* unfurl in front of us. In the darkened theater, I was aware that George was mouthing all the words, particularly for Wotan— I catch myself in the same habit when watching George's roles even now. I heard him whisper, "Do it, do it" during decisive moments, or grumble audibly if someone made a mistake. I don't think people sitting next to us were too pleased, for George's whisper carried well around us.

In the end, he was satisfied. The singers came through with moving performances and during the last measures of *Götterdämmerung* we both had tears in our eyes. There was a huge ovation for the cast and for the director who had all worked so hard.

These summer days were among the happiest and most relaxed in many years. George was able to enjoy his success and look forward to other achievements. At last the future looked safe. He had left for Seattle with the knowledge that upon his return to Washington, he would be involved in work which would give him great satisfaction.

In the spring of 1975 George had meetings with Christine Hunter, the daughter of his good friend, the Maecenas William Fisher, who had grown into a great lover and patron of opera in her own right. Chris and Bill Hunter had settled in Washington with their three little boys and she had been asked to become the president of the board of trustees of the Washington Opera Society. Chris told George that she would accept on the condition that he become director of the company. George later told the press that his decision to take the job was due to the fact that "I feel she is somebody I can work with in a most congenial way and someone who is supportive of my ideas." Indeed, during the next two years, the two were to work together in perfect harmony.

At the next board meeting on May 5, Chris simply announced that she accepted the presidency and that George London would be the new director.

George was thrilled to have his own company at last, although he did not have any illusion about its size. He quickly announced that he would revise the unpopular plans of his predecessor, who favored contemporary works. He was planning for three operas in the 1975/76 season, the same in 1976/77, and would expand to four operas in the 1977/78 season.

He realized that plans had to be made well in advance because of booking problems and the operas chosen with great care because of casting and financial problems. He could not, for example, stage an *Aïda,* which required bank-breaking sets, a chorus, and crowds of supernumeraries. But the modest budget of the Washington Opera

Society permitted outstanding performances of works that did not require elaborate sets and a huge chorus, such as *Madame Butterfly* or *L'Italiana in Algeri*. "We must have both great international artists and productions which will feature young American singers among whom are the stars of the future," George announced in the May 7, 1975, *Washington Post*. Through the Opera Institute he was in touch with the best young singers in the country, and now he would be able to cast them in vehicles that would show off their talent.

One of his early decisions was to change the name of the company by removing the word *Society* and calling it simply the Washington Opera. He said the word *Society* reminded him of a meeting of old ladies around a tea table. "It doesn't sound professional," he told me.

At the Opera Institute he had had a most capable and efficient associate, Ruth Sickafus, but at the beginning, to save money, he did not even have a secretary at the Washington Opera. He did his own typing with two fingers, describing himself as a diligent and well-meaning but not very competent secretary.

Later George was able to get a few rooms in another part of the Kennedy Center specifically for the opera company. They were tiny rooms without windows, like most of the offices in the building; George referred to his office as "a broom closet."

George brought two key employees to Washington. First he engaged a serious and industrious young man, Gary Fifield, as business manager and managing director. Then he asked Jerry Shirk to join the company. Jerry had worked with George for the *Walküre* staging in Washington and had proved to be a gifted and resourceful helper; he became stage manager and technical director. They worked together with great success during the next two years, and Jerry wrote me a letter containing his fond recollections from this period:

> Our system was that George would make the arrangements, then Gary would issue the contract. I remember at least one occasion when George worked out an engagement for an important artist and the moment would arrive when George would call Gary and say, "I have just engaged Miss X to sing the role of Y in our production of Z. Her fee is $5,000, so please send

off the contract." At this point, Gary would have a fit of apoplexy over the amount, and would say, "Do we have to pay that much? I'm sure we could have gotten her for less." George would merrily respond, winking at me as he said, "Of course, I could have gotten her for less, but that happens to be exactly what she's worth!"

Especially in the area of artist fees, he often expressed his conviction that managements and agents so often take advantage of artists, that he was determined to be on the artist's side. "Maybe it won't make any difference," he would say, "but maybe this artist will be a little happier to be here, and maybe she (or he) will be a bit more willing to cooperate with our difficult situation, and *maybe* she (or he) will sing just a little bit better, knowing that this is a good job, not some kind of favor for George London."

George especially loved to engage the young American artists whom he knew from the auditions that he heard in all of his capacities. Many of them did not have agents, and he always got a special charge in sending them contracts, unannounced, not negotiated, just as a surprise in the mail. In the days when I typed the contracts, I recall one situation where he instructed me to send a contract to a singer for a fee of $600 per performance. Since I was quite sure he had not actually negotiated this fee with anyone, I asked if this was a definite agreement. He assured me, "She will accept this, and we will hear from her the day she gets the contract and my letter."

Predictably enough, he was right, and she was thrilled. Also predictably, Gary wondered if it might not have been possible to get her for less, but by that time, of course, the contract was already out.

In everything he undertook, George always strived to accomplish it in the classiest and most honest possible way. Whether it was in the casting of the tiniest bit parts, or in the style with which international artists were met at the airport, he refused to try to cut corners. Once committed to a project, he would consider his commitment final and total. He said, "I would pawn the family silver if that would make a difference to this production."

In view of his past, it was normal for George to favor the artists. He needed some big names to sell the season, but he knew he could lower the budget of any production without harming the quality of the show by engaging many unknown artists commanding lesser fees. He was able to look at a score and calculate in minutes how much it would cost to produce the work.

During his first season the Washington Opera presented *Otello* with such established stars as Evelyn Lear and James McCracken and also introduced young singers such as Rockwell Blake, Nöelle Rogers and a young conductor, James Conlon. The following year, George persuaded his friend Nicolai Gedda to do his first *Werther* in Washington with the promise that George himself would stage it. He engaged a young Japanese artist, Yasuko Hayashi, to do *Butterfly* and asked Frank Rizzo, a gifted young director, to stage it. Frank joined the company and stayed as artistic director for ten years.

George was making plans for years ahead. Every night he brought home the score of another opera, which he studied with intense pleasure. I sat next to him on the bed while he exclaimed, "Such a wonderful aria" or "What a great part for a mezzo." Then I asked, "Can you do this opera in Washington?" and he answered, "Maybe, perhaps in a few years, if I can find the right artists." He only wanted to present a work if he felt that he had the necessary performers for its roles. George foresaw the renewed interest in French opera and scheduled two Massenet operas, *Thaïs* and *Werther*. Then he tried without success to put together a cast for *Carmen* with the thought of persuading Shirley Verrett, a beautiful singer, to play the title part. He loved Russian opera and was familiar with lesser-known repertoire. He started talks with Mstislav Rostropovitch, director of the National Symphony, concerning the possibility of doing Rimsky-Korsakov's *The Czar's Bride* starring Rostropovitch's wife, Galina Vishnevskaya. This project was finally realized in 1986.

In spite of his enthusiasm, he could not get to his office before nine-thirty; his metabolism was geared to late hours forever. He would stay late, rarely coming home before seven. He said, "When I work, I work with total concentration and accomplish as much as anyone on a given day."

In fact, he took his work home with him. I was just as involved with programs and casting as he was and always ready to discuss his plans until late at night.

We were both enjoying our life. On December 31, 1975, he wrote to his mother, "This is the last day of what was in many ways a good year for us and for that I am very grateful."

As planned, the first three operas of George's season at the Washington Opera were *L'Italiana in Algeri, Otello,* and *Thaïs,* given during February, March, and April 1976. He wrote to his mother: "I have my first short season of opera behind me, and I believe I have made the public aware of a new style and new standard of opera in Washington. Plans proceed for the next two seasons and look very good indeed. I am optimistic."

The whole tone of his letters was different. He could visualize a future with a rewarding and secure place for himself. At fifty-five, had he been singing, George would be nearing the end of his career. Some of his contemporaries were slowly leaving the stage. I was relieved to see that he no longer hurt so cruelly.

We came to the conclusion that we were in Washington for good and that it was foolish to keep renting houses. Bethesda was too far away if George wanted to come home to change for a performance at night. Marc would graduate from high school in June 1976 and had been accepted to a six-year medical program at Northwestern University. So we were free to move anywhere.

After some searching, I found an attractive brick house in an excellent neighborhood, near Fox Hall Road, just "eight minutes from the Kennedy Center," as George proclaimed. We liked this house at first sight and decided to buy it even though it was a bit more than we had planned to spend. It was not huge but had enough rooms to accommodate my mother, now living with us, Marina and Marc when they came home, and our housekeeper, Ricilia, who followed her restless employers everywhere. The living room was not as large as in Edmunds Street but there was a spacious dining room.

We had to give up the pool table, as there was no basement, and the dogs had to be content with the laundry room or the couch in the den; but we felt that was a small sacrifice compared to all the conveniences.

We were due to move in the beginning of April 1976. A few weeks earlier I discovered a small lump on my throat under my chin, which was diagnosed as a tumor on the parotid gland. It had to be removed, because there was a small chance of malignancy. The surgeon warned us that, since the tumor was close to the facial nerve, there was the slight danger that the operation would result in partial facial paralysis. Every physician consulted gave the same answer but there was no choice; the growth had to be removed. I entered George Washington Hospital with apprehension. How would George react if I was disfigured? I did not dare talk about it.

Philip and Marc stayed with George while the operation was performed. He controlled himself with difficulty. They kept reassuring him, hoping that all would go well. I remember waking up in the hospital room, looking at George's smiling face. "You will be fine," he said. "It is benign. I love you more than ever." Reassured, I closed my eyes and returned to a half-sleep full of George's love.

Two weeks later, with a bandage on my neck but hardly noticeable traces on my face, I supervised the movers. George was busy with the opera, which was just as well, as Ricilia and I were more efficient without him. But during the previous weekend George and Marc proceeded to hang our paintings in all the rooms. Every wall was measured exactly and each painting hung precisely in the center at the same distance from the floor as all the others.

He enjoyed this task and I let him decide where each work was to go. It did not matter too much for I knew that a few months later I would find him one night changing everything around, including the furniture, to give our house "a new look." "Much better, don't you think?" he would say.

As soon as we were settled, I gave a party that coincided with the opening performance of *Thaïs*. There was a big crowd but the buffet table was loaded with delicious dishes from Ricilia's kitchen, which satisfied the appetites of the cast and all our friends.

It was a good period for us. I went to the rehearsals with George and sat next to him with my yellow pad, as in Seattle. Now that he was dealing with his own company, he was even more particular about everything. Although he was not directing most of the time, he was still responsible for the final product. He made sure the wigs were becoming, the men's coats the right length; he checked every detail, down to the size of the buckles on the women's pumps. Always there were long rehearsals for lighting, which he considered so important. He made sure that the musical preparation was thorough before the show came on stage, because orchestra rehearsals in the hall were costly and had to be kept to a minimum. He engaged conductors familiar with the style of the works he was presenting, such as a French conductor for the Massenet operas.

In May he went to Cincinnati to perform the speaking part of Moses in a concert version of Arnold Schönberg's *Moses and Aaron*. He gave a profound, moving performance. However, he was not satisfied with the quality and volume of his voice and decided to go back to Dr. Rubin in California for another injection in his paralyzed cord. He told George not to use his voice for a few weeks and warned him to be careful about not catching any food in his throat, because the passage was somewhat reduced now due to the rigidity of the injected cord.

George met me in Switzerland where I had preceded him with the children. We spent an idyllic month of July. He reported to his mother, "The mountains were clear, the Mont Blanc was out in all its glory, it was just heavenly. I'm so happy we have this place. It's just good for the soul."

The Geddas, with whom we were close friends, had visited us some years earlier and had been so delighted with the landscape that they had bought a beautiful house with a swimming pool in the next village. We spent many joyous summer days with Nicolai and his wife Stacey, whom Marina and Marc loved like a somewhat older, beautiful sister. George, taking advantage of their proximity, had arranged rehearsals at our house for the forthcoming *Werther*.

For a couple of weeks Nicolai and Joann Grillo, who was to sing Charlotte with him in Washington, came every day, and George staged all the scenes in which they appeared together in the opera. The high walls of our living room resounded with the passionate oaths of Werther's love against a background of vineyards, lake, and white mountain peaks. It was a perfect setting for the opera and I felt privileged to hear it this way.

George was irritated because his speaking voice sounded hoarse much of the time. I called Dr. Rubin for advice. He assured us that the harshness would pass, and indeed it went away at the end of the month. When George left for Graz to give two weeks of master classes there, he was well rested and in excellent disposition.

After the summer, we would be without children for the first time in our lives together. Marina returned for her senior year at Yale and Marc was off to Northwestern as a freshman. George knew he would miss them, and went on last-minute shopping sprees with them. He bought all kinds of fancy stereo equipment for Marina, which they smuggled secretly into the house to avoid my objections. But they giggled so much that I could not fail to notice. Eventually I admired the perfect sound of their purchase and was touched by their obvious delight with each other. After Marc's departure, George wrote to his mother, "Marc was a bit sad to leave, just as we were. But when the family is that close, that is the price one pays when separating."

He did not have much time to think about the void left by the children. In November he went on his yearly circuit to Los Angeles, San Francisco, Houston, and New York for the National Opera Institute's auditions. In December, the 1976/77 season of the Washington Opera started auspiciously with successful performances of an early Verdi opera, *Attila*, with Justino Diaz in the title role.

On January 2, 1977, George wrote to his mother, "With a bit of luck, a few smiles of Providence, the new year can move us closer to some of our goals. I persist in being optimistic and I believe there are good reasons for being so. The one important thing is good health."

In February *Butterfly*, directed by Frank Rizzo with Yasuko Hayashi, the young Japanese soprano, in the title role, was a triumph. This Italian-trained singer had a beautiful voice and moved with inimitable grace in her own splendid Japanese kimonos. President Carter heard about the success from his elder son, Chip, and decided to come to the performance with Mrs. Carter and Amy.

The news spread quickly. The whole company was tremendously excited and outdid itself. Afterward the president and his party came backstage, guided by George, and congratulated all the performers. Mr. Carter had obviously enjoyed himself and demonstrated his knowledge of the story. He congratulated Ermanno Mauro, the tenor, who had played Pinkerton, adding jokingly, "You've disgraced the U.S. Navy, but you're an asset to opera."

The newspapers were full of accounts of the president's visit, and of course it was great press for George as well. Unfortunately, his enjoyment of this acclaim was marred by problems with the Kennedy Center. La Scala and the Paris Opera finally came to Washington in the fall of 1976 under the guidance of Martin Feinstein, George's successor as director of the Kennedy Center. Evidently these performances kindled a desire in Martin to have his own opera company, and he made plans for his company to be part of the Kennedy Center.

George was thunderstruck when he heard of this scheme. He realized that if the Kennedy Center sponsored an opera company it would mean the end of an autonomous Washington Opera, which depended on the Opera House of the Kennedy Center to stage performances. Even without this new competition, it was always difficult to get the house's schedule of availability far enough in advance. (The intimate Terrace Theater, ideal for small-scale productions, did not exist yet at that time.)

I saw that George was worried and distressed, and I felt deep resentment against those who caused him such anguish. I tried my best to reassure him but I too felt depressed. Would there never be a peaceful life for us? We had finally settled down and now there was more turmoil.

George was nervous and somber and I was afraid for him. But he had proved to me again and again that he was tough and incredibly resilient; he was not going to abandon his little opera company so easily. He told Chris Hunter about the rumors. She was disturbed. They decided to see Roger Stevens together and confront him with the story. Apparently Roger did not deny it but assured them that Martin would not be given the means to transform his plans into reality.

Chris and George left somewhat reassured, but they had not been able to finalize the dates for the 1977/78 season at the Opera House. Without the dates, George could not sign contracts for the artists he wanted to engage and everything remained up in the air.

More rumors kept spreading. Martin Feinstein had involved Lorin Maazel in his plans; Maazel was choosing the operas to be given; he was sounding out some singers; and so on. I pointed out that such large-scale plans would require a six-million-dollar budget, and I doubted the monies would be available. George went directly to Martin and challenged his plans. Suddenly there were talks of associating George and the Washington Opera into the venture.

Meanwhile Chris Hunter scheduled another meeting with Roger Stevens to ask for a definite commitment of dates for the next two seasons. I had gone to Switzerland for a week to prepare the house which we had rented out for a year, and George wrote to me at the end of April:

> I met with Chris for a talk before the meeting. . . . Chris is prepared to tell Roger that if the Kennedy Center insists on proceeding with Feinstein's plans, we are prepared to pay off our contract obligations and cancel our next season. Chris persists in believing that Roger is, au fond, too sensible to preside over the destruction of this company in order to extend Feinstein's power base. It would be a major scandal, and she and I believe he doesn't want that.
>
> It's a risk we have to be prepared to take when we go into that meeting. And apart from the gamble, there is no doubt that if the Kennedy Center announces their own future operative plans, we will have a desperate job to raise our money for next season.
>
> I agreed with Chris, and when our talk was over I felt as though a stone had dropped from my heart. I am confident that I will always find productive ways to use my talents. But I will not work under such dreadful conditions. As I write this I feel more relaxed than I have in many months, and it's a good feeling. I love you. Your George.

I answered from Vufflens-le-Château on May 1, 1977:

> Your letter disturbed me. I wonder if the threat to cancel next season is the right approach. How can you give up all you would eventually accomplish for opera in this position, all that you love and do so well.
>
> Such difficult times, such agonies, perhaps being here all by myself has helped to give me a better perspective. I love it here but I realize now it is too remote, too far away from all my children and in the long run an impossibility unless one has

plenty of money to travel back and forth, and even then what? Well it is not possible to have everything. If I sound sad, it is not so, just reflective, and after all my duties here are rather full of memories of times past, and closing a piece of our life without knowing where we are going next.

I do know that I love you as ever with unfailing admiration, respect and passion, such a wondrous feeling after these many years. How lucky I am to be with a man like you. I wish you with all my soul to be well and happy, I suffer with your pain and I am happy with your joys. I love you. Your Nora.

These were our last letters to one another.

In the midst of this anxiety, George staged *Werther,* which was a solid success and a personal triumph for our friend Nicolai Gedda. But George could not rejoice in his achievements while agonizing about the very existence of the company.

Then, possibly prompted by George's steady successes with the opera and by fear of a big deficit for the Kennedy Center, Roger gave George firm commitments for the dates at the opera house for the coming years. Chris and George felt like celebrating. Later we heard that the board of the Kennedy Center rejected Martin's plans; they were not willing to finance an opera company. Some years later Martin Feinstein resigned.

George bounced back with his usual resiliency, but it all took its toll and I thought he looked tired. I insisted he have a checkup. He wrote to his mother: "We are all well, no complaints. The doctor found the results of my recent physical 'superb.' Nothing wrong at all, with blood pressure at 120 over 70. So that, too, is something to be very grateful for."

Now he could concentrate on the planning of the future seasons and at the end of April he wrote, again to his mother:

I am busy these days setting repertoire and casting for the season after next and hopefully soon we will know what periods we can have in the Kennedy Center in 1979/80. One has to plan that far ahead in order to be able to get the artists and conductors one wants. We have established strong ties to the Washington public, and with a little luck and cooperation I think the future looks very good. I will be gone for the first two weeks of May. I will be staging *Don Pasquale* in Grand Rapids, Michigan, again with a cast of outstanding young artists. You may recall I did *Così fan tutte* there two years ago which was a big success and gave me a lot of pleasure.

In a rare reflective mood, he remembered singing the role of Dr. Malatesta in *Don Pasquale* many years ago at City College. "Imagine, I was only twenty-one years old. It is a long time ago!"

We went in good spirits to the Opera Ball in June. It was hosted by the Swedish Ambassador and Mrs. Wachtmeister in the enchanting gardens of the embassy. Everyone applauded when George arrived. He was radiant and I was just as delighted to hold the arm of my tall and elegant husband.

He had to make conversation left and right with patrons of the opera. But he made sure to dance with me several times during the evening.

George's plans for the season 1978/79 were the most ambitious so far. There would be four operas, *The Magic Flute, Elisir d'amore, The Seagull,* and *Tosca.* The production of *The Magic Flute* was being borrowed from Toronto, and George decided that he had to see it before leaving for Europe, where he was to give some master classes, to make sure that it was right for Washington.

He flew to Canada, saw the performance, was quite pleased with it, and returned to Washington Thursday morning, July 28. He had to leave for Munich the same evening, on his way to Graz, where the classes were to be held.

I picked him up at the airport and took him to his office where he had last-minute matters to attend to. The director he had hired for *The Magic Flute* canceled. George was very annoyed but decided that if he could not find anyone else, he would direct it himself.

I thought he looked drawn and begged him to stay overnight. He argued that he had to be in Graz by Sunday and could not disappoint the people there. He promised that he would rest on the two days he would spend in Munich. I wanted to go with him, but he was leaving for only two weeks and it seemed unreasonable for me to go. Moreover my mother had suffered a slight heart attack recently and I did not feel that I could leave her. Sometimes decisions that seem inconsequential turn out to be terribly important. If I had traveled with George, we would have stayed together in a hotel in the center of town and his fate might have been different.

That day George took a short rest at home, and in the late afternoon Marina and I drove him to Dulles Airport. It was a warm July evening. George was dressed in a red plaid blazer, white shirt, navy tie, and light-gray pants. I thought he looked refreshed and as handsome as ever. He was as happy as I had seen him in a long time, relieved that the Washington Opera was secure. We walked with him as far as was allowed before he boarded the shuttle bus that takes passengers to the planes.

We kissed good-bye as passionately as twenty years earlier; then he embraced Marina and walked toward the bus. I called him back, something I never did before, and begged for "one more kiss." He turned around, gave me a kiss, laughed his joyous musical laugh and said, "I'll be back in just two weeks." Then he was gone.

16

The Illness

In me there is an endless scream
and I can't tell what's crying.
Whether it is my broken heart or my bowels.
—RAINER MARIA RILKE

The telephone in my room rang at three o'clock in the morning. I lifted the receiver with shaking hands. The caller was Max Lipin, the friend with whom George was staying in Munich. Max could hardly talk. He said George had suffered a heart attack; he was in the hospital; they did not know how serious it was. I must come at once.

It was Sunday morning, three days after George's departure from Washington. I called Pan American, made sure that my passport was valid, and threw some clothes into my suitcase. I had no further details of George's illness and no idea how long I would be gone. I called Andy in New York and asked him to inform the rest of the family. Marina helped me pack and together we told the news to my mother, minimizing the seriousness of George's condition so that she would not worry too much. Marina gave me a book for the trip.

All night I sat in my seat on the plane, staring at the open pages on my lap, unable to make sense of a single line.

After what seemed an endless night during which I wavered from the worst expectations to feelings of confidence, I arrived in Munich the next morning blinded by the bright sunshine of a beautiful summer day. I thought briefly, "How can there be tragedy on such a day?" but as I entered the airport I was confronted by newspapers with George's picture and headlines in big black letters: "George London has heart attack." "London in a coma." For a week I would see them all over town. I could not deceive myself; something terrible had happened.

Max picked me up and drove me to the Hospital Medizinische Klinik Rechts der Isar where George was. I entered the room. He was lying completely still, attached to a respirator. His eyes were closed; he seemed lifeless. I took his hand. The touch was so familiar, the skin so soft and warm, that I regained some hope.

On the way Max had told me the story of what had happened. It would be repeated many times, and I would tell it many times, yet I was never able to verify it completely. On Saturday George had listened to a few young singers and, as usual, could not help coaching them for a while. In the evening he had gone out to dinner with old friends, among them Franz Spelman, who had been a witness at our wedding. Franz found George in great form. He told wonderful anecdotes and seemed more cheerful and relaxed than he had been in years. Franz, who knew him well and who was very perspicacious, concluded, as I had, that George had overcome the grief of losing his voice.

They talked quite late and George and Max drove back to Max's apartment, which was some distance from the center of town. At six o'clock in the morning, Max was awakened by George, who said apologetically that he had been having terrible pains in his left side for the last few hours. Max immediately called a doctor, but shortly before the doctor arrived George said he was feeling better.

Each time I go over this story I think if only they had driven to the hospital immediately, he might have been saved. Obviously George had first had a mild heart attack. Had he been in an emergency room, the outcome of the next attack might have been quite different. But over the years I tried to prevent myself from thinking of "ifs and buts"; it would have driven me crazy and I needed my sanity most of all.

When the doctor came, George was sitting at the breakfast table. He took George's blood pressure, which I am told was normal, and he was about to speak, when George fell forward stricken with cardiac arrest. The doctor immediately started mouth-to-mouth resuscitation while Max called an ambulance and paramedics. The doctor was a little man and could not do much physically; by the time the ambulance came Max was hysterical. He told the paramedics that George was a prominent opera singer and that they must save him. They tried to revive him for a long time—varying accounts say from ten to twenty minutes—until finally George's heart started beating again. It seems this took place in the ambulance on the way to the hospital.

I was never able to speak to the doctor to ascertain the exact amount of time George's heart had stopped, a crucial factor in estimating how long his brain had been without oxygen and how severely brain damaged he would be. At the hospital, a doctor kept telling me if only he had been there when the heart stopped, George could have been saved without any damage to his brain. If only . . .

But at first I did not know these details and did not yet understand the implications. The doctors could not say whether George would live and, if he did, how long he would be in a coma. I was stunned; the magnitude of the catastrophe had not yet penetrated. I explained to the doctors that George had an injured vocal cord and therefore a somewhat narrowed air passage in the throat. They duly noted my declarations, which did not seem to make any difference since they had already done a tracheotomy on the patient. I sat next to him in silence for a long time, until Max persuaded me to go.

We left the hospital and he guided me through an assault of journalists and fans to whom I could say nothing new. We drove back to Max's apartment without a word. I felt as if all this was happening to someone else; it could not be me. In George's room, Max gave me a box; he said George had bought this present for me two days ago. I opened it and found a silk blouse in a print of my favorite pale-green colors. His first purchase abroad had been for me. I felt again surrounded by the aura of love that George had woven around me. How could anything serious happen when I was loved this way? I felt sure he would wake up and everything would be all right.

Then I touched his clothes, which still bore the marks of his body, and leafed through his appointment book, filled with plans for weeks to come. When I realized that I was expected to pack George's belongings, the tears finally came. I cried silently for a long time, alone in the room, as I would many times over the years. The tears were always there, close to the surface, but I did not wish to exhibit any sorrow to the world; this was my private grief. I determined then and there to hide the depth of my despair from my family and my friends and to show my determination to help George's condition. I sensed at once that I would function best this way.

Two days later Philip came to Germany so that I would not be alone, and when he could no longer stay away from his business, Marc came and remained in Munich until college started. Without exchanging a word, the four children established an extraordinary support system for me, which never weakened during the years to come. Andy helped consistently with the paperwork; Marina immediately started taking care of the household and shopping. Philip handled all our housing dilemmas. All four had their own problems and suffered their own loss in various degrees, but they did not let their worries and grief interfere with their devotion to me. Every weekend, when we were back in the States, one of them, most often Marina, was there to keep me company. Their love gave me strength. I never felt alone in the face of trials.

After four days George was taken off the respirator and he was able to breathe spontaneously thereafter. Otherwise, there was no change in his condition. We called in a specialist, a renowned neurologist from Vienna, but alas he could do nothing but confirm what the Munich doctors said. George's heart had suffered a grave injury but the cardiograms showed no further problems. He was in a deep coma, but it was possible to wake up from such a condition and recover. I asked how long the coma might last; the specialist had no answer. In the meantime he prescribed intravenous injections of a mysterious medication that he promised would nurture the brain cells.

Thus I entered the world of doctors and hospitals where I would eventually feel more at home than in my own house. For there I was with George and at home there was emptiness.

Contrary to what one hears, I had generally excellent experiences with the physicians I dealt with. As soon as I arrived in Munich, I communicated with my Washington friend, neurologist Dr. Margaret Abernathy, who supported me for the following years with positive and constructive advice without ever sending a bill. At a distance she could not help too much but encouraged me to hope.

Philip put me in touch with Dr. Elisabeth Kübler-Ross, the author of *On Death and Dying,* and I called her in Chicago. She knew who George was and after I explained his condition, she told me: "Play music for him, play his favorite pieces and records of his own singing and talk to him. People in a coma can hear. Tell him that if he wants to go, you will understand and you will be able to take care of yourself. Tell him that if he comes back, you will take care of him."

This advice, together with Margaret Abernathy's encouragement, kept me going. I believed Dr. Kübler-Ross's credo and from then on I carried on a monologue for George, convinced that he could hear me and understand me.

A young pupil of George lent us her Munich apartment while she was in the States. Every morning I dressed carefully and made up my face, hoping this would be the day George would wake up and I wanted him to see me at my best. Then I took the streetcar, which stopped just in front of the hospital.

The month of August was exceptionally cold that year. Covered with hastily bought sweaters, I sat in a corner of the trolley car and watched the town's citizens rushing to work. The headlines about George were replaced by still larger headlines about Elvis Presley's death. I was relieved not to see George London in capital letters anymore but felt sad for the rock singer who died so young.

At the hospital everybody knew me. The halls and the cardiac unit were spotless; the nurses, who worked in teams of two, were pleasant and incredibly efficient. During the entire two months George was there, he was not able to move or eat, or even open his mouth. The nurses turned him every hour, checked his feeding tube and his trache tube with perfect timing.

When I entered his room in the morning, I switched on the tape recorder and played some of the tapes I had bought or others that friends had given me: recordings of George himself, or of Mozart concertos, Schubert's Unfinished Symphony and Beethoven's Ninth Symphony conducted by Furtwängler, all favorites of George.

Every day I straightened his hands so that they would not stay contracted in a fist. Then they would remain flat, beautiful, like a young man's, motionless next to his body. I stroked and kissed his hands and talked to him. Following Dr. Kübler-Ross's instructions, I told him how much I loved him, how happy I had been with him, but that I would understand if he wanted to leave this difficult life. I said I was well and able to handle everything and I promised to stay with him always if he needed me.

Whenever the nurses came to turn George, I had to leave the room and went to talk to the doctors. The residents sat in front of a panel monitoring the heartbeats of all the patients in the cardiac unit and every day I would ask about George's, which had returned to normal. The two physicians who were on duty most of the time had studied in the United States and, after two weeks, I began asking them if they thought that George could withstand the trip back to Washington.

They told me that George's heart had been badly injured but that he now seemed stabilized and there was no reason why he could not travel in another four weeks. The problem was that he could not be moved except on a stretcher and that ruled out any commercial flight. The German doctors seemed eager to discuss their difficult patient with me, but they could not offer a solution.

In the late afternoon I left the hospital, after a tender goodnight kiss on George's cheek, and promised to return the next morning. I had dinner with Marc, sometimes in the gaudy anonymity of a local McDonald's, often with dear friends who came from all over Europe to spend a few hours with me and comfort me. This was a specially difficult time for Marc, who was allowed only short stays in the hospital room and was left to roam by himself in a strange city. He was distressed when he had to leave to go back to college, but even though I missed his tender presence, I was glad that he could go on with his life.

I found that in this period, where life seemed to have stopped for me and where I seemed to be floating in a timeless, farcical bubble, I felt better if I concentrated my energy on one specific goal. So I decided that I would find a way to get us back to the States. I discovered that the army had a hospital flight every week to repatriate sick and injured soldiers from Frankfurt. Normally this plane took only army personnel, but on special occasions civilians were transported. All our friends in Washington were approached. I had no rest until progress was made. Our old friend from Vienna days, Si Bourgin, had connections at the State Department and was able to help. Eventually word came through the American vice-consul in Munich that George could be flown in the military plane.

During the weeks of negotiations, I continued to spend my days at the hospital, sitting next to George's bed, holding his hand, listening to the music and carrying on the monologues.

One day, as I sat there as usual, I noticed a quivering of George's eyelids. As I watched him slowly open his eyes, I could not move; an immense wave of hope came over me. Finally I mustered the courage to get up. He did not turn his head; he was looking at the ceiling. His eyes were clear, black and shiny, and they had no expression.

I was shattered. The miraculous awakening was a myth which would not come true for us. I swallowed my tears and called the doctor who took note of the change and assured me that this was a sign of real progress. I did feel somewhat encouraged, and redoubled my efforts at George's bedside. He started getting physical therapy every day and I began showing him some pictures of himself and the family and talking to him about his career and about himself.

During the entire time in Munich I spoke every week with Dr. Abernathy, who supported my decision to bring George to the States and promised to arrange for his admission at Georgetown Hospital as soon as we got to Washington.

At long last word came that George would be taken by the army hospital plane, but there was no provision for me. Now I begged the American vice-consul, Mr. Ira Levy, to make it possible for me to travel on the same plane. I explained that it was essential for me to be with George to take care of his needs, that he could not talk and that I would have to explain his condition to the medical attendants on the flight. Mr. Levy understood. Eventually we received permission to travel together on condition that I pay my way, which of course I agreed to do, never expecting it to be otherwise.

At last, six weeks after my arrival in Munich, we were able to leave. I carried George's hospital records and a letter from Dr. Rolf Emmerich, the attending physician of the hospital, which included the following words: "We anticipate a gradual recovery over a period of 3 to 6 months with hospitalization required during this period . . ."

I felt immensely encouraged as I said good-bye to the entire staff of the cardiac unit. Then we were helped into the ambulance that drove us from Munich to Frankfurt. Again it was a beautiful day, but this time it seemed to hold some promise. I was sitting squeezed between the stretcher and the I.V. stand next to my immobile husband while the ambulance sped across the countryside. George was being fed intravenously, and on my lap I held the precious box containing plastic bags with his fluid nourishment for the entire trip.

When we reached Frankfurt it was dark, drizzling and cold. I was glad that I had forced the nurses to put an undershirt and socks on George. We arrived at the U.S. army base and hospital, where our first trial awaited us. The army doctors had to examine George to decide if the patient could withstand the nine-hour trip to Andrews Air Force Base near Washington.

I had to fight to accompany George into the examining room. This would be a constant problem wherever we went. Medical personnel did not realize that George could not speak, and I always feared they would subject him to some painful tests, which he did not need. This time I could not prevent them doing a cardiogram, which, I was told, was required for the flight. It took two people to turn and undress him, but at least I could beg them to be gentle.

Watching the doctors' reactions, I realized more fully how terribly ill George was. I wondered if it was not folly to attempt taking him to the States, yet I was afraid the doctors would not permit his transport. I was told they would let me know in the morning if we could leave. In the meantime George had to stay in the hospital and I had to go to a small hotel nearby for the night.

It was nearly midnight when I finally got to bed, after making sure again and again that George was reasonably well taken care of. I walked the gray halls of the huge hospital and felt terribly forlorn and abandoned. Nobody seemed to care that in this place lay everything that made my life worthwhile.

I slept fitfully. At dawn the phone rang and I was told we were leaving within two hours. Greatly relieved, I rushed to the hospital. I made sure that George was well covered and accompanied the stretcher to the ambulance that took us to the armed forces plane. There were a number of other patients in the ambulance and quite a few more once we got on the plane.

It was a huge aircraft, probably a former troop carrier, now transformed into a hospital plane. Toward the front on each side were cots, some in tiers. In the center there was a large table at which three nurses and the plane's crew were sitting. Still a little farther back were about six rows of seats for other passengers. I was assigned one of these while George was put on one of the cots toward the left. I barely had time to check if he was attached safely and covered when I was ordered to my seat with a stern command not to move.

The plane lifted off safely, but the noise in the cabin was deafening. It could not be compared to the comfort of commercial airlines, but on the other hand, there was a great deal more space. Anyway, I was infinitely grateful to be there.

In the course of the nine- to ten-hour trip, I was allowed to visit George only a few times and then only briefly. It was very cold and I asked for and received additional blankets, but the brown army covers were made of thin, harsh wool and provided little warmth.

Later on in the trip I noticed that George's I.V. needle had come out. I begged the nurses to attend to him. There was one other cardiac patient aboard who also needed attention, but the other patients were all ambulatory and required no care. There were three nurses on the plane and I felt sure that they could take care of George's emergency. During the remaining three hours I went from one nurse to the other, begging for attention and explaining the gravity of the situation. Each one replied curtly, "Don't worry, we'll take care of it, please remain seated." Each time I staggered back to my seat amid increasing turbulence. I was unable to see the cots from my seat and could only hope that at least one of the nurses would keep her word.

At last the aircraft touched down in the United States. I ran to George's berth and was horrified to see that the I.V. had been put in improperly and was not functioning. I was indignant about this gross negligence, but what can you do when you are a guest of the U.S. Army?

When the doors of the aircraft opened, I was relieved to see a young resident, Dr. Eugene Madonia, who identified himself as Dr. Abernathy's assistant. He had been allowed inside the plane by special permission. I was almost hysterical with worry and could barely speak.

I managed to explain George's condition, the cold, the loss of the I.V., and how frantic I was. The young doctor reassured me, told me that he had come with an ambulance and would take us directly to Georgetown Hospital.

I walked down the steps from the plane and saw Andy's good face and Marc's shiny black eyes smiling at me and I was able to smile back and pull myself up very straight. I was not alone; I had my family to back me up. Now they would be near me, and I was not going to disappoint them and be a whimpering mother. The trip was one of the low points of these years, perhaps the lowest because I was so alone. I would never feel alone quite that way again, even at times when I experienced utter despair. I realized that at any time I could call my children and one of them would come to me. They knew how much I suffered but I resolved to make them feel that their own lives would go on and that George would have wanted it that way.

I climbed into the ambulance while Andy and Marc followed with our bags in my car. George was already warmly wrapped in blankets and the I.V. had been reinserted. The ambulance sped away, sirens blaring. In less than fifteen minutes we turned into the emergency entrance of Georgetown Hospital.

It was September 9, a warm and sunny summer day. Dr. Abernathy was waiting for us in front of the door with Marina. She knew how difficult this first contact would be for our daughter and wanted to be there with her besides wanting to care for George as soon as he arrived. She told me often later on how impressed she was with Marina's behavior.

I was apprehensive. Marina, Daddy's little girl, was now twenty-one. She had been closest to him during the last years. She had the same vitality and sense of fantasy that he had, and they would go out together to movies that I did not like or on shopping sprees for things that we did not need. Over the coming years, Marina was to feel an insurmountable sense of loss. She felt George's illness like "a fall, the end of a personal golden age and a shock that would diminish the value of all subsequent experience," to quote Isak Dinesen.

But that afternoon Marina stood there silent and composed. She looked at George as he was removed from the ambulance and told me that to her relief she found his face not much altered. I held my daughter tightly in my arms as we came closer. Suddenly George raised his hand. I looked on in disbelief; the others were not aware that this was the first time he moved his arm. I was very excited and told Dr. Abernathy. She agreed that this was an encouraging sign. Now I no longer felt the fatigue of the trip and walked briskly into the hospital.

Later on, the news was not so good. George was severely de-hydrated and had contracted pneumonia. His life was in danger for the second time in six weeks. I began another daily shuttle between this hospital and our house. But now I could use my car and the trip took only five minutes.

I was glad to be back in our own house. Every evening, in our bedroom, I looked at our double bed with sorrow and hoped fervently that someday George would be able to come home. At least I was comfortable. Ricilia cried about George, whom she adored, but cooked all my favorite dishes for me and the children, and friends kept me company and made the days seem shorter.

The greatest trial upon returning was the meeting with my mother. She had recovered from her heart attack in the spring and, aside from arthritic pains, she was fairly mobile. She had a large bedroom and bath in our house and a companion who attended to all her needs.

After her original objections to my marriage to "an artist," she had turned into George's greatest fan. Over the years she was often jealous of my devotion to him; she complained that I spoiled him, but she too worshiped him and he could do no wrong in her eyes.

After my return, I walked into her room and sat on the edge of her bed. She kissed me tenderly with tears in her eyes. She was so glad that I was home. "What will become of you?" she moaned. She could not bear to see my happy marriage threatened and could not understand George's illness. She added, alluding to herself, "How can you take care of two sick people?" I explained George's condition as best I could and assured her that I was full of hope that he would improve.

My mother was never able to accept George's condition and could not face him when he came home. She loved me dearly and must have known how much her attitude upset me but she could not help herself. Eventually I established schedules that prevented George and my mother from seeing each other in the house.

He improved slowly, and was taken off the critical list at Georgetown Hospital. Once he left the intensive-care unit, however, he needed private nurses around the clock, for although he was now able to move his arms freely, he could not move his body and still could not open his mouth or swallow. He was being fed through a nasal tube and breathed through the trache tube. However, his eyes seemed alert now and I thought that he recognized me when I came in every morning.

The foremost question was to know how severely brain-damaged he was. Every possible test was done. The EEG was not conclusive for it was impossible to keep his head immobile during the test. A scan seemed to show that the brain was normal; doctors still knew very little. Dr. Abernathy ordered therapy and every day the nurse and I wheeled George to the physical therapy department, where he was helped to sit and eventually stand with two people holding him up. It was a tremendous task but I could see some progress.

Eventually we kept the trache tube closed most of the day and I could see that George breathed spontaneously through his mouth. I called Dr. Henry Rubin in California and he assured me that George had enough room in his throat to breathe freely in spite of the immobilized vocal cord. Dr. Leo Reckford in New York agreed with the diagnosis, and the neurology resident felt that George could do without the tracheostomy tube.

I was convinced that if George got rid of that metal contraption in his throat he would feel freer to use his voice and would try to speak. Dr. Abernathy was not in favor of my plan but finally agreed to it. The tube was removed and within a day George opened his mouth and started to say no and then yes. I was jubilant. He also could swallow some liquids, and I was able to fend off the stomach specialists who had warned me that George could not be fed by nasal tube much longer and would need an operation to permit him to be fed direcly to the stomach. I was determined that I would not allow this; somehow I would make him eat again.

In time George was able to answer questions reasonably with a yes or no. He sat up in a chair and was able to swallow some soup. I was optimistic for further progress when all hopes were shattered again. He developed heavy breathing and a strident sound in his throat, and it became clear that he needed another tracheostomy. I was dejected and felt guilty. Perhaps I had been wrong to encourage the removal of the tube. A new trache tube was inserted in his throat. It was terrible to think of the desecration of his throat, which had meant so much to him.

I decided to have his throat examined by a specialist, one who was familiar with George's special condition before the cardiac arrest. So I called Dr. Max Som, whom George had often seen after Dr. Rubin's injections. I called Dr. Som and he agreed to admit George to Beth Israel Hospital in New York. With determination, I transported him by ambulance to New York, accompanied by the ambulance attendants. I held his hands during the trip. His eyes were open but he did not make a sound. He had clearly regressed. After the five-hour trip, I was relieved to see the familiar face of the doctor. George was examined. Apparently the original incision in Germany had been made somewhat too high. Another operation was required to improve the tracheostomy as much as possible.

I sat huddled with Andy and Philip in the gray hallway of the hospital, waiting for the doctor to come out of surgery. Finally he came up to us followed by his aides. This physician, who had decades of experience of the worst illnesses, had tears in his eyes. He told me that he had done all he could for my husband. He would never be able to breathe safely without a trache tube. George had been without oxygen too long after his cardiac arrest and had suffered irreversible brain damage.

Dr. Som turned to me compassionately. "You must make some plans for the future and think of yourself."

I was crushed. I was forced to face the fact that George's infirmities were irreparable. For a moment I felt as if the ground was sinking under my feet and there was nowhere to hang on. But I vowed that I would not give up so easily and that no matter what, I would always take care of George. Anyway, for the time being, he was so sick he had to remain in the hospital. Everyone was extremely supportive and helpful. The president of the hospital as well as the chief neurologist loved opera, and were great fans of George and tried to make things as easy as possible for us. I needed nurses around the clock and spent a long time in the nurses' office explaining that George was a big man and that a small woman, no matter how capable, could not turn him.

At the end of each day I felt drained. The children took me out for dinner and tried to divert me in the evenings. My friends came to my rescue. Hope Miller, whose husband, an obstetrician, also practiced at Beth Israel, offered a room in her house five minutes from the hospital where I could stay as long as I wished. She had been my first friend in the United States in 1940; we had always kept in touch through the years and now she and her husband, Arthur, gave me their help and their comfort. All my New York friends came to see me. We met at a restaurant across the street from the hospital, which became the headquarters for my visitors.

No one could see George yet except for me and the children. Winter had come, and I remember my first New Year's Eve with him in the hospital. I let the evening nurse leave early so she could be with her family. The hospital halls were dark and quiet. I sat next to George watching a television broadcast of *Fledermaus* from Covent Garden. It was a charming and spirited performance. My ailing husband was breathing heavily and suddenly I knew that we would never enjoy such performances together again. The tears rolled down my face uncontrolled for a long time. I clutched his thin hand in mine. The pain, the sorrow was terrible, but I would endure again and again.

———

Since we had left Washington, George's mouth was clenched tight, and it was essential that he open it and start eating. Several times he had pulled out the dreadful feeding tube from his nose and each time it had to be put in again. I asked for a therapist's advice and she gave me a small curved spoon with instructions to push it in the side of George's mouth. I was determined to succeed. I decided to use ice cream because it was one of George's favorite foods, it needed no chewing, and it was easiest to swallow.

Every day, in the middle of winter, I went to the nearby Baskin-Robbins and brought back different ice-cream flavors for George. First I got no more than a drop into his mouth, but at last he seemed to recognize the familiar taste, and little by little he opened his lips. In a few weeks he was able to eat regular portions. Then he managed to swallow some juice, a difficult task for a patient in his condition. Still the doctors felt he was not able to eat enough to sustain himself without the feeding tube.

The physicians at Beth Israel decided that they could do nothing more for George and that he was well enough to leave the hospital. Dr. Som tried to suggest that it would be difficult to take care of him at home and that I should consider putting him in a nursing home. I bristled at this and answered that I had sworn to George when he was in a coma that I would look after him always and that is what I would do. The physicians accepted my decision. Even though I knew that it would be difficult, I planned to take George back to Washington and to care for him myself.

Dr. Hyun Cho, who was Dr. Som's assistant, taught me how to take care of the trache tube and how to change it. Eventually Marina discovered that we could replace the metal tubes with plastic ones, which were much lighter and better tolerated by the patient. The physical therapist showed me how to move George, although we still needed two people to get him into an armchair. Once again Dr. Abernathy helped me with encouragement and preparations in Washington, and at last we set forth in another ambulance going south to the capital. George was coming home after seven months.

Once more I sat next to the stretcher for the five-hour trip. This time I was calmer. George was no longer in danger.

As soon as we were on the way, I pulled out the feeding tube and said, "George, you have to eat now. You must swallow your food, otherwise I cannot take care of you." I gave him a portion of ice cream that I had brought along and he swallowed well. From that day on he started eating, first puréed food, then within weeks solid food.

He began to have as much pleasure eating as in the past, favoring the sweets he had always liked. Bolstered by this victory, I faced our return with more courage. The bedroom of our house was upstairs and there was no way to get George there. So we transformed the living room into a bedroom with a hospital bed, chair, and all the necessities he required.

For the first time since I returned from Munich, George was living in the same house with me, and even if we did not share a bed, he was close by, night and day. I did not have to run out to him every morning fearful of what I would find. I started the habit of greeting him and talking to him when he first woke up, for I realized that his mind was most alert at that time. I would never go to bed at night without giving him a last good-night kiss.

It was wonderful to have him home, even though at first I was not used to the responsibilities and was afraid I would not know how to handle all the problems. I could no longer rely on the hospitals to find me nurses; from now on I had to find them by myself.

In spite of some progress, George could not move himself, could not speak, could not feed himself. He improved significantly in the next months but essentially he would need constant help in the following seven years. During all those years I had to make sure that he had nursing care around the clock. I got in touch with various agencies and eventually came to know about nurses through recommendations. The biggest problem was George's size and weight, even though he was very thin. I knew how to take care of the trache tube and could give him his medicines; but he had to be lifted into a sitting position and moved from place to place, jobs most women were not strong enough to do. The various lifting contraptions were of no help; we tried them all. The only useful appliance was a Burke chair, with a seat that lifted mechanically and thus raised the patient to a standing position.

Even with this chair, most women found it impossible to take care of George. I could employ only exceptionally strong females or else I had to have male nurses, and these were hard to find. This was an unending problem. We had to have three shifts each day and usually different nurses on weekends, for most nurses worked only five days. It turned out that the night shift, 12:00 to 8:00 A.M., was the easiest to fill, for this nurse only had to turn the patient in bed, and a well-trained woman could do it. Actually, I could turn George in bed at first, but later I injured my back and could no longer do it by myself.

While I was still in Germany, Andy had begun to examine all of George's insurance papers. He had established that George had some disability insurance, about $1,000 a month altogether, and that through the Washington Opera he had an excellent health insurance policy that fortunately also provided for private nurses.

So I learned to fill in insurance forms and to keep perfect records of every amount spent. The fees for the nurses started at sixty dollars a shift and eventually went up to seventy-five and eighty dollars for registered nurses. Thus the insurance paid an average of two hundred seventy-five dollars a day in nurses' fees, and I felt temporarily relieved.

The Washington Opera generously paid George's salary for one year after his illness. I watched the operas he had planned so carefully being performed with great success at the Kennedy Center by the artists he had chosen with knowledge and love. His place was taken over with devotion by his assistant, Gary Fifield, who came to see me often, always hoping to hear that George was getting better and would come back to his job in the future.

As the days went by I understood that any real progress would take months to achieve. The financial burden of the household plus supporting our two younger children, who were still in college and graduate school, were enormous. Consulting with Andy, I came to the conclusion that I could not keep the house in Switzerland, and so I sold it. I never went back there. Andy made all the arrangements and sent back the few pieces of furniture and the paintings I wanted. I needed the money but above all I could not go to this house without George. It was George's house; it was the symbol of his achievement; it was *his* terrace in front of his living room; it was *his* view of the lake and the Alps and the castle. It was the house he built, and if he could not be there then I no longer wanted it.

I was left with the very pleasant house in Washington. However, it became impractical since there was no proper room and bath for George on the main floor. Too, Margaret Abernathy told me that George needed more therapy in order to improve further and suggested he go to a rehabilitation center, but there was no such place in Washington. Again I would not agree to put George into such a center without my being there, as long as he could not speak. During his entire illness, I had nightmares in which George was mistreated by someone when I was absent. I searched for a place where I could take him on a daily basis and found the Burke Rehabilitation Center in Westchester County, New York. I went to White Plains to visit the center and was assured that George would be accepted as a day-care patient.

All I needed to do was to move our whole household from Washington to near White Plains. Knowing me, my children realized that nothing would persuade me to change my mind. Furthermore, they admitted that it would be easier to manage our affairs if I were closer to New York where Andy lived. Marina went to graduate school at Columbia University and Philip did much of his television work from nearby Connecticut.

Philip was able to find a ranch house with a separate apartment for my mother on a two-acre wooded plot in Armonk. I sold the house in D.C. and proceeded to move two ailing people, three dogs, two cars, and all our furniture from Washington to Westchester in one day.

We settled George in his new room while a crew of painters directed by Philip was putting on the last coat in the living room. The house was completely geared to George's needs. Everything was on the same level and could be reached in his wheelchair. He had a closed porch where he could exercise winter and summer; he had a tub with a Jacuzzi, and a small swimming pool close to the house, for which Philip had built a wide access ramp.

When we were settled and George seemed used to his new surroundings, I called Burke and made an appointment to visit. I had bought a station wagon with an extra-roomy front seat and easy storage for the wheelchair in the back. With the help of the nurse, we took George up the ramp to the day-care section where he was examined by the therapists in charge.

Within minutes I was told that George "did not perform on command" and that therefore he could not be accepted as a regular day-care patient. His case was too serious and did not conform to normal stipulations for their patients. "But," I said, "you had promised on the basis of the physician's report." They answered that upon seeing the patient, they could no longer agree to take him. If I insisted we could try some occupational therapy there from time to time. As suggested, we brought George to Burke a few times but there were always long waits and he responded poorly to the therapists' commands.

I was deeply disappointed and very irritated. It seemed that these institutions, which were supposed to help the handicapped, were geared only to help sick people who were guaranteed to improve.

In spite of what I had been told, I was determined to help George. I found a remarkable physical therapist, Bill Anderson, who worked with George with incredible devotion in the years to come. He helped me to find a tilt table so that George could stand up every day; he recommended the armchair with the lifting seat and found a contraption that permitted us to lift George into the swimming pool on hot summer days. Little by little, with Bill's unflinching support and the help of nurses who became attached to George—such as Judy Jones, who stayed six years—I think I was able to give George a somewhat bearable life.

I constantly asked myself what he would like and what would please him. I made sure that he was well dressed every day. I cooked his favorite dishes, I played his favorite pieces of music. I obtained videotapes of his own television shows and of operas from the Met. I took him for rides in the countryside by car and for walks in the wheelchair. I was aware that the exercise program on the mat and the tilt table was painful for him, but I knew it was essential that he move his body if he was to remain healthy and free from bedsores.

He learned to sit up by himself and to stand up when helped, and to bear his weight. I remember my joy when, after months and months of sitting, he stood tall and slim, towering above me. He seemed pleased and I felt extraordinarily hopeful. I was convinced that soon he would be able to walk.

However, the New York neurologists were not encouraging. We consulted Dr. Fred Plum, head of the neurology department at New York Hospital. Dr. Plum was very attentive but could not give me much hope. He tried to help by enrolling George in a special research program for brain-damaged patients, but it didn't seem of much help. Various new drugs were tried by Dr. John Blass, who was kind and supportive, but none made a significant change.

Yet I continued to think that additional progress was possible. I knew that I had more communication with George than the doctors believed. I spoke to him constantly as if he were perfectly well. At first I hired a speech therapist but George did not respond to pictures of apples and oranges, but he did look with interest at pictures of himself in costumes of his various roles. He reacted most of all to the operas I played for him and to records of himself singing.

As the months passed, the thing I missed most was hearing him speak. Shortly after we moved to Armonk, his medication was changed. He screamed for days and I thought I would lose my mind; then the new drug took effect, but total silence followed and I thought I almost preferred the shouting. Then one day while playing an aria from *The Flying Dutchman* I discovered that he was saying the words along with the music perfectly in German. So he could speak! These words were printed in a part of his brain with the music and were still there. As the days went by I played other arias from his records and regularly he would say the words. His voice sounded perfectly natural, warm and strong. I basked in the sound.

Since we had replaced the heavy metal tracheostomy tube with the small plastic one, he could eat very well and drink with little difficulty. In the morning, when his mind was most receptive, he could feed himself pieces of toast with jam. His somber expression changed to one of enjoyment, though he had not smiled yet. Now he again answered yes and no when I asked him whether he wanted something, and I considered this a great improvement.

I told him every day that the children were doing well, that I was able to take care of him, that he need not worry. I never failed to tell him how much I loved him, and every evening I came to kiss him good-night and make sure that he was lying in a comfortable position.

Then one morning, in Armonk, as usual I said, "Good morning, George, how are you?" He looked at me and said clearly, "I love you," and smiled a big sweet smile.

It was a magical moment which made years of effort and frustration a thousand times worthwhile. It is hard to describe the joy and the feeling of fulfillment. Here at last was the sign of approval I had so desperately worked for all these months, taking care of him day and night, never knowing whether he heard me, whether he really knew me or even wanted my efforts. Now I knew, I knew for sure, that he still loved me.

I went over to him and hugged him and he hugged me in his strong arms. He had broken the walls of silence erected by the dreadful illness, and once again we were like one.

17

Last Years Together

CONFUTATIS
"I pray, suppliant and kneeling
My heart contrite as ashes
Take unto thy care my ending."
—Bass part, Verdi, *Requiem*

In the following months George repeated quite often that he loved me and smiled every now and then; but he never talked more than that, he never laughed, and he never learned to walk again.

The physicians asked me periodically how I was holding up and if I would consider putting George in a nursing home. I was adamantly opposed to the idea. For me, he was present and alive and I wanted to take care of him. I could see him whenever I wanted to, I could touch him, I could be sure that he was comfortable and treated with warmth and respect. I could look forward to his rare smiles and the few words he spoke each day. I could always hope.

The help of the nurses was still essential. George still could not turn in bed, nor dress, nor get up, nor do any of the simplest movements. Only his arms and hands could move freely, but not always with perfect purpose. He could not brush his hair or feed himself.

Every day he was dressed in an attractive shirt, with a silk cravat to hide the trache tube. Clean shaven, his hair brushed and shiny, he would sit in his armchair. About once a week there were visitors for him. I felt he was pleased when close friends came to see him. After all, he had been an extremely gregarious person, a man with close bonds to his friends, and now he was surely bored and lonely.

On the other hand, visits were a trauma for me. Even though I prepared his friends, the shock at what they saw was so tremendous that many could not bear it and they often left the room in tears. Here was this man who had been the essence of life reduced to sitting silently looking at you with burning eyes, his arms stretched out to hold you.

I saw men cry and suffered anew with them, yet I wanted George to have the company and so I continued to encourage visits. Some could not bear to come back and I understood, but some came regularly, women and men, talked to him, brought tapes, held his hand, brought him the gift of friendship and affection.

When three years had passed the insurance company warned us that the premium was running out; within a few months the company would no longer pay the nurses' fees. I was in a panic. How could we afford payments of eighty thousand dollars a year for nurses alone, not counting food, mortgage, and transportation? I felt I was standing in front of an abyss that I could never fill. And then I found out what extraordinary friends we had.

First, the American Guild of Musical Artists, whose president George had been for four years, had a pension fund program, and voted to support his care generously each year. But in spite of great efforts, they could not provide such staggering sums. Then all at once Chris Hunter, Bill Blair, Matthew Epstein, from Columbia Artists Management, and great singer after singer organized a benefit program to help their ailing friend and colleague.

The benefit took place on November 4, 1981, at the concert hall of the Kennedy Center, which had been donated by Roger Stevens. The concert was televised nationwide. The funds it raised provided security for George's care and taught me how much George was beloved by his colleagues, those with whom he had performed and those he had helped to start their careers.

Beverly Sills was the master of ceremonies for the telecast. She had met George in 1946 and recalled the circumstances of their meeting:

> There was a lady on the West Coast whose name was Mrs. Burnstein and there was another lady living on the East Coast whose name was Mrs. Silverman. Mrs. Burnstein had a son whose name was George. Mrs. Silverman had a daughter whose name was Beverly. Neither of the children was married, they were both singers and they were both Jewish and both mothers thought they were made for each other.
>
> So they arranged a blind date, and George invited me to lunch at a little restaurant on West 57th Street called "Vim and Vigor Vitamin Bar." I think he was a little nervous how it was all going to turn out because he brought along an old buddy with him and his buddy's name was Mario Lanza. The three of us really hit it off and we had fabulous times together. But I think George always knew there was going to be his wonderful Nora and I always knew there was going to be my wonderful Pete, so nothing really came of it and we all went our separate ways.

The program was composed of performances by great operatic stars of our time, accompanied by foremost conductors and pianists. Behind each magnificent performance was a personal story of generosity and friendship, which was being returned to George a thousandfold on that night.

I remember Marilyn Horne telling me in her dressing room, "It is a measure of your husband's character that not a single singer canceled tonight."

I felt deep gratitude and humility to find out that his name had rallied such support. During my lonely daily struggle I had never forgotten to love my patient, but I sometimes forgot what he had meant to so many others.

With financial security assured, I now muliplied my efforts to give George as much distraction as possible. I showed him the videotape of the gala in small portions to suit his short attention span.

After the gala I went to Los Angeles to visit George's mother who was in a nursing home. She was past ninety but fairly well physically. However, her mind was wandering. She recognized me, then confused me with Marina. She refused to watch the telecast of the gala. She could not admit George's illness. For her, the beloved son would remain eternally young, healthy, and successful. She died in 1986.

In the summer of 1982 we attempted a treatment for George using Dr. Moïshe Feldenkrais's method, which was based on repetition of gestures and reflexes. This was supposed to stimulate the brain in a manner comparable to the development of infants' brains. In order to give this system a good chance, we spent three weeks in Amherst under most difficult conditions. George had special exercise sessions every day at Hampshire College, where Dr. Feldenkrais taught and treated people. I reasoned that if it had been up to George, he would have tried it.

Unfortunately, the result was negative and we moved back, worn out from the effort of transporting him back and forth during stifling summer days.

After our return from Amherst I felt a terrible let-down. I finally admitted to myself that I had exhausted every avenue for improvement. I dreamed at night that George talked to me, that he walked with me hand in hand across the fields in Vufflens. When I woke up I realized that this would never happen again. I had known it for some time, but I had kept busy with constant plans for improvement. Little by little the hopelessness of our situation covered me like an iron mantle. Revolt and bitterness were useless and counterproductive. I had to accept the facts and concentrate on maintaining George's condition as it was. This meant daily physical therapy, regular meals, frequent outings, conversation, and musical stimulation. It was an unending cycle, but up to the last year there were precious moments of recognition that made it all worthwhile for me.

My mother died in September 1982 just before her ninetieth birthday. Her passing relieved me of the burden of her care but as she had said, "With whom will you talk when I am gone?" I spent long winter evenings in silence, isolated by a grief that no one could share.

All my four children were married the same year. In June 1983,

George witnessed his daughter's wedding day in our garden although he could not lead her to the altar.

Those were bittersweet days for me. I had always imagined how delighted George would be, how he would love his new son and his new daughters, how proud he would be at his son's graduation from medical school. On all those days I stood alone in a festive dress, sad yet joyful and grateful to see my children happy and whole.

The long illness had taken a heavy toll on the children. Their efforts to spend some time with me every week forced them to disrupt their lives. I tried to tell them that I could manage alone, but they sensed that I did in fact need their company. Marina felt the heaviest obligation; her husband was very sympathetic, always ready to come with her.

The children's visits to Armonk were difficult. They were expected to spend some time with their father, and this was heartbreaking for them. They did not have a close daily relationship with George and they only saw a shadow of the man they loved and admired. They did not believe that he understood what we said to him. I was painfully aware of their agony and yet I felt if their presence provided George with just an instant of pleasure, their sacrifice was justified.

Another year went by. Our routine did not change. Once a week I went to the city visiting friends or going to the opera. Once with much help and enormous effort we had taken George to a rehearsal of *Fidelio,* but the trip was too long and too tiring for him; when he got to the box he could hardly absorb what he saw, and so we did not try again.

At the beginning of 1984 I began to worry again about expenses. The nursing fees were constantly rising; simultaneously it became more and more difficult to find personnel. Our friends in Austria heard about our problems and about the tribute in Washington. So in June 1984 a concert dedicated to George took place in Vienna. Again his friends and colleagues gave generously of their time. Our friend Gottfried Kraus, who had been a fan of George's since 1949 at age thirteen, was the organizer.

I traveled to Vienna to be present at the concert and I was deeply moved. For their fellow artist the chorus of the Vienna Opera sang Beethoven's prisoners' chorus from *Fidelio,* which George loved so much. Then Leonie Rysanek, Catherine Malfitano, Tatiana Troyanos, and Nicolai Gedda, among others, sang for him for the second time. The magnificent huge baroque concert hall was packed with George's Viennese fans who came after so many years, as if he had just performed for them yesterday. The love affair between Vienna and George continued. As Gottfried said: "Vienna would never forget George London." When the singers pulled me in front of the audience to bow in place of George, we all had tears in our eyes. I knew the ovation was for him, for all the joy he had once given to this public.

A great wave of love engulfed me and I wished desperately that George could have been there and experienced this homage.

When I came home I tried to describe it all to him. I told him how admired he was and that he would always be remembered, but I knew that he no longer understood much of what I said.

At Christmas 1983 George had had a slight stroke. I called our family doctor, Dr. Robert Silverman. He was on vacation as was Dr. Cho, who was always ready to come when there was a throat problem. I needed help and called Marc, who was a physician now, resident in neurology at Mount Sinai Hospital. Marc felt that it was a heavy responsibility and a great strain to take care of his father, but I explained that in case of emergency it was a relief for me to know that I could count on him. From then on I often asked his advice about various problems or dosages of medicines and found his advice helpful, accurate, and very supportive.

George recovered once again but his left side was slightly affected and now he stood up only with great difficulty. Worst of all, he never spoke again. I hoped in vain for a smile and a last word. I wanted so much to hear his voice. I played his records, a mixture of pleasure and pain for me, but he no longer spoke the text.

After my return from Vienna, every week brought slight changes for the worse. George no longer enjoyed his food so much. Even the famous Sacher torte, which friends sent from Austria at regular intervals, hardly tempted him. He had more and more problems drinking and had long coughing spells that I could not bear to watch.

He became terribly thin and developed a sore on his hip. He slept for long periods during the day, and when he was awake each movement seemed more and more difficult. I no longer insisted that the children visit him when they came to see me on weekends. It was too much of an ordeal for them and I could not be sure that he recognized them.

As the winter months went by he seemed to spend more and more time in his chair. Often I sat on the armrest, bending over him, my arm around his shoulder until he dozed off. In spite of his silence I felt that he knew me and wanted my presence. I sat next to him in utter despair day after day, while dusk was falling on the bare trees outside his window.

He was pale and his cheeks were sunken; only his eyes seemed bright and alive. He looked at me beseechingly and I understood his message. I could hear his voice in the prayer of the Verdi *Requiem:* "Take unto thy care my ending." I told him, more than once in those last months, what I had learned in Munich. "It was all right for him to go." I told him that he had done enough for me, that I would be safe and that his family was well.

On Sunday evening March 24, 1985, I was alone in the house. The day nurse had left and the night nurse was not expected until midnight. As usual, I went into George's room for my evening visit to make sure that he was comfortable. His hand was cold and limp, and I realized suddenly that he was not breathing. I took his wrist and could not feel any pulse. I rushed to the phone. Our doctor was not available and an anonymous answering service took the call. Then I reached Marc in New York. He came as quickly as he could. He confirmed that George had died in his sleep.

I sat next to him for the last time. There were so many things I wanted to tell him once more: feelings and promises and foolish nothings that suddenly seemed important. I thought I heard his voice as Amfortas, imploring: "Death! To die!/Unique mercy!"

I understood. Now he was liberated and whole again. I held his hand in mine and kissed him for the last time.

With shocking haste, the undertakers came before the night was gone, but that is the law, and the body I loved so passionately was taken away forever.

I refuse to think of him as he lay that night, pale and emaciated. I think of him radiant after a concert, or arms outstretched in front of the curtain in Bayreuth, or triumphant after the *Boris* in Moscow.

I remember him smiling proudly in the crowd at Marina's graduation and laughing tenderly at our last good-bye in Washington.

I know that in spite of the vocal torments and nearly eight years of torture, his life was a success. He achieved what he wanted; "he made his mark" and reached most of his goals. He gave joy, support, and inspiration to those around him.

To me, George gave the greatest gift of all: he gave me a sense of self in addition to his love and respect. Through his artistry, his humanity, his vitality, I discovered new dimensions to life. Through his courage and fortitude I found unexpected strength and compassion. I became the woman he expected me to be, but my life without him will be forever incomplete.